THE COWBOY WHO CAUGHT HER EYE

Lauri Robinson

MILLS & BOON

First published in Great Britain 2013
by Mills & Boon, an imprint of Harlequin (UK) Limited.
Harlequin (UK) Limited, Eton House, 18-24 Paradise Road,
Richmond, Surrey TW9 1SR

© Lauri Robinson 2013

ISBN: 978 0 263 89840 8

Harlequin (UK) policy is to use papers that are natural, renewable
and recyclable products and made from wood grown in sustainable
forests. The logging and manufacturing process conform to the
legal environmental regulations of the country of origin.

Printed and bound in Spain
by Blackprint CPI, Barcelona

Lauri Robinson's chosen genre to write is Western historical romance. When asked why, she says, 'Because I know I wasn't the only girl who wanted to grow up and marry Little Joe Cartwright.'

With a degree in early childhood education, Lauri has spent decades working in the non-profit field and claims once-upon-a-time and happily-ever-after romance novels have always been a form of stress relief. When her husband suggested she write one she took the challenge, and has loved every minute of the journey.

Lauri lives in rural Minnesota, where she and her husband spend every spare moment with their three grown sons and four grandchildren. She works part-time, volunteers for several organisations, and is a diehard Elvis and NASCAR fan. Her favourite getaway location is the woods of northern Minnesota, on the land homesteaded by her great-grandfather.

Previous titles from Lauri Robinson:

HIS CHRISTMAS WISH
  (part of *All a Cowboy Wants for Christmas*)
UNCLAIMED BRIDE
INHERITING A BRIDE

Also available in Mills & Boon® Historical *Undone!* eBooks:

WEDDING NIGHT WITH THE RANGER
HER MIDNIGHT COWBOY
NIGHTS WITH THE OUTLAW
DISOBEYING THE MARSHAL
TESTING THE LAWMAN'S HONOUR
THE SHERIFF'S LAST GAMBLE
WHAT A COWBOY WANTS
HIS WILD WEST WIFE

To my sister-in-law, Berta.
Gotta love those cowboys!
Love you,
Lauri.

Chapter One

~~~~~~

Dakota Territory
August 1884

Carter Buchanan kept the hat pulled low on his face and his feet propped on the seat across from him, waiting for the others to gather their bags and bundles and head for the exit. He was as ready to get off the rumbling box on wheels as the rest of them, but he never let anything show—feelings or thoughts. That was how he liked it.

He did let out a pent-up sigh and cast a little glance around, checking how many other passengers still had to depart the Chicago and Northwestern railcar. Several, including the woman with a dozen kids. True, it wasn't a full dozen, but she had a horde. With red hair and freckles.

Irish. He was, too. Black Irish. That's what they called him all those years ago when he roamed the streets of New York. His hair was still black, his eyes still blue, but no one had called him that for years now. Not that it mattered. It hadn't then and it didn't now.

Once the commotion slowed, he pushed back his hat, planted his boots on the floor and gathered up the bedroll he'd tucked his well-worn dictionary in earlier. Sampson would be glad to see him. The gelding hadn't been impressed with his accommodations. Neither had Carter. What the railroad advertised and what he'd just experienced were as far apart as the east and west coasts. He knew. He'd been to both. Coasts, that is.

Right now he was smack-dab in the middle of these good old United States of America. The land his father never got to see. Mother, either. The trip over from the old country saw to that. Carter had seen this country though. Lots of it. And now he was in Huron, South Dakota. Named after the Indians that once roamed the prairies, founded to become the headquarters of the western division of the C&NW railroad, and where his latest case took him.

The only place bills had surfaced from last year's train robbery was right here in Huron. Ironic, that's what he'd called it. Told Mr. Pinkerton that himself. The man agreed and told him good luck.

Good luck. That, too, was ironic. What other kind of luck would you wish upon someone?

The outside air wasn't a whole lot better than inside the train car. Hot and heavy. He drew in a good portion anyway and set off in the direction of his horse.

Full of muck and mud, a recent rain no doubt, the ground surrounding the depot platform stunk from droppings left about, which he stepped around as if sashaying a woman across a dance floor. Not that he did that too often. Unlike dancing, sidestepping piles he was used to.

Sampson was nickering before the gate to the stock car dropped and upon bounding down, the palomino made his own offering to the stench and muck.

"That happens every time," a young kid said, handing over Sampson's reins.

"I'm sure it does," Carter answered, giving the curly-haired boy a coin for his troubles.

"If you're hungry, there's a restaurant in the hotel, or the mercantile sells breads and such, if'n you want to make your own." The boy waved a hand toward the buildings lining both sides of the muddy street. "It's a bit farther away, but I'd recommend the mercantile. Miss Thorson makes the best cinnamon rolls you'll ever eat."

"Obliged," Carter said, tying his pack behind the saddle. He led Sampson away then, but just far enough to examine the surroundings. A cinnamon roll did sound good. He'd always had a soft spot for pastries, and the mercantile was one of the places he'd visit, but first he'd get a feel for the town.

This assignment didn't require him to be undercover—he was using his own name—but that didn't mean he wanted anyone to know who he was, what he was doing. One never knew how folks would relate to a Pinkerton man. Some were impressed, others angered, and there were always a few who really didn't care. He'd be one of the latter, if he was in anyone else's boots. Plenty of Pinkerton operatives, even some he knew well, were little more than thugs with a cross to bear.

Carter took to walking again, down the muddy street, giving Sampson a chance to get his bearings while surveying the buildings on both sides. Connected, one to the next, they went on for half a dozen blocks. Several were stand-alones, had little walkways—muddy ones—between them, and most had two stories, a couple with balconies. Some were made of bricks, even had the dates they were built—last year—displayed in the top row below the crowning eaves. Others were made of wood, but painted. All in all, it appeared to be a well-laid-out and prosperous town.

The line outside the hotel suggested most of the train passengers had decided on a meal at the restaurant. It was close to noon. He'd get himself one of those cinnamon rolls later, but just now he was moseying. He was good at moseying, and liked it, too. It was amazing what a man learned just by keeping his ears open, walking about, and Carter set a slow pace, doing precisely that.

It was close to an hour later when he found himself at the edge of town. The sun was high, drying out the ground, and Carter was satisfied he knew enough particulars to dig in to his assignment.

Thorson's Mercantile, a big wooden structure, and a stand-alone one, was at the end of the main street, a considerable distance from all the other buildings, making him wonder if it was one of the first ones built several years ago, before the railroad bought up the land on the west bank of the James River for their western division headquarters. The store looked as if it had been a house at one time that someone had added a big front room to, complete with plate-glass windows and a sprawling porch to display odds and ends for sale. There was a barn and a couple other buildings nestled around it, as though the original owners were building a ranch, but changed their minds.

That's what he'd decided was in his future. A ranch. He'd have it someday. Soon. Just had to decide where. That's one of the things he'd come to like about being a Pinkerton man. Assignments rarely sent him to the same place twice, giving him a chance to explore where he wanted to finally hang his hat. It paid well, too, being a Pinkerton operative. He had no complaints on that either.

Carter swung into the saddle, ready to ride, give Sampson a chance to stretch his legs. There'd be plenty of time to get that cinnamon roll, see Ted Wilcox and then settle in the hotel before nightfall.

The thunder of hooves had Molly Thorson lifting her head and resting a hand on the end of the hoe handle. Cowboys were nothing new, they rode through town, even visited the mercantile on a regular basis, but the horse this one sat upon deserved a second look. Big and glistening like a gold coin in the sun, the palomino was magnificent. The never-faraway longing in her heart sprang to life; however, this time it was quickly overshadowed by a unique fluttering in her stomach.

Molly pressed her free hand to her abdomen, held it there. Waited.

The movement didn't repeat itself and she went back to hoeing. It was too soon. At least she thought it was, and there was no one she could ask. No one to tell her what to expect, what to do. It was only here, when she took an hour after lunch to hoe the garden, that she could even let herself think about the baby.

That wasn't true. She thought about the little life inside her all the time, but it was only here, when she was alone, that she could pretend things were different. That being pregnant was something to behold and cherish.

Time was ticking by and soon everyone would know about the baby. They'd be telling her what to do, too, and what they thought. Especially of her. A harlot. An unwed mother. A woman like that.

Hoe in hand, Molly attacked the weeds, releasing frustration all the way to the end of the row.

It didn't help. Only made her sweat and brood over things more intently. Loathe herself.

Disgusted inside and out, she blew out a breath. If she lived forever, she'd never take another sip of Afton Smith's cherry wine. She'd never been so sick in her life and now she knew life could always get worse than what a person thought it was. If only she could have that day back. Things would be different, that was for sure. But she couldn't have that day back, and she had to find her backbone instead of her wishbone, figure out a way to live with what she'd done.

Her anger renewed itself, or maybe it had never left, she'd just forgotten about it for a moment. With vigor, she took after the weeds in the next row until a little beet got caught on the end of the hoe. Pausing, Molly took a moment to stretch the discomfort from her back before leaning down to stick the tiny bulb, stringy root down, back in the earth.

As much as she loathed herself for what had happened, she loved the little life growing inside her. If it was just her, she'd face down the entire town, not really caring what they thought, but more often than not she witnessed the residents' reactions to those they considered were beneath them, saw and felt it when people looked upon Ivy. They'd do that to her baby, too.

"Molly!"

Lifting her gaze, she waited for Karleen to shout the rest of what she had to say from the side of the store.

"Mr. Ratcliff needs your assistance!"

Molly waved a hand, signaling she'd heard, and then dug out the last two weeds trying to grow at the end of the row. She also carried the hoe to the barn before making her way toward the store. It was their livelihood, the mercantile her father had started back when there was nothing out here except a few farmers and some Indians—Ivy's tribe. Father's plan had been to start a horse ranch when they'd left Ohio all those years ago. It hadn't happened—a ranch—being a merchant had been more lucrative. The store was still profitable—barely—since the railroad opened a dry-goods store that was always well stocked. Their shipments were never delayed.

The weight on her shoulders was too heavy to shake off. Of course it was. There weren't just the worries of the store weighing her down. There was her sister, and her ward, little Ivy—a treasure for sure—the baby growing in her body, and a slew of other things she couldn't pull up right now. There was work to be done. Her hour of solitude was over.

As she walked along the pathway from the barn to the store, Molly couldn't help but glance down the road, in the direction the palomino had galloped. The days of saddling a horse and riding for hours with no real purpose other than pleasure were gone. Long gone. But they still called to her. Stronger than ever.

She increased the speed of her steps.

As old as some of the trees on her property, Mr. Ratcliff met her on the store's wide porch, rubbing his bushy mustache. Without a word of greeting and as pleasant as a hornet, he informed her, "I got an issue with those nails you sold me."

His lack of pleasantries didn't disturb her, she wasn't overly agreeable either. Hadn't been for some time. "Oh, what's wrong with them?"

"They're rusty."

If rusty nails were her only problem, the world would be a glorious place. Molly pressed her tongue against the back of her teeth, telling herself to stay calm. They needed every sale to make ends meet. "Did you leave them in the rain?" she asked, keeping her voice even.

Mr. Ratcliff hitched one thumb under a suspender strap while stomping his walking stick against the porch boards with his other hand. "I just bought them last week."

Staying calm didn't come easy, and deep breaths weren't cutting it any longer. "I know when you bought them. I asked if you left them outdoors, in the rain."

Little more than five feet tall, Mr. Ratcliff lifted his chin, covered with several shades of stiff gray whiskers, as if that made him taller than her. It didn't. So he stretched his neck. "Your papa would never have sold rusty nails."

"I didn't sell you rusty nails, Mr. Ratcliff. I'm positive they were just fine when you purchased them. However, once left outdoors, in the rain, nails will rust. Rather quickly."

"They're rusty, all right. Come take a look." He turned around, which took several steps considering he had to get both feet moving and his cane all at the same time.

Molly had no choice but to wait, and then followed behind his shuffling feet, all the way across the porch and into the store. Karleen was making herself look busy by rearranging the bolts of material on the table Mr. Ratcliff slowly made his way past and Ivy was dusting the set of shelves holding shoes—of which no one had bought a pair in over a year. Molly managed a tight grin for the child as she continued to follow the disgruntled customer—growing that way herself with each footfall—all the way to the far wall where on the counter sat a small rusted and dented can.

Once there, nerves thoroughly frayed, Molly skirted around to the backside of the high counter her father had built by hand, and plucked a wet and rusty nail from the pile in the bottom of the can.

"See?" Mr. Ratcliff said as if it was utterly unbelievable.

"I see the water in the bottom of the can," she pointed out.

"Now, listen here, missy. I know'd your pappy

when he first moved to this here county. You weren't no taller than a weed back then. Your sister still creeping on all fours. I helped put up that barn out back and even worked on this here storefront when the time came. Didn't use no rusty nails either. No sirree. When Niles Thorson sold a man nails, they were good ones." Along with several thumps of his stick, he loudly declared, "I want new nails. Ones that aren't rusty."

Several things were vying for the tip of Molly's tongue. She knew exactly when her family had moved here and was more than ready to tell Mr. Ratcliff exactly what she thought of his demand; however, someone else spoke first.

"What are you building with those nails?"

In no mood to be interrupted, Molly turned her glare toward the door. Spurs jingled as a tall man made a direct path toward the counter, but it was the gun belt hanging low on his hips that kept her silent. A Peacemaker, which should make her nervous since they weren't good for much except killing a man, but the gun didn't make her uncomfortable. It had her adding up receipts. So did the Stetson on his head. Both the pistol and the hat were things she'd like to stock, but couldn't. They were too expensive to sit on the shelves, therefore could only be sold by special order. Men buying Peacemakers and Stetsons didn't hang around town waiting for their order to come in. The railroad's dry-goods store kept them in stock, and made a hefty profit on each one they sold.

Mr. Ratcliff had shuffled around to look at the stranger, too, and the old man asked, "What you want to know that for?"

"Just curious."

The newcomer's voice was low and slow, subtle, and the gaze of his cobalt-blue eyes was steady, unwavering. Molly kept hers just as solid, even when their gazes snagged. He nodded toward her and then the can. She dropped the nail amongst the others and pushed the container toward the stranger as he arrived at the counter. Little intimidated her, and though she couldn't quite say this man unsettled her, he had a commanding way about him few probably ignored.

After thoughtful surveillance of the can and nails, the man asked, "You were seasoning these, were you?"

"Uh?" Mr. Ratcliff asked, easing his way over to peer into the can.

"Seasoning the nails." The stranger looked at her again. "May I?"

Molly had no idea what he was asking, but nodded nonetheless. Strangers weren't uncommon, not with three trains rolling through town most days, and when she saw the same man twice, she remembered. This was the cowboy who had ridden out of town on the palomino. A quick glance through the store, out the front window, proved it. The horse was tethered to the hitching post.

The cowboy pulled a handkerchief out of his back pocket, and started lifting the nails out of the can, drying them off one by one. "You wouldn't have a container of axle grease, would you?"

His question was directed toward Molly. Not completely convinced she should, but curious, she walked the length of the counter to where the hardware items were located and carried back a good-size tin of grease.

The stranger dipped a corner of his kerchief in the grease and started rubbing it over each nail. Turning those dark blue eyes toward Mr. Ratcliff, the cowboy said, "Smart man, Mr...."

Bobbing his head, the old man answered, "Ratcliff. Owen Ratcliff."

"Smart man, Mr. Ratcliff," the cowboy repeated. "Seasoning your nails like this. Now when you use them, they won't be as susceptible to rust."

Owen Ratcliff went from grinning to frowning in a flash. "Uh?"

Laying the last nail on the counter, the cowboy asked her, "Would you have a different container for Mr. Ratcliff's nails? Even a piece of paper to wrap them in would be fine."

Once again Molly followed his request, retrieving paper and a length of string. She was still curious, but also a touch intrigued, as was her sister, who'd inched closer. No one pleased Mr. Ratcliff. Leastwise she never had. Not even when she tried. Yet this cowboy, with his slow, even voice and even slower movements, had placated the man through and through.

The nails piled on top of the paper looked as good as the ones in the pail on the other side of the store. She'd never heard of seasoning nails, and suspected it was a ruse, but chose not to say anything. A sale was a sale and every return went against her bottom line.

With precise, dedicated movements, the cowboy wrapped the paper around the nails and secured it with the string. "There you are, Mr. Ratcliff. These nails will now be the strongest ones you've ever set a hammer to."

Mr. Ratcliff took the package, and Molly had to bite her lips together. A smile was trying to form—that hadn't happened for months, but the dumbfounded expression on Owen Ratcliff's face was something no one in town had ever seen. She'd swear to that.

Never speechless before now, the old man barely muttered a humph as he started his slow shuffle toward the door. Molly was still staring, half expecting Ratcliff to spin about and start spouting off before he reached the porch, when a quiet giggle drew her attention.

"I wouldn't have believed that if I hadn't seen it with my own eyes," Karleen whispered, walking around the counter to edge in beside Molly. Her sister, usually too engrossed in a book to notice anything going on around her, held one hand over the top of the counter. "Hello, I'm Karleen Thorson, and this is my sister Molly."

"Carter Buchanan," the cowboy replied evenly, shaking Karleen's hand.

"It's nice to meet you, Mr. Buchanan," Karleen continued with a bright smile. "I do believe you may have just performed a miracle. No one's ever silenced Mr. Ratcliff."

The cowboy, or Carter Buchanan—Molly had never heard of any Buchanans in the area, and couldn't help but wonder where he was from and what he was doing here—turned and eyed the doorway Mr. Ratcliff was shuffling through.

"He's probably just lonely. Doesn't have anything to fill his time, so he thinks up things to complain about." Turning back, he touched the brim of his hat. "It's nice to meet you, too, Miss Thorson." He then extended his hand toward her. "And you."

A shudder traveled down Molly's spine. "Maureen. Maureen Thorson," she answered, without shaking his hand. She would never, ever so much as touch another man.

"Wasn't that amazing, Molly?" Karleen asked. "I've never seen Mr. Ratcliff speechless. I really should go tell Mr. Franks. He'd want to write an article about it in the weekly post."

"No," Molly said, "you won't go tell Mr. Franks, you will finish unpacking the freight." Too young to know better, Karleen was too friendly with strangers, no matter how many times Molly cautioned her on it, and that had the past five months of irritation coming to a head. Searching for something, anything, she could control, Molly pointed toward the doorway that led to the living quarters. "Ivy, it's time for you to go finish your lessons."

Instant regret shimmied up her spine. Two big brown eyes and a quivering lip told her just how snippy she sounded. Softening her tone, for Ivy didn't deserve any wrath, Molly added, "I'll come see how you're doing in a few minutes."

"Come on, Ivy," Karleen said, walking around the counter while flashing Molly a quick shot of disdain. "Let's go see how far you've gotten in your reader." With another sharp glance, she added, "I'll finish unpacking the crates afterward."

Molly wanted to scream, mainly because

she knew her sister was right. The freight could wait, but Karleen didn't have the responsibilities she did, or the worries. And shouldn't. Karleen was only sixteen—she, on the other hand, was twenty-three. Plenty old enough for responsibilities. And to know better.

Drawing a deep breath, Molly told herself to count to ten. If she voiced her opinion right now she'd tell the stranger, greased or not, those nails weren't any stronger now than when they'd been sitting in rainwater, but Mr. Ratcliff, still shuffling across the porch, might hear, therefore she counted. She had counted to about five when the cowboy spoke.

"Why aren't they in school?"

Spinning, she leveled a dull gaze on the man. Still conscious of listeners, she kept her voice low as she pointed out the obvious. "Because Karleen graduated last year, and Ivy is an Indian."

His face was expressionless, but he might as well have been stomping one foot. A person full of antagonism sees it in another. "So? She's still a child. Still needs to learn."

"That's true," Molly said, wondering where the sudden urge to mollify him came from. For months she'd fought the town council, who refused to allow Ivy to attend school, but had gotten nowhere. She'd have been at this month's meeting, too, but fearful someone might notice her growing girth, she'd pretended to have forgotten what night the meeting had been held. "But Indian children are not allowed to attend Huron's public school."

"Why?"

She picked up the tin of axle grease and carried it back to the shelf. "I was told it's because the school is funded through the tax system and Indians don't pay taxes."

The cowboy—only cowboys wore guns and spurs—was leaning on the counter, watching her, which had her sucking in her stomach, though it was well covered with a dress two sizes too big and three underskirts, and all the sucking in the world wouldn't flatten it. His, however, was as flat as the counter. The tan shirt tucked into his black pants didn't have a single ripple.

The idea she'd noticed so much about him made her skin tighten. "Is there something you needed?"

He cocked a brow. "Actually, yes."

She thought about waiting it out, but didn't have the patience. "What?"

"One of those cinnamon rolls."

With a piece of paper, she picked up a roll from the plate on the corner of the counter and folded the edges around the pastry so he could carry it out the door. Not eat it here. The price was posted and he slid the correct change across the counter. Usually, no matter who it was, she'd thank a customer for their purchase, but not today. Not him.

"Could I speak to the owner?"

Molly walked to a crate sitting at the other end of the counter, started lifting things out of the sawdust. "You are," she said, experiencing the first bout of pride she'd felt in months.

"You?"

"My sister and I."

Carter held in his surprise. He hadn't overheard that while walking around town. Then again, besides the boy at the train depot, no one had mentioned the mercantile and he hadn't asked, knew he'd be stopping by and would learn all he needed to know. His plan had included getting a job here, at the mercantile, so he could watch the money flowing in and out, but he'd expected a man to own the establishment. Not a snooty woman, younger sister and little Indian girl—who, in his opinion, should be on the other side of town in the brick building with all the other kids. He didn't have a lot of tolerance for kids, but had even less for people mistreating them.

The woman, Maureen, she'd called herself, though the tiny splattering of freckles covering her cheeks made her look more like the name her sister had called her—Molly—paused while unloading the crate. Gave him another uppity stare.

"Did you have a complaint?" she asked.

He had plenty of complaints, but voicing them wouldn't help his case, so he pulled up a grin. "Nope. Just wanted to say your reputation precedes you."

Her glare turned omniscient, and said she didn't like what she thought he knew. Which meant he had more to learn. Picking up the pastry, he nodded. "Your cinnamon rolls. I heard they're the best around."

She didn't believe that any more than he did. Interesting. He tipped the brim of his hat with one hand. "Ma'am."

He was out the door, but heard her growl nonetheless. That was one ornery woman, and irritating her had a smile wanting to crack his lips. He didn't let it. Took a bite of the cinnamon roll instead, and then leaned one elbow on his saddle. The pastry was tasty, might be the best he'd ever had, and he ate it right there, watching the front door of that mercantile, coming up with a new plan.

When the roll was gone, he folded the paper and stuffed it in his saddlebag—never know when it might come in handy—and then he patted Sampson's neck while untying the reins from the post. "Time to visit Ted Wilcox. We need more information before we set our plan in place, boy. Then I'll get you some oats." Keeping his voice low while conversing with the horse—as he often did on cases—he added, "Molly Thorson is hiding a secret as big as you, and my gut says money is involved. Stolen money."

Chapter Two

Ted Wilcox was at the train depot in his office on the second floor, and upon seeing him, the man nodded toward the steward sitting behind a desk in the outer room Carter had entered moments ago.

"J.T.," Wilcox said, "go reserve a room at the hotel. There's a guest on the next train that will be expecting it. Put it in the railroad's name."

"Yes, sir," answered J.T., who was little more than a boy with round glasses and long brown hair, who just might be afraid of his own shadow.

Carter returned the young man's nod, knowing Wilcox was reserving a room for him but didn't want anyone to know that. He waited until the assistant was gone before crossing the room to shake the railroad man's hand.

Average height and stocky, Wilcox displayed

an attitude that said he expected to be listened to. "Mr. Buchanan, I presume?"

"Carter," he answered.

"Ted," the man offered in return. "Let's step into my office."

Carter followed through the thick wooden door. If the railroad had spent as much money on their passenger cars as they had this man's office, they'd have a lot more happy travelers. Then again, maybe folks out here weren't used to the plush cars the trains back east had. He hadn't heard many complaints on his trip, but no one heard much over that brood of redheaded kids.

"The room I sent J.T. to reserve is for you," Wilcox said as he walked around his big mahogany desk. "I was going to see to it during lunch, but since you hadn't stopped in, I wondered if you'd been on the train."

Carter questioned holding his explanation. This was the one thing he didn't like about being a Pinkerton man. It was expected he should instantly trust his connections when on assignment, but he liked getting to know people first. In this instance, there wasn't time. He needed to learn as much as possible, fast, to determine how—besides working there—he could watch the coming and going at the mercantile. Therefore, he'd have to give a little to get a little. "I wanted to get a feel for the town first."

"Good idea," Wilcox said, gesturing to a chair.

Once Carter sat, the man pulled open a drawer and handed a bill over the top of the desk.

"This is it, the only bill that's surfaced," the man said. "The serial numbers match those the mint confirmed were in the shipment stolen last year."

A five. Crisp and new. Not so much as a corner bent. The numbers did match. Carter had memorized them. "In May?" he asked, verifying that's when the bill was discovered.

"Yes. J.T. is who got it. He'd bought some things at the mercantile. The poor lad has a crush on the youngest Thorson girl, they went to school together. He showed it to me because he'd never seen a bill so new. I paid him ten dollars for it."

Carter let a lifted brow express his thoughts.

Wilcox grinned. "The railroad paid him ten dollars for it. I recognized the serial numbers right away." He took the bill Carter passed back across the desk and replaced it in the drawer. "J.T. thinks I just like new bills, so he's on the lookout for more." The man propped his elbows on his desk and laced his fingers together. "Nobody knows about the robbery, and the C&NW wants to keep it that way. Having people believe we lost that kind of money would damage our reputation. That wasn't a passenger train. Not a single person boarded after it left Chicago, and no one got off until it arrived here. But the loss was noted in Nebraska."

None of that was new information. Carter had read the inside report, knew how the railroad had covered the loss and tried to solve the inside caper themselves, without any luck, and now the owner wanted it completely investigated and resolved. Carter had also memorized the manifesto of passengers. Railroad men and soldiers.

"The money had been in a locked box in a private car," Wilcox said. "The box was still there, just empty, and one man couldn't have carried that amount out without being noticed, not with a hundred pockets. He'd have needed a carrying bag of some sort, and every man on that train was searched."

None of this was new, and that's what Carter needed, new information. "How'd the Thorson sisters end up owning the mercantile?"

"You've been there?"

He tipped his hat back a bit. "Had a cinnamon roll for lunch."

"That's what keeps people coming in their doors. The older sister came up with that idea."

The way Wilcox leaned back in his chair and folded his arms said he wasn't impressed. Carter waited, knew the man would say more.

"The Chicago and Northwestern Rail needs to own this town, Mr. Buchanan—Carter. We opened a dry-goods store three years ago, and little more than those cinnamon rolls keep people from buying everything they need from us instead of those sisters."

"A little competition makes good business." Normally he wouldn't have voiced his opinion, but the situation merited it.

"Usually," the other man answered, "but laying new lines is costly. What the railroad makes here is invested in more rails heading in all directions. Once the tracks are all constructed and C&NW trains are flowing, competition will be welcomed. Until then, it's up to me, and now you, to see that every dollar spent in Huron flows through the railroad's coffers."

That wasn't new either. Mining towns were the same. The trouble was greed. By the time the tracks were all laid, the railroad would have another reason why they needed to own everything. They always wanted more. And the man was wrong. It wasn't up to Carter to see people spent their money with the railroad. He was a Pinkerton man. Solving a crime was his job.

"We almost had it," Wilcox said. "Thorson's Mercantile. The old man had never wanted a store, he was set on ranching. Raising horses for the army. Story is he found more money was to be made in selling supplies instead. We have the army's business now, and thought after the man and his wife died the girls would close up shop. Instead they started selling those cinnamon rolls, and have kept a steady business going ever since. 'Course, we haven't hit them too hard—town folks like those girls, feel sorry for them, and we need to act accordingly. Keep it all undercover. You know how that is."

Carter refrained from commenting. He did know how it was, but that wasn't why he kept quiet. Molly Thorson was. He didn't want to like anything about her. That snooty attitude of hers had set a frost deep in his bones, but, being an honest man, he had to admit he held a touch of respect for her. She had backbone, and finding a way to keep her doors open—fighting against the railroad—took pure gumption.

She was scared, too. He'd seen it in her eyes when he mentioned her reputation. Stolen money was a reputation killer.

All in all, every instinct Carter had told him he had to revert to his original plan. Get a job at the mercantile.

A knock sounded and Wilcox rose and walked across the room to crack open the door.

"I'm sorry, Mr. Wilcox, but the hotel is full up. Seems that woman with a passel of kids that got off the 11:10 is Mick Wagner's mail-order bride."

An involuntary shiver raced over Carter's shoulders.

"Seems it took up the hotel's last three rooms just to find enough sleeping room for all of them. They'll be there for a couple days, too. Walt Smith went to tell Mick she's—or they've—arrived, but it'll take him three days to ride out there and back."

"Thanks, J.T.," Wilcox said, closing the door. When he turned, he shrugged.

"How many kids did that woman have?" Carter hadn't meant to say that aloud.

Wilcox laughed. "I couldn't count them all, not with the way they were running around like heathens." He shrugged again. "I didn't know Mick ordered a bride."

Carter's tongue stayed put, but sympathy did cross his mind. Had to. Any man had to feel sorry for another one getting in that position. A wife and a passel of kids. All at once.

"There is a boardinghouse on the east edge of town, but the widow Reins runs it, and she's as nosy as a coon."

"That's all right," Carter said. "I'll find a place to bed down for the night."

"What about tomorrow?"

"By then I'll have a job at the mercantile. It'll come with room and board."

Wilcox let out a cynical laugh. "Thorson's Mercantile?"

Carter didn't nod, but did let a tiny grin emit.

"You Pinkerton men must be brave," Wilcox said. "Or crazy."

Carter held his opinion on that, too.

By noon the next day he was back at the mercantile, buying another one of those cinnamon rolls. Molly Thorson wasn't any more pleasant today than she'd been yesterday, but the rolls were just as good. Leastwise it smelled that way, he'd yet to buy and eat one.

"What do you want?" she demanded while glaring up at him from where she stood behind the counter unpacking another crate.

Nothing to do with you, he almost snapped in return. She looked about as friendly as a thunderstorm, and that was before taking in account her ugly gray dress. But a white apron covered up most of the dull color, and he had a job to do. "I'm working my way to Montana," he said.

Her snarled "So?" was quickly followed with "Oh, good grief."

He'd never heard that reaction to the territory. Yet Montana had nothing to do with her response.

"It's broken." She was growling again and holding up a fancy teacup. "Mrs. Rudolf ordered a set of six cups and saucers," she said, turning that nasty glare on him again. "My best sale all month, and one is broken. She's going to be furious. Her garden party is this weekend."

Her eyes were the palest blue he'd ever seen—
not even the sky held that shade—but it was how
she was blinking a massive set of eyelashes, as
if not wanting to cry, that made his throat get
thick. He hadn't thought of the orphanages from
his childhood in years, yet he was right back
there. Seeing the faces of all those unwanted little
souls. "You still have five," Carter said.

"What good will that do?"

He didn't know. It had been all he could think
to say. She'd gone from snippy to sappy as fast
as an alley man flips a coin. That thought—alley
men, thieves really—sent his mind in another
direction.

That's how he'd become a Pinkerton agent.
Allan Pinkerton himself had learned that Carter
had gained access to the den of several alley
thieves, and had hired him as an inside infor-
mant. It had been shortly after he'd arrived in
Chicago, still just a kid really, and he'd thought
joining those thieves might be his only way of
making money. He had a lot to thank Allan for.
Whether the man knew it or not, he'd nipped
Carter's thieving days in the bud. Changed his
whole outlook. If not for Allan, Carter might
have been walking on the other side of the law,
and it was best he never forgot that.

Carter spun on one heel, but hadn't made it
more than a yard away from the counter when a

gasp had him turning around. Those faded blue eyes were locked on the doorway and he twisted slowly, curling one hand around the handle of his gun, not sure what he'd see.

The tension gripping his spine dissolved. It was nothing more than a woman, one who might outweigh Sampson, but a woman no less. He let his gaze wander back to Molly Thorson, where it stuck. She'd gone pale and the hand over her mouth had him wondering if she was going to chuck her lunch all over that crate of dishes. He'd seen that look back at the orphanages, too, after kids had eaten some of the slop forced on them.

Growing whiter than her apron, she whirled around and shot through the open doorway the sister and the little Indian girl had used yesterday. He waited a moment, but when no one re-appeared, Carter glanced back toward the open doorway. The big woman was about to barrel over the threshold and instinct told him this was Mrs. Rudolf, the owner of a broken cup.

A Pinkerton man was an actor, could hop from one character to the next just by changing his hat. Carter did that—removed his hat and his gun belt, put them both on a shelf on the back-side of the counter and was gingerly setting pink-and-gold cups upon matching saucers when the woman arrived, eyeing him critically over the rim of her round glasses.

"Good afternoon, Mrs. Rudolf," he said with all the pleasantry of a store clerk.

Her frown left indents on her face the size of those he'd seen in the dried-out ground down in Arizona.

"Carter Buchanan." He gave a nod over one shoulder. "I'm helping out the Thorson sisters." Drawing the woman's attention to the cups, he continued, "Got some mighty fancy cups here."

The deep wrinkles on her forehead softened as she picked up a cup. "Oh, my, they are absolutely beautiful, aren't they?"

"Yes, they are. I've never seen anything like them." He wasn't lying. There'd never been a reason for him to take much interest in teacups. Wouldn't be now if one of the Thorson sisters would step through that doorway.

"I was getting worried they wouldn't arrive in time for my party," Mrs. Rudolf said, still gazing at the cup as if it was gold instead of just painted that way. "They were supposed to be in last week, you know."

No, he didn't know that, but he could imagine how displeased this woman was going to be when she learned one of her treasured cups was broken. Therefore he said, "I know. Miss Thorson is very upset over that, and she's even more disturbed by how carelessly her order was handled. Tore off for the back room just moments ago." Though he doubted it, he added, "Probably to pen her correspondence."

"What correspondence?"

"To the freight company, over the shoddy way they treat merchandise. The way they treated you." He refrained from specifically naming the railroad, having to balance things as carefully as a beam scale weighing gold dust.

"Me?"

"Yes, ma'am," he said, remaining in character. "I don't see the cause to get so riled up, but you know Molly." The name slipped off his tongue as if he'd been saying it for years. Maybe he had—he'd worked with a lot of people, and remembering every name would be impossible.

Mrs. Rudolf nodded. "Yes, I do." Leaning closer, she whispered, "She never used to be this way. It's only been recently."

Doubt was settling hard again, but he agreed with a nod. "I'm sure it's things like this. Too many mishaps wear a person down."

"Things like what?"

"I know someone as reasonable as you would never let anything this silly upset them." He paused then, as if taken aback for a moment. "You are a reasonable woman, aren't you, Mrs. Rudolf?"

"Of course I am."

Her insistence proved she wasn't, but he'd already figured that out, so he smiled. "I thought so." Going a step further, which he did only when the situation called for it, Carter gave her a touch of flattery. "Anyone with eyes as tender as yours is very reasonable."

It worked. Her weathered cheeks turned as pink as the roses painted on her cups.

"I knew one broken cup wouldn't disrupt your garden party," he said brightly.

"Broken cup!"

The women around here sure did anger quickly, not so unlike everywhere else in the world. Keeping his tone even, and adding a sorrowful look, he said, "Yes, ma'am. That's why Molly is so flustered. Over the way the freight company treated you." He patted the old woman's hand. "And I'm glad you don't blame her. I'm sure your guests will understand. Besides, it's only one. You won't have more than four guests, will you?" A woman with this disposition couldn't have many friends. Then again, birds of a feather flock together.

"Well, no, there'll just be the four of us. Wives of the town council." Her tone implied the importance of that. Or at least she thought it was significant.

"Good." He'd been wrapping the cups and saucers in paper from the shelf next to his hat and gun belt, and now bent to pick up a small crate he assumed was for this purpose. "You'll even have an extra to spare, then." After piling the dishes in the box, Carter picked up the broken cup. "I'll keep this one, to prove it's damaged, but feel free to explain to the women what happened and how Molly is assuring you'll receive the sixth one as soon as possible." Before Mrs. Rudolf could answer—it was obvious she was thinking through everything he'd just said—he glanced around, continued, "Now, where did I see that bill?"

Her silence said she was still contemplating things, so he ran a hand through his hair as if growing frustrated. "I know I saw it. I don't want to upset Molly more by—"

"I remember how much it was," the woman said, digging in her little lace-covered wrist bag.

"Thank you," he said, exaggerating his supposed relief. "You certainly are a reasonable woman, Mrs. Rudolf, and for that, take ten percent off what you owe." Eyeing her pointedly, he added, "You can pay the balance when your sixth cup arrives."

The bills she laid on the counter were old and wrinkled, but he still took a moment to glance at the serial numbers. That was, after all, why he was here. They weren't close to the stolen ones, and after he'd set the money next to the big engraved box he assumed was the cash drawer, he picked up the crate of dishes. "I'll carry these out to the porch for you. I'd hate to see you stumble on that step and break another cup. That would ruin your party."

She let out a tiny giggle as he followed her to the door. "I dare say it might." When he handed over the box after she'd stepped down, Mrs. Rudolf asked, "What was your name again? I can't remember."

"Carter Buchanan, ma'am. And it was a pleasure doing business with you."

"You, too, Mr. Buchanan. Do tell Molly I said hello, and there's no rush in getting that settled with the freight company." Waddling along, she glanced over her shoulder. "I am a reasonable woman, and do understand how these things happen."

Carter held his opinion on that, but spun back toward the doorway when someone asked, "Who are you?"

He barely noted the sister before glancing over her shoulder. Molly was the one he'd expected to see, but there wasn't any sign of her. He'd imagined her charging through the doorway like a freight train the entire time he'd been dealing with Mrs. Rudolf and her silly broken cup.

"What, Carter Buchanan, are you doing in Huron?"

He shifted his stance at the skepticism in the

girl's voice. If Karleen was sixteen, he'd guess Molly, or Maureen, to be twenty or so. Young still, but more defined by life. Their names sounded a bit Irish to him, not that it made any difference. Neither of them looked Irish. Both of the Thorson sisters had blond hair tucked neatly into buns on the backs of their heads. Molly's—Maureen's—had hints of brown in it, making her pale blue eyes more prominent. Karleen had blue eyes too, they just weren't as unique.

Carter shut his mind off then, or attempted to. Nothing good came when a man started thinking too much about a woman. He'd seen that before. If a fella wasn't careful, next thing he knew he'd have a passel of kids as big as that woman's on the train—like that poor sap that had ordered her as a bride. An event that horrendous would take a while before it quit churning about in the back of his head. How a man could want a woman so badly he'd order one was unbelievable. Even to him, and he'd seen a lot of unbelievable things in his life.

"I was in the storeroom," Karleen said, her gaze going to Mrs. Rudolf waddling down the road. "You could have gotten hit with that broken cup."

He'd agree to that, but said, "I'm working my way up to Montana."

"Montana?"

"Yep, gonna start a ranch up in those parts." He flipped roles again, pulling up his cowboy jargon and nodding to his horse still tethered to the post. "Sampson and I are looking for a bit of work in these parts, to earn enough money for the next leg of our trip. I was thinking of asking your sister if you folks needed a hired hand."

The girl planted both hands on her hips, as if that made her appear older, and gave him a good solid once-over. "Have you ever worked in a store before?"

"Sure have. I've done most everything at one time or another." He had even built coffins over in Minnesota while undercover one time, just to make sure they were burying the right man. This job looked to be about as pleasurable.

"Actually, Mr. Buchanan, we do need help around here, and considering the way you took care of both Mr. Ratcliff and Mrs. Rudolf, it would behoove me to hire you."

Behoove. That was a good word. Couldn't say it had ever come up in conversation before. He knew it though, from his dictionary. The well-worn book had been his constant companion for years—his only true education. A man learned a lot looking up words, thinking about how they related to people and places.

"The barn needs attention—is that something you could see to, as well?"

"Yes, miss, I could. But wouldn't your sister have to be the one to hire me?" He wanted the job, all right, needed to examine every bill that came through, but being fired as soon as he was hired wouldn't give him the chance and the older sister was surely the one in charge.

"We are equal owners in the store. I can hire as easily as she can." Karleen Thorson stepped onto the porch then and lowered her voice, "Molly wasn't always as ornery as she is right now. She's only been that way for the past few months. I think it's the dresses she keeps sewing for herself. They're two sizes too big and as unflattering as Otis Zimney's milk cow."

Carter wouldn't admit he'd noticed the drab dress. Nor would he admit he'd noticed Molly's face. Other than those few freckles, her complexion was unmarred and the graceful arch of her cheeks left her looking about as delicate as Mrs. Rudolf's china cups.

There he was, thinking too much again. He always thought about his cases, thoroughly, deeply, but usually not the people involved in them.

"If you tell her I compared her to a cow, I'll fire you," Karleen whispered.

Carter let out a chuckle, and found himself wishing the older sister was as pleasant to be around as the younger one. That single notion had him picturing the money, making it front and

center in his mind. He needed more clues. That's
what the problem was. Didn't have enough solid
evidence to set in and ponder all the intricacies
of the case. Once that happened he'd quit thinking so much about Molly Thorson.

"There's a small cabin out back," Karleen said.
"It has a bed and stove. Help has lived in it a
time or two, but for the past couple years Ivy's
just used it as a playhouse. You can stay there if
you want. That'll save you even more money for
your ranch in Montana."

"I'd be obliged," he said. "You're sure your
sister won't mind?" Carter had his reservations,
but needed to get his foot in the door.

"Oh, she'll mind. She minds everything
lately."

There was no doubt she'd mind. He didn't
need more evidence in that part.

"But," the girl said a bit on the sly side, "if we
team up, she won't have a choice. We need help,
Mr. Buchanan, have for some time, but Molly's
too stubborn to admit it."

Carter's insides churned. Undercover was one
thing. Deceit another. He understood that and
balanced it out as needed. There was no reason for this job to be different, but deep down,
this time it struck a chord. He had to ignore it,
that's all there was to it. Completing his assign-

ment would be impossible without working at the mercantile.

"Why don't you get settled?" Karleen wiped her hands on her yellow skirt, nodding toward the road. "We have another customer coming, but Pastor Jenkins is always pleasant. He's a bachelor, like yourself, and several women in town think he's rather handsome, except Molly. She doesn't like men with dark hair." Smiling, the girl then said, "There're empty stalls in the barn for your horse."

Molly wanted to rush out the door, proclaim there weren't any empty stalls and that Carter Buchanan could not work here, but Pastor Jenkins was almost on the porch, and she couldn't endure his questioning looks. Or his persistence. Which was why she'd told Karleen she didn't like men with dark hair—just to stop her sister's questions. The pastor had suggested he'd like to call upon Molly, and she'd told him no, even before Robbie had returned to town. Before…

It happened again. The fluttering in her stomach. Strong enough to capture her full attention. Molly inched her way back into the living quarters while she waited this time. Wondering if she truly had felt something. She hadn't been ill for several weeks, and was still shaky at how it had suddenly come on, which had left her with no choice but to flee. Holding it in hadn't been an option. By the time she'd returned to the store, Carter Buchanan had been behind the counter, placating Mrs. Rudolf, even making the woman blush. That was as uncommon as Mr. Ratcliff's silence.

Carter Buchanan was good at what he did. Telling lies, making people believe them. Like all men.

Karleen passed through the doorway just then. "Oh, there you are. Pastor Jenkins is here for his daily roll. I told him you were keeping one warm for him."

Like a horse tied up to a post too long, Molly snapped against the confines, the invisible ones that kept her tied to the store, to her life. "I'm not keeping one warm for him, and you had no right to offer that man a job."

Her sister didn't so much as glance her way as she walked to the stove and took the pan of rolls out of the warming oven, but she did say, "It doesn't hurt to be kind to people. You used to tell me that all the time."

That was true. At one time Molly had felt that way, even lived that way, but not anymore. "We're attempting to run a business, Karleen, not make friends."

Cutting the rolls apart, Karleen sighed heavily. "That's what I'm trying to do, Molly, run a business. Why aren't you?"

"Why aren't I?" she huffed in return. "That's all I have been doing. Without much help, I might add."

Karleen had the most expressive eyes, and right now they said Molly's words had hurt. Painfully so.

Molly cursed her temper that simmered right below, boiling continuously. Karleen was young, had so much to learn, but did do her fair share. "Go give Pastor Jenkins his roll," Molly said, but that truly was all the comfort she could offer her sister. "Then go tell that cowboy you changed your mind. That you can't hire him."

"But I *can* hire him, and I did."

Her moment of mercy vanished. "No, you can't."

"Yes, I can."

Holding her breath, for it was too hot to be released, Molly pointed out, "You are only sixteen, too young to know who to hire and who not to." She wanted to add who to trust, but that held too much ridicule coming from her.

"You said when I graduated we'd become equal partners. That happened this spring. I work as hard as you do in this store. I did even while I was still in school." Karleen could be as feisty as their mother when riled, and was so now. Without taking a breath, she continued, "I'm tired of being treated like a child. I deserve more respect than that. I've earned it."

As much as it infuriated her, Molly had to admit a portion of that was true. They'd never have kept the doors open as long as they had if it wasn't.

"Now," Karleen said, putting the pan, minus one roll, back in the warming oven above the stove. "You know as well as I do we need the help around here. The barn is a disaster, the fence line is down again, the storeroom has a leaky roof and there's that lovely hornets' nest on the backside of the outhouse." Spinning around, she finished her rant with, "If you want to go fix those things yourself, go fire Carter."

All her sister said was true, but one thing snagged at Molly's ire more than the others. "His name is Mr. Buchanan. You don't know him well enough to call him by his first name."

Karleen didn't answer, simply stared at her with a somewhat amazed expression as she crossed the room, roll in hand.

"I will fire him," Molly declared. It was beneath her to spat with her younger sister, but Karleen had challenged her, not so unlike when they were younger.

"Fine," her sister replied. "Have fun with the hornets, too. Which shouldn't be too hard. You're about as pleasant to be around as they are."

Molly was still conjuring up a response when Karleen paused in the archway leading to the hall. "Just remember, if it wasn't for *Carter*—" her sister said the man's name with great emphasis "—we'd have lost Mrs. Rudolf's sale this morning. With the mood you're in, you'd have smashed every cup. And how would that have affected our profits?"

Nose in the air, Karleen marched down the hall, and the way she greeted the pastor, with honey-laced cheerfulness, provoked every last nerve Molly had. She'd fire Carter Buchanan all right, and she'd paddle Karleen's behind, just as their father used to do.

Some of her steam dissolved. Papa had never paddled any of his children, and Molly wouldn't either. Not because she didn't want to, but because deep down, she knew Karleen was right. Not in hiring Carter—Mr. Buchanan—he still had to go, but in everything else, her sister had hit the nail on the head. Rusty or greased. All those things did need to be seen to, and Karleen was an equal partner. As would Ivy be someday.

She might only be sixteen, soon to be seventeen, but Karleen had the head of a merchant. Papa always said that. He'd said Molly was the worker bee, his way of complimenting her, too. She had been a worker bee and didn't mind it in the least. In those days, when her parents were alive, she'd completed any chore requested because afterward she'd been free to do as she'd pleased. Ride. All afternoon at times.

Karleen, on the other hand, never rode. She'd rather sit in the corner reading a book. That's how she knew how to handle customers, from watching their father. Though back then, all Molly had noticed was how her sister batted her big blue eyes at people. That's what her sister still did. Something Molly insisted had to stop. At sixteen, Karleen didn't know the consequences of it.

There was a dangerous ledge between being a girl and becoming a woman, and Molly had to make sure Karleen didn't fall off it. Not the way she had.

Right now, on the edge of that cliff was Carter Buchanan, and the man was going down.

Chapter Three

Carter got Sampson settled first, and the horse was grateful, nickering his thanks before trotting out the back door of the barn. It was sad, a barn of this size almost empty. Besides a couple of milk cows grazing, there was a donkey and a few horses near the far side of the fenced-in area. Carter waited, making sure Sampson would get along with the other animals. After some head tossing and grunting, all seemed fine, so he picked his belongings off the floor—that was in desperate need of some attention, as was the fence out back—and set out to find the cabin.

Exploring as he walked, he noted the broken door on the chicken coop and an almost empty woodshed. Fall would be here soon, then winter. That shed should be full. Seeing such things neglected irked him. When you grow up with nothing, you tend to notice how some folks don't take care of what they have. Not everyone, but enough that he'd become conscious of appreciating what he had. Right now, it was mainly his bank account, because that's what would get him to his final goal. Once there, he'd be set. Live out his life in a simple fashion that didn't matter to anyone but him.

The cabin was set back a ways from the other buildings, a little sod shack, but it had a wooden door and real windows. Besides the bed and small stove, there was a child-size table, complete with little dishes and a couple of dolls sitting in pint-size chairs.

He left it be as he set his saddlebags and other items on the bed and then stretched his arms overhead. Sleeping in a real bed would be refreshing after sitting on the train all the way from Chicago. He could have purchased a sleeping berth, but a cowboy working his way to Montana wouldn't have done that, so he hadn't either.

"Don't get too comfortable. You're not staying."

He didn't have to turn around to know the older sister had found him. Snippy really did get on his nerves.

"Here's your hat and your gun belt. Leave."

He turned, took the items she held. After putting on the hat, he settled the belt around his hips. There'd probably be no use for it, but just the same, he secured the metal buckle and tied the strap to his thigh.

"Did you hear me?" she asked.

It took a lot to get a reaction out of him, but Molly Thorson made ire inch up his back like a slow and steady caterpillar climbing a branch. "The people on the train heard you," he said. "The one that left an hour ago."

She opened her mouth, but then as if she'd forgotten what she wanted to say, she snapped it shut. Her eyes, however, could have fired bullets faster than his pistol.

Finding the slightest bit of humor in how easy it was to get a reaction out of her, he said, "Your sister hired me."

Her cheeks were bright red now, or maybe they already had been, and she planted both hands on her hips. Trying to appear as wide and formidable as a woman the size of Mrs. Rudolf, she informed him, "Karleen had no right to hire you without consulting me first."

The sister had been right, Molly's dress was too big, not even the long white apron hid that fact, and the dull drab color was unflattering. How she chose to dress, or look, made little difference in the scheme of things. Staying here did, and he wasn't about to leave. "Then you probably need to go talk to her."

"I have spoken with her."

"And?"

Her face turned redder. Even her neck, where the dress was tightly buttoned, took on the hue.

Having Karleen on his side, though she was younger and he had to admit shouldn't have the authority to hire anyone, looked as if it might be enough. "Since she was the one to hire me," he said, "I'll leave when she fires me."

"You will leave now."

She reminded him of a snake, all coiled up and hissing, and full of bad attitude. "You don't have a very good disposition, do you, Miss Thorson?" Steam was practically coming out of her ears, and he couldn't help but add to it. "Molly."

Molly didn't know if she'd ever been so enraged in her life. Every inch of her being was furious; even the hair on her head felt as though it could snap in two at any moment. She had enough to deal with, but having Karleen all of a sudden take an interest in a man—one as appalling as him—was the last straw. He'd break Karleen's heart into so many pieces it would never be whole again.

"You know, if you were a bit more like your sister, more on the pleasant side, you might just have a few more customers," Carter Buchanan said in that slow, drawling way.

"You stay away from my sister," Molly seethed.

The somewhat startled expression on his face took her slightly aback. It was gone, the look of surprise, when she glanced up again, making her wonder if she'd imagined it.

"Your sister, Miss Thorson, is a girl. As are you. And I have no interest in girls. I am interested in mending your fence, cleaning your barn and filling your woodshed, along with a few other chores, including helping out with irate customers, but only because I want to earn enough money to make it to Montana before the snow flies."

His little ploy may have worked on Mrs. Rudolf and Karleen, even Owen Ratcliff, but it wouldn't work on her. She couldn't be placated. There was too much ire inside her for that, even as she imagined all those chores being completed before the snow flies, as he'd put it. Something else would arrive along with the snow, and she'd been more focused on that lately than becoming prepared for winter. Unable to find fault in what he'd said—other than her being a girl—she went back to his earlier statement.

"I have plenty of customers, Mr. Buchanan."

"You won't if you keep up that attitude much longer," he said. "Most people don't like temper tantrums."

Something did snap, and unable to think beyond the fury it sent rolling inside her, Molly screamed, "Get out!"

His expression never changed as he kept looking at her, calmly, thoughtfully.

A bit of embarrassment overcame her and oddly, slowly, some of her anger eased. Some. She was still fuming. "I know you heard me, Mr. Buchanan." She pointed to the open doorway. "Leave."

He plopped onto the edge of the bed, crossed his arms not so unlike a stubborn child. "Make me."

"What?" She'd heard him, just couldn't believe a grown man would act so.

"Make me."

If he wasn't twice her size she'd drag him out the door. Since that wouldn't work, Molly searched the room for something to throw at him. There wasn't much. Just Ivy's toys.

"I suspect Ivy would be upset if you broke her dishes," he drawled. "Mrs. Rudolf was certainly displeased by her broken teacup."

"Which was none of your business."

"I know. But you'd scattered for the high country."

He'd have to bring that up, wouldn't he? For a moment she'd imagined he was her biggest problem. Her only problem. Wishful thinking. A unique tenderness had welled up inside her, washing away a good portion of her anger. That happened frequently, as if the baby was saying she wasn't alone in all this. At times, that made her teary-eyed, and now happened to be one of those times. She'd sneaked a peek at a medical book on the store shelf, read how pregnancy altered a woman's emotions and found it overly tiresome. As was the fact the book had sold before she'd had a chance to read more. It didn't help that as of yet she hadn't found an excuse to order another one, either.

"I didn't scatter for the high country," she said. "If you haven't noticed, there is no high country around here."

"I noticed."

She took another drawing breath, sensing the little life inside her was calm and well. "The broken cup just upset me," she said, though there was no reason to explain her behavior to this man.

"You shouldn't let that happen."

She shouldn't have let a lot of things happen. "We can't always control everything," she muttered.

"We can the important ones," he said, "if we try hard enough."

It was apparent he was attempting to manipulate her with that gentle tone as easily as he had Mr. Ratcliff and Mrs. Rudolf. It was useless. She wouldn't ever be influenced by another man. Yet, she wasn't nearly as riled as she had been. "Don't unpack your bags, Mr. Buchanan. You are not staying."

With that, Molly spun around and walked out the door. There, in the warm summer sun, she took several deep breaths, though she really didn't need them. How did he do that? He'd not only calmed two of her most irritable customers, he'd calmed her, and her baby.

A noise behind her set her in action, marching forward. To where, she had no idea. Karleen was still assisting Pastor Jenkins. If anyone in town were to pick up on her sin before it was revealed, it would be Caleb Jenkins. He had a way of looking at her that left her feeling as if she'd committed murder. Perhaps he knew she'd considered it. She'd thought about shooting Robbie Fredrickson if she ever saw him again. She wouldn't, of course—she hoped she never saw Robbie again. If he ever learned about the baby, Lord knows what would happen.

She had enough worries without dredging that one up, and she'd just have to wait until Pastor Jenkins left. Then she'd tell Karleen to get rid of Carter Buchanan, and this time she'd make her sister listen.

Right now, she'd find Ivy. She hadn't spent enough time with her lately, and her littlest sister always raised her spirits. The girl had gathered her schoolwork and skedaddled upstairs earlier. When Molly had run through the kitchen, heading for the outhouse.

Guilt, frustration and all the other things that lived inside Molly lately had her throat burning. She just couldn't do anything right. Little Ivy had only been a toddler when she'd been left at the mercantile. Terribly ill, it had taken the entire family, and Dr. Henderson, to keep the child's heated skin cooled, and to dribble fluids into her tiny mouth around the clock for several days.

Ivy had survived, and had been a part of their family ever since. Almost her little sister and almost her daughter—at least since their parents had died—Ivy was as near and dear to her heart as Karleen. Molly often wondered—especially lately—about Ivy's mother. Years ago she'd concluded the woman must have died, and believed it more strongly now. No woman would give up her child. A little life that had formed and grown inside her. It was too precious. Though she had yet to meet her child, she already cherished him or her. The little fluttering she'd experienced the past few days was fascinating and something she wished she could share with someone. Tell them how tender and miraculous it felt.

Molly entered the house and climbed the stairs. A single brave had come to the mercantile the spring after Ivy had joined their family, and though their father never voiced what had been said between him and the Indian, he had told the family that Ivy would continue to live with them, forever. Karleen—her mind always full of the stories she read—had several theories on what had transpired, but when asked, Father would simply say it didn't matter how or why, Ivy was there, she just was. Molly agreed with that, still did. Other than the school issue, most of the town had accepted Ivy, too.

If only things were that simple now.

Molly found Ivy in her bedroom, sitting on the floor and practicing her letters on the slate balanced on her lap.

"I can help Karleen in the store if you need to work in your garden," the child said, looking up with a touch of worry in her generous brown eyes.

Molly sat down on the floor and looped an arm around the tiny shoulders. "Maybe later," she said. "Thank you for offering."

Ivy nodded and then drew a perfect lowercase *e*. Molly couldn't help but recall how Carter Buchanan had said Ivy was a child and deserved to learn. She agreed, and once again wished things were different. If her father had still been alive, Ivy would be in school. He would have seen to it. Molly had tried, but she just didn't have the persuasive way her father had. She was more like her mother in that sense. Not necessarily by choice. She'd like to be more domineering, but that wasn't how she was raised. It wasn't until after her parents died that she'd had to learn to make decisions—was still learning in some instances—and how to live with them.

Molly picked up the book near Ivy's knee. "Could you read to me for a few minutes? Karleen's minding the store and I'd love to sit up here with you for a bit."

When Ivy smiled as she did right then, it made the entire world brighter. Molly tried to swallow the lump in her throat—the one that told her life was far from awful—and then leaned over to plant a tiny kiss in the center of the part that separated Ivy's long black hair into two braids.

"I believe you're ready for a new reader," Molly said a short time later as the child closed the book. "You've mastered this one without a single mistake. I believe Karleen ordered a few extras. They're on a shelf downstairs."

"Karleen says books are the most wonderful thing on earth," Ivy said. "And that someday I can borrow hers."

"I have no doubt you will soon be borrowing Karleen's books," Molly answered, withholding the rest of her opinion. She enjoyed reading, always had, and could think of one particular

night she should have sat down with a book, but
she'd been too shocked that night to see Robbie. "Have you finished your other lessons?" she
asked, though her mind had slipped again, and
she was now thinking of Carter. He'd said he
wasn't interested in Karleen, but Karleen might
be interested in him, and men were fickle.

"Yes."

"Well, then." Molly stood and helped Ivy put
the book and slate on the table in the corner.
"Would you like to pick some beans?" She and
Karleen could teach Ivy many things, but there
was no one for the child to play with during the
long hours the store was open, and Molly knew
that was as important for a child as books. "Just
enough for supper, then you can have a tea party
with your dolls."

Ivy agreed as they left the bedroom hand in
hand. The soddy was Ivy's playhouse, one more
reason Carter Buchanan had to leave. There was
no room for him here.

It appeared nothing was on Molly's side all
afternoon—not that she expected there to be.
Life couldn't change that quickly. Ivy picked a
large bowl full of beans, and then played happily with her dolls in the soddy, but the opportunity to speak with Karleen about firing Carter
never appeared.

From what she heard, Mrs. Rudolf had wasted

no time sharing the story that the mercantile had a new employee. Even Mr. Wilcox from the railroad stopped in, requesting to see Molly. She left the back room and met the gray-haired man at the counter, fully prepared to hear that the rest of her order wouldn't be in for weeks, and ready to tell him exactly what she thought about that. Instead, she was utterly shocked when he earnestly proceeded to apologize to her for Mrs. Rudolf's broken cup. He not only insisted she order another complete set, which he personally promised would arrive undamaged, but he vowed to assure future shipments would arrive on time. The railroad, he said, did owe all customers the same excellent service it provides its own investments.

Molly was speechless, and had more things to ponder by the way Mr. Wilcox tipped his hat toward Carter as the railroad man left the store. Carter was behind it, that was for sure, and Karleen would never fire him now. That was irksome, but what bothered her more was how he was embedding himself so deeply into their business.

By the time they locked the front door that evening, she'd bet they'd sold more merchandise than any other day since her parents had died. It was true, Molly concluded upon totaling the receipts and the cash in the drawer. Their best day ever.

Questioning what that meant, a sound, or a sense, had Molly lifting her gaze from the store's daily journal.

"You shouldn't leave that money in the cash drawer overnight," Carter said from where he leaned against the doorway that led into the house portion of the building.

"It's called a cash drawer because that's what it is," she said, closing the book and placing it on the shelf beneath the counter.

"I know that. But so does everyone else."

She didn't like when he did that, talked slow and deliberate, making people think, therefore she didn't bother looking his way again.

"Anyone could break in here, steal the money. They'd be long gone by the time you heard anything."

That was highly unlikely, yet she asked, "And where do you suggest I put the money, if not in the cash drawer?"

"Hide it. Somewhere only you and Karleen know about. Every night and take it out every morning."

The hair on her arms had started to quiver. Her father used to do that, but over time, she'd forgotten. What else didn't she remember? The sound of their voices? No, she'd never forget how Papa's laughter had echoed through the house like joyous thunder, especially when he was telling one of his famous jokes. Molly tried for a moment, but couldn't seem to recall even one of his many stories. But she could remember how it felt to know he was in the house, how his presence chased away all her childhood fears. Fear was with her now constantly, and his laughter was gone.

Shaken, she gathered the bills out of the cash drawer and blew out the lamp on the counter. Walking past Carter, she hissed, "You're still leaving."

She could hear his laughter, and it rattled her very being.

Molly got up twice and moved the money to different locations—out from beneath her bed to behind the wood box in the kitchen, and then to the top drawer of her bureau—but still couldn't sleep. Counting sheep didn't help, neither did rehearsing how she'd insist that Karleen fire Carter. Therefore, when she crawled out of bed the next morning, she was groggy and irritated—more so than normal.

It was while Molly was pulling the third batch of cinnamon rolls from the oven that her mood hit rock bottom.

"Goodness," her sister commented while entering the kitchen. "The store is busier than yesterday. We're going to need another batch of rolls. People who hadn't gotten a good look at Carter yesterday are trying to today." Karleen started placing rolls on a plate. "Actually, some who had seen him yesterday are back for a second look." Grinning, she added, "He is so very handsome, don't you think?"

"That's disgraceful, Karleen," Molly snapped.

"What? Licking my fingers?" Karleen asked, doing just that.

"That, too," Molly said, setting the heavy pan on top of the stove with a loud thump. "Carter Buchanan is not staying here."

"Yes, he is," Karleen insisted. "He's not only good for business, he's exactly the help we've needed. The cows were milked, the eggs gathered and the animals fed before I even got up. You, too. No boy from town would manage all that."

Her sister was pointing out how last week Molly had suggested they hire a boy from town, which increased her irritation. Shoving the last pan of rolls into the oven—not caring if they ran out before the noon train or not—Molly slammed the door. "Those are simple, everyday chores that don't hurt us a bit to accomplish. Having someone else do them is just plain lazy."

"Well, maybe I want to be lazy for a while," Karleen said. "Lord knows working in the store all day and baking dozens of rolls and breads isn't enough for us to do."

"Don't take the Lord's name in vain," Molly scolded. She was a fine one to be preaching Bible lessons, but couldn't stop the reprimand from coming out.

"I didn't take his name in vain," Karleen insisted. "I said he knows how hard we *do* work around here." Sighing, she rested both hands on Molly's shoulders. "You never used to be like this. Even just a few months ago you'd have been happy to have the extra help. Carter's a wonderful salesman. He's even sold two pairs of those shoes that peddler unloaded on us. That alone should have you dancing. What's happened to you, Molly? Even Ivy is afraid you're going to snap her head off like a bean stem for the tiniest mistake."

Molly shrugged out from beneath her sister's hold. She couldn't handle anyone touching her, but more because the truth hurt. "Because I grew up. And it's time you did, too."

"I have grown up, Molly. I may not be as old as you, but I haven't been a child for a long time. Not since the day Mother and Father died. It wasn't my fault, Molly. It wasn't my fault they died and we had to learn to run this place."

"I never said it was," she insisted.

"You act like it is."

"I do not," Molly retorted. "Now, hush up, the customers might hear you." For good measure

Molly waved a finger at her sister. "And don't be snippy with me."

"Snippy? Me?" Karleen all but snarled. "You're the snippy one. Ask any of the customers, they'll tell you. You act like everything is someone else's fault, including why Robbie Fredrickson wouldn't marry you."

The last bit of starch left her knees—the small amount she'd held on to all this time—but other places, Molly was still seething. "I didn't want to marry him."

"Because no man wants to marry a woman with two younger sisters to take care of."

Her hands squeezed the chair harder. "I didn't say that," Molly corrected.

"Well, Robbie did," Karleen said. "I may only be sixteen, Molly, but I know some things, including that if a man really loves a woman, he doesn't care how many sisters she has."

Karleen was right, she herself had told Robbie those exact words, but her sister didn't know everything. "You don't know anything about love. You're just a child."

"I know more than you think." Karleen leaned across the table. "I know Robbie only courted you to get this store for the railroad."

"We didn't court," Molly seethed. "And I know exactly what Robbie wanted." She did know, and she'd known it five months ago, but she'd wanted things to be different. Not just for her but for her sisters.

"Then get over it," Karleen snapped.

Molly bit her tongue, refused to answer. She was over it all right, but Robbie was not the problem. The result of that night was. It had seemed no matter how hard she worked, there was no hope of things changing. She'd hated everything about her life that day and wanted out.

Karleen and Ivy had gone to Ralph and Emma Walters's wedding party at the hotel. The whole town had been there, and she'd planned on going too, except the freight had arrived ten minutes before it was time to leave. It couldn't be left out for anyone walking by to pilfer, so she'd stayed home, carrying box after box inside until it was good and dark. It had rained, too, exacerbating her sense of misery, and had made her recall how fast everything had changed. How that violent spring storm had hit two years prior, causing the James River to flood its banks, washing away buildings and stealing the lives of people so quickly the entire town was in shock for months afterward.

Safe, here at home, she and Karleen and Ivy hadn't known what had happened to their parents until the preacher arrived and explained how the bridge had collapsed beneath their wagon.

"Molly?"

Things had changed that fast again five months ago. Molly pushed Karleen away and stumbled for the door, needing much more than fresh air.

"Molly, I'm sorry," Karleen shouted, but Molly kept moving.

If she stopped, she might collapse.

Chapter Four

Carter moved toward the door that led to the living quarters, where the scent of cinnamon rolls filtered into the store. The sisters were squabbling again. This in itself was nothing new, but Karleen's apology said it was worse this time. Not that he was surprised. He had a harder time than usual holding his tongue when it came to Molly's attitude, too.

He was disgusted, mainly because the two might start pulling each other's hair out, not that it was any of his business, but there was enough going on without them fighting. "I'll be right back," he told the only customer left in the store.

"Take your time," the preacher said.

Carter couldn't decide whether to leave the man alone or not. Most folks trusted a man of the cloth, but he didn't. Religious folks—men and women dressed in their black-and-white clothes—had been the ones who kept plucking him off the streets in New York and plunking him down in orphanages. Until he'd been old enough to make a clean getaway. A westbound train, with two other boys his age.

Karleen, once again shouting Molly's name, had him glancing toward the little girl perched on a stool and writing the alphabet in a tablet with a stubby pencil. "You keep an eye on him," he said.

Ivy nodded, and then giggled as she glanced at the preacher. The other man laughed too, and Carter had to let his guard down, admit the store and the girl were safe. He darted through the doorway and down the hall that led to the kitchen, where he asked, "What's wrong?"

Turning from the open back door, Karleen shook her head. "I've upset her."

"What else is new?" Carter asked, though he didn't feel any humor. Molly Thorson woke up as ornery as she went to bed. He'd testify to that. Had wondered if she was going to throw the eggs he'd carried into the kitchen this morning at him.

"No, I really upset her this time," Karleen said, clearly despondent. "And I shouldn't have."

A part of him would rather not, but still he said, "You go see to the customers, I'll go make sure she's all right." He'd long ago learned people were easier to deal with when they were rational, and worked long and hard on mastering his ability to put people where he wanted them so he could get the information he needed. But he wasn't overly confident anything he'd learned would work on Molly Thorson.

"Maybe we should just leave her alone," Karleen whispered.

That would work too, except the pleading look in the girl's eyes said she was sincerely worried. It wasn't as if he was responding to her silent plea. No girl—or woman—would ever make him do something he didn't want to. The bickering had to stop. That's what it was. There were more important things at hand. Like his latest bit of information. With a nod, he moved toward the door. "I'll just go make sure she's all right, and then I'll leave her alone."

"Thank you, Carter."

"You just don't let those cinnamon rolls burn," he said. Being a friendly cowboy with a never-ending grin was already getting old, but he had to keep it up. And would. "We're going to need them when the next train arrives."

He'd played a lot of roles in his life, but this was the first time it included dealing so closely with women. It had to be done, though, as had his conversation with Wilcox yesterday. The railroad man hadn't been impressed, or happy to offer an apology, but Carter had told him if there was any hope more money would surface, people needed to be filtering in and out of the store regularly. Locals, not just the few passengers looking for cinnamon rolls. No one was making big purchases, but they were spending money. Cash, and he checked the serial numbers on every bill.

There'd been one that matched in the drawer this morning. It was in his pocket now. He'd replaced it with one of his own. Trouble was, he had no idea how it got there. He'd watched every transaction, knew who'd handed over bills and who'd paid with coins, and not one person had used a five-dollar bill. Yet that's what had turned up.

A touch reluctant—for he did want to be in the store, watching that drawer—Carter stepped off the back porch. After a quick search of the yard, he entered the barn and blinked, adjusting his focus after the bright sunlight. He'd cleaned the barn last night—something that had sorely needed to be done—after supper. That's where he found Molly, sitting on a pile of fresh straw he'd pitched down from the hayloft and scattered into one of the empty stalls.

She jumped to her feet when she noticed him and ran toward the other end of the long walkway.

"Molly," he said calmly. Someone knew how that bill in his pocket got in the drawer. Karleen was too talkative to hold a secret of that magnitude, and Ivy was just a babe, which only left one person. Therefore he had to find a way to have a normal, calm conversation with Molly.

He said her name again as she started to climb the ladder leading to the hayloft, but when she turned, looking at him over one shoulder, he shouted it, and ran. In all his years of living, of chasing people and capturing them, he'd never truly seen one go completely colorless. But she had, and her eyes had rolled upward.

His heart was galloping inside his chest. He was thankful he'd arrived in time and caught her just as she'd slumped. Slowly, gingerly, he lowered her onto the extra mound of hay he'd thrown down last night for today's feeding and crouched beside her.

Visions flashed before his eyes, as they had been doing since he'd arrived in Huron. Times he'd forgotten, or buried so deep he thought they were gone. Things back in New York, when he was just a kid. Right now it was Amelia he was remembering. She'd only been ten when she'd died, and she had been the one reason he'd stayed at that last orphanage as long as he had—almost two years. He'd left after her death, and never looked back.

Giving his head a clearing shake, Carter whispered, "Molly?"

She didn't move, but she was breathing, had just fainted. He'd never seen that either. Heard of it, of course, but never seen it, and wasn't too sure what to do about it. On more than one occasion, he'd seen a man get knocked out, so he checked her head, in case she'd bumped it in her rush up the ladder.

Amelia had fallen out of a tree. A broken rib punctured her lungs. That's what one of the nuns had said.

Carter tossed the sudden thought aside and let his hands roam over Molly's arms and then checked her ribs. When his exploring touch went lower, ran over her midriff, he froze. Every last part of him, and all his thoughts collided like bees swarming into a hive. He sat there for a moment, too stunned to think and then, darn close to being afraid, he touched her again. Felt her stomach from side to side, top to bottom.

Drawing his hands away, he stared, as if he could see through her white apron and gray dress.

Most men his age, somewhere around twenty-seven, knew a woman's body, and he did, too. She wasn't big and round like some he'd seen, but Molly Thorson was pregnant.

Pregnant.

Not quite believing it, he reached over, touched her stomach again. There were layers of material between his palm and her skin, but he'd bet every last dollar he'd ever earned he was right. That firm little bump he was feeling was a baby. She was pregnant.

No wonder she was so ornery. She was pregnant and didn't want anyone to know. But this took two. Where was the father? Who was the father?

A tiny moan sounded and he drew back his hand, but then pressed it to her forehead. "Molly?"

She opened her eyes but closed them again. "What happened?"

"You fainted." He grasped both her shoulders, and a large part of him wanted to shake some answers out of her, but he wouldn't do that. Just touching her had his fingers tingling, telling him just how spooky this was. Not that he scared easily, but pregnant women, they were scary. "Can you sit up?"

"No," she said, shaking her head. "Not yet. Everything's still spinning."

"All right, just lie there for a moment." She was probably spooked, too. An unwed pregnant woman had to be. Leastwise he assumed she was unwed, and believed that assumption to be true. He never catered to others' assumptions, he liked proof, but his own were another matter. Right now he assumed something else, that she was scared spitless. "Do you want some water or something?" he asked.

She licked her lips. "No, it'll stop in a minute."

"This has happened before?" A new dimension had just been added to his case, one that had him wondering if he should wire headquarters and ask for a different assignment. That thought had never crossed his mind before, and was more than a little out of character—any character he'd ever played—but an assignment had never put him smack-dab in the middle of a scandal of this proportion. The town was going to tear her apart when her condition was revealed, which was bound to happen. If he was still here, still working at the mercantile, he'd have to defend her. Pinkerton man or not. He already felt it welling inside him, and he wasn't so sure he was comfortable with it.

"Yes." Her sigh was heavy enough to hold water. She opened her eyes then, stared at the ceiling overhead. "It's happened before."

His assignments were to solve cases, catch robbers or track down murderers, not protect people—other than himself—which is how he liked it.

"Does Karleen know?" he asked.

Fear flashed in her eyes before she closed them. She swallowed too, like a gulp of someone set to hang at noon. He'd witnessed that more than once.

"Know what?" she asked.

She hadn't even told her sister. Karleen had said there used to be a time when Molly laughed and was a joy to be around, but that lately she wouldn't even talk and was irritated about everything. Having held secrets, personal ones, for many years, Carter could relate. It had taken him years to learn how to make his past work with him instead of against him. She, however, didn't know how to do that, and didn't have much time to learn it.

"That you've fainted before," he said. "Maybe you need to see a doctor."

"No," she said, scrambling to sit up.

"Slow down," he scolded, helping to ease her into a sitting position.

Pushing his hands aside once she was sitting, she snapped, "I don't need to see a doctor." She tugged at her apron then, fluffing it away from her stomach. "So don't be telling Karleen I do. And don't be telling her I fainted, either."

She was back, all grouchy and grumpy, and in a way, he was happy. A grumpy Molly he could deal with. However, now that he knew why, things had changed. There hadn't been anything in the *Pinkerton National Detective Agency's Investigative Training Manual*—which he had memorized—about pregnant women, and he doubted his dictionary was going to help in this situation either.

"Come on," he said, tucking his legs beneath him to stand. "I'll help you into the house where you can lie down for a bit."

"I don't need to lie down, and I don't need any help."

He stood and crossed his arms. Was reminded of being in the cabin, when he'd challenged her to make him leave. It had been childish, but she'd been behaving like a child then, and was again now. She scrambled to her feet, which goaded him a bit. He did want her to need help. His. Just to prove his point.

She flounced her skirt and her apron again before turning about and, nose in the air, marched toward the doorway.

Carter watched her go, all the way out the door and into the sunlight, where she stopped, turned to see if he was still watching her. He was, and tipped the brim of his hat up, just so she'd see how closely.

She tilted her head slightly, but didn't move, just stared back at him.

It was a showdown of sorts, a duel, where neither of them had guns, just a challenge to see who'd make the first move, look away for even a split second.

She was going to get awfully hot standing in the sun; he could stare down a rattler.

It took about that long before she finally spun around and stomped off for the house, and Carter let out a long, slow breath. He removed his hat then and wiped away the sweat. This woman had him on rocky ground, and there was no wondering about it. He didn't like it, not one little bit.

Thoughts of quitting no longer floated around either. He'd never not solved a case and he'd solve this one, too. The only thing he'd ever run away from was New York. That's how it would remain. Though he just might move on to Montana sooner than later. It might be time.

Carter left the barn, but made it only as far as the corral. Sampson was there, tossing his head. They'd been together eight years now, the only family he'd ever had.

Right from the start, he'd told Allan he wouldn't promise to be an agent for years. He couldn't. He hadn't known if Chicago was where he needed to be, and since then, even with all the traveling he'd done, he still didn't know.

The only things he remembered about his father were words. Sometimes they still echoed in his head. Like right now. He didn't know how old he'd been—somewhere around five, close as he could figure—and they'd been boarding the boat with a crowd of others heading to America. *"That's where we need to be,"* his father had said.

There were other words, too, that his father had said, then and in the days that followed, about how he'd feel it when they arrived, how he'd know when he found the one place in the world he was supposed to be.

Carter was still waiting to feel it, still believed he would someday. That his father had been right. Work with the agency had taken him across the nation and back again, and the closest he'd come to a connection was up in Montana while searching out cattle rustlers. Something about the land there, how it met the sky, had him contemplating exactly what his father had been talking about.

The cattle-rustling assignment had been five years ago, and standing here now, looking over a horizon that was somewhat familiar, Carter questioned if it was time to go back to Montana.

He spun around, took in the customers wandering into the mercantile. Should this be it, his last assignment? Is that why this case had him pretending to be a cowboy working his way to Montana? Why it had memories surfacing that hadn't been there for years?

Irony or fate? Things happened like that at times, fell into place, and he accepted them. Both into his work and his life.

It took work for things to fall into place, though and that's what he needed to focus on. Find the money, and find who stole it. One person knew, and he was going to have to put everything into getting the information out of her. If she hadn't told anyone about her pregnancy, finding out where she came up with new five-dollar bills was going to take finesse.

Good thing he'd had years of practice.

Molly was going to be sick, but for the first time in months, it had nothing to do with the baby inside her. The laughter coming from the store was enough to make anyone sick to their stomach. She'd had to listen to it for days now. Karleen laughing. Carter laughing. Even Ivy was laughing more than not.

She didn't mind that. The past few months Ivy had grown somber, and Molly knew why. She'd tried harder the last couple days, attempted to smile and be more pleasant, especially to Ivy, but her irritability hadn't gone away. If anything, it had grown. Carter Buchanan was to blame. Not even weeding her garden, as she was doing right now, helped.

Karleen had to say his name a hundred times a day, and Ivy fifty. Even customers asked for him by name. Molly was so tired of hearing that one single name she could scream. She didn't scream; however, she did refuse to say his name. She called him Mr. Buchanan when she had to speak to him. He, on the other hand, called her Molly. Only family called her Molly, she'd told him that at a moment when she was speaking to him. It hadn't helped. He still called her Molly.

She wanted that to bother her, but, truth was, there was no reason for it to. Very few people called her Maureen.

"You shouldn't be out here without a hat on."

Molly closed her eyes against the increased thudding of her heart and kept on hoeing. Not that ignoring Carter would make him go away. She'd tried that, too.

"You're going to get too hot, might faint again."

"I'm not going to faint again," she said without lifting her head.

"How do you know that?"

Planting the hoe in the ground, she turned, but the reply she'd gathered scattered like a flock of birds shooed from the branches of a tree. Her mouth went dry, too, and all sorts of things fluttered inside her.

"Where are you going?" she asked, and then wanted to bite the end off her tongue.

The slow grin on his face only added to the overall upheaval inside her. Carter was a handsome man, as several women whispered when they thought no one was listening as they pretended to shop. They did make purchases, but just little items, excuses to be in the store, to moon over Carter. There was going to be mooning today, no doubt about that. He had on new black pants, stiffly creased from hem to waist, and a crisp-looking white shirt—Karleen had probably ironed it for him—and a black vest. There was also a string tie around his neck, and his Stetson sat as prominently on his black hair as ever.

If she didn't know better, she'd think he was going to a wedding—as the groom.

The way her insides somersaulted probably made her baby dizzy, and she curled her other hand into a fist, just to keep it at her side. She really didn't want to like him—and didn't—but she was getting used to him being around, and that was almost as bad.

"I'm not leaving town, if that's what you're hoping," he said.

That was exactly what she should be hoping, but wasn't. "Too bad," she said, pulling the hoe out of the ground.

His deep chuckle had her lips quivering, wanting to grin. He'd made a habit of that, laughing at her remarks, twisting them around as if they were joking or teasing each other.

They weren't.

Carter had changed, though. Or maybe she

just saw him differently. It wasn't anything she could describe, but she was no longer concerned about him and Karleen, and that disturbed her more. It left her with little else to believe other than he really was a cowboy working his way to Montana.

"Here, let me do that for you," he said, wrapping a hand over hers, holding the hoe handle.

The touch, the heat of his palm should have her pulling her hand away, but it didn't. There was nothing uncomfortable about him touching her, no matter how hard she wished there was. She still didn't want him here, but mustering up the ability to hate him was growing harder day by day.

"I can do it," she said. "I like hoeing."

He didn't remove his hand. "Just let me finish this row for you."

"Why?"

"Because it's hot out here."

Of course it was hot out here, but it was hot inside the house, too. August was like that. Finding that argument useless, she said, "You'll get your clothes dirty."

"I'll be careful."

His fingers were moving, not pulling the hoe from hers, just rubbing the back of her hand. It was attention grabbing, that was for sure. He was good at coaxing people into doing what he wanted with mere words and subtle actions. She'd witnessed it, and as hard as it was to admit, admired it.

"Do you know the difference between weeds and turnip leaves?" she asked, trying to sound aggravated.

"I'm sure you'll tell me," he said.

Snapping her head up, prepared to say she didn't have time to tell him, the words dissolved on her tongue. Amusement twinkled in his eyes, and for the life of her, it wouldn't let her look away.

"Won't you?" he asked.

In the space of a single heartbeat a stimulating bout of mirth overtook her from top to bottom. It was so unexpected, Molly was unable to fight it, and had no choice but to give in, enjoy the moment.

"You should do that more often," Carter said.

"Do what?"

"Smile."

The moment of bliss faded as fast as it had arrived, leaving additional gloom in its wake. "Maybe I don't have anything to smile about."

"What about Ivy and Karleen?" He caught her chin, used a fingertip to force her to look up at him. "They make everyone smile."

"Do you have a family, Carter?" she asked, truly wanting to know.

He didn't respond, not so much as a blink of an eye.

She sighed. He'd never share such things with her, and she'd never share her problems with him, but she would tell him one thing. "Family are the very people we need to protect."

He still didn't speak, but his dark gaze was strong, penetrating, and Molly wished she could deny how deeply she felt his compassion. He was so much more than a hired hand, he was a man. A real man. He did all the heavy chores, and he'd fixed the loose barn door, the leak in the roof over the back porch, and got rid of the hornets, but none of that meant as much as how he treated people. He not only knew how to handle customers, he was kind and caring toward Ivy. Claiming they didn't bother him, he assured Ivy her dolls could stay in the cabin, along with the table and tea set, and that she could play in there anytime she wanted. He'd even joined in, pretended to drink tea and converse with the dolls one day.

Molly had seen all this while hanging clothes on the line, and right now she felt the same kind of compassion he showered on Ivy raining down on her, as if he understood their plights in life. Ivy's early loss of her parents, and Molly's hidden burdens.

What she wasn't sure about was whether his compassion was laced with pity or not.

"Let me hoe, Molly," he said quietly. "Just this row. You can watch, make sure I don't dig up anything except weeds."

He was already digging things up inside her. Things she'd sworn would never come to the surface again. The hoe left her grasp as she stepped back, ready to flee, but Carter reached out, took her hand with his free one. "Show me the weeds, Molly, and I'll dig them up for you."

His words held double meaning. Even with all the turmoil erupting inside, Molly comprehended that, and a tiny little part of her—she had to wonder if it was the baby—asked her to give in to him. To let Carter help. Not necessarily her, and she certainly wouldn't tell him about the baby or about what she'd done, but he had made things easier on Karleen and even Ivy. And on her as well. She'd never have gotten the fence fixed, or the roof, or a dozen other things, including increasing sales. She couldn't help but wonder how he'd react when the truth came out.

Not that she was hoping he'd still be here when the baby was born, but he might be when her condition was revealed. It was bound to happen soon. At the rate the baby was growing, extra-large dresses wouldn't hide her belly much longer. He'd already been protective of her sister and ward. She'd witnessed it when seedy-looking characters—train passengers or those traveling through—entered the store, and Carter always insisted upon waiting on them.

The fluttering in her belly happened again, as it had more and more lately, and she couldn't help but wish her baby would someday know someone like Carter. A real man. Like her father had been.

"Is this a weed?" Carter asked, still holding her hand, but kicking at a tiny plant with the toe of one boot.

Molly swallowed, inwardly toying with the thought that she wished he'd protect her, too, as he did her sisters. It had been a long time since she'd had someone to share her burdens with, and secretly she wanted to accept what he was offering, even if she truly didn't need help hoeing. She tried to reroute her thoughts, tell herself Carter didn't belong here. But he was here, and she couldn't deny how comforting that was.

"This one, Molly," he said, "is it a weed?"

Tired of fighting in so many ways, Molly nodded. "Yes, that's a weed."

"Then I'll get rid of it for you." His gaze locked on hers as he asked, "All right?"

There were so many things she had to combat, maybe she should give in this once. It might conserve her energy for when she really needed it. "Yes, you can get rid of that one."

They progressed slowly, with Carter asking

which ones were weeds and Molly explaining how they differed from the vegetables that still had some growing to do. It took a couple rows, but soon they were talking about other things. Plants mainly. He told her about the cotton fields he'd seen down South, the apple orchards out west and the fields of wheat in Kansas.

"You've certainly been a lot of places," she said as they neared the end of the last row. He'd done it again, lessened her anxieties, and for once, Molly didn't fight it, just accepted how nice it was to have a normal conversation about inconsequential topics.

"Yes, I have."

"Why?"

"Because I wanted to see all my choices before I decided on one."

He hadn't looked up, and she'd wished he had, though she couldn't have voiced why. "And you chose Montana?" she asked.

"Yes."

"Why? What's in Montana?"

They were at the edge of the garden, with no weeds left, not a single one. Carter stood the hoe upright and rested an arm on the handle. "Land," he said, "a lot like this. The first day I was in town, I rode out there." He nodded toward the horizon, where the blue of the sky met the green of the earth in one long unending line. "Good land, goes on for as far as a man can see, kind of like the ocean."

"And you like that?"

He picked up the hoe and gestured toward the barn. They started walking at the same time, side by side. "Yes, I do. Don't you?"

She let her gaze wander the land for a moment. "Yes, I do." The wide-open space was much more appealing than the scene on the other side of the store.

"Why?" he asked.

Because the land certainly wouldn't judge her like the town would, but Molly couldn't voice that. "I don't know."

"I do."

She snapped her head his way. There were times he made her wonder whether he knew everything there was to know about her. This was one of those moments. Her breath broke into snippets as she drew in air.

"Because there's nothing there," he said. "Nothing to obscure your view. Not of where you're going or where you've been. And there's nothing to hide behind, either."

They entered the barn while she contemplated what he could possibly have to hide from. Not a single possibility came to mind. She, on the other hand, couldn't hide in a forest at midnight.

"Everyone has secrets, Molly," he said while

hanging the hoe in the corner near a few other tools, rakes and shovels and such. "If anyone ever tells you they don't, they're lying."

Her gaze was still on the long-handled tools. He'd built the rack to hang them all on yesterday. Had asked her to come stand out here so he wouldn't hang it too high, and when she'd refused, Karleen had gone.

Molly turned, looked up at him, too curious not to ask, "Even you?"

His grin was a bit devilish. "Even me." He took her hand then, rubbing the back with the pad of his thumb and her palm with his fingers.

It wasn't in the least intrusive. Her fingers wanted to curl, fold over his. For months she'd wished there was someone who'd take her hand, lead her through the days when she felt small and lost, assuring her everything would be all right, but it couldn't be him. Not Carter Buchanan, a cowboy working his way to Montana. There was no hope in that.

Yet her fingers folded around his as he lifted her hand. She watched, almost as if she was a fly on the wall, spying on people, as Carter drew her hand all the way up to his face. He kissed the back of her hand—a tiny, soft peck that penetrated into her bloodstream.

"Thank you for letting me hoe your garden, Molly."

Molly nodded, but her eyes were on the hand he still held near his lips. She didn't feel like a bystander any longer and was considering what that meant.

Carter lowered her hand to her side before letting go.

"I have to leave now," he said, "or I'm going to be late."

A smidgen of fear twirled in her chest, relatively close to her heart. "Where are you going?"

"I can't tell you. But I'll be back."

He'd taken several steps toward the door when she said, "I saw you that day." There wasn't anything significant in the statement, other than she'd wanted to say it.

Stopping, he tilted up the brim of his hat before he turned around. A couple steps later, he was in front of her again, close enough she could once more smell the bay rum shaving soap he used each morning.

"I saw you, too. You were hoeing your garden and watched me ride past."

A pinch of embarrassment stung her cheeks as he gently laid a hand against one. There was also a drawing inside her, a deep powerful one that had her heart quickening.

"I have to go, Molly, but I'll be back. Don't worry."

She stepped back, suddenly frightened. "I'm not worried."

He stood there, watched her closely, as if he expected her to run. She wanted to, but didn't. Her legs weren't strong enough.

Carter grinned again, and then winked. "Good."

This time Molly didn't say a word as he walked away, out the door, but she did reach for something to help her stand. There wasn't anything, so she lowered onto the floor, not caring it was the barn. Her breathing was irregular and a definite chill made her skin clammy.

She didn't even like Carter Buchanan, yet, all the same, the things she was feeling right now scared her to death.

Chapter Five

Carter hadn't turned around since he'd walked out of the barn. Walking away from an adversary, leaving them thinking, wasn't new to him. What was new to him was the way several parts of him were no longer looking upon Molly as an opponent. The woman had flustered him since the day he hit town, and that was still happening, but in a different way now. He'd been way too close to kissing her back there in the barn, and not on the hand. Plenty of times in the past he'd played the gentleman, used false charm to persuade a woman to tell him what he needed to know, but he'd always drawn the line at kissing.

Molly was bringing up his past, too, more often than he liked. Not in words, but little actions. Like when her lips had curled up, forming a little smile, his past had flashed another image.

Amelia again. She'd been so tiny and alone way back when, and he'd fought kids and adults to leave her be. They'd only been children, and he couldn't say exactly what they felt for each other, but Amelia was the only person he'd cared about way down deep inside, and he'd hurt when she died. Hurt terribly. That had been fifteen years ago, and he hadn't thought of her for a long time, and had no reason to now.

Other than Molly. She reminded him a lot of Amelia. Little, lost and alone. Sure, Molly had a home and family, but in some ways that made it worse for her—she had that much more to defend.

That was goading him too, how he wanted to defend her, keep her secret. Keeping those girls safe was foremost in his mind. There had been times the past few days he'd almost grabbed customers by the backs of their shirts and hauled them out the door. He hadn't needed to, though. One look from him and the men understood they either treated those girls with respect or they'd answer to him. There had been one or two who hadn't grasped that readily enough, and he'd sent the girls into the house. He'd waited on those customers himself, who, he'd bet, would never make the same mistake a second time around.

Knowing that wasn't very satisfying though. It only had him wondering who'd protect the Thorson sisters after he left. That shouldn't be his problem. He was here to solve a case. Nothing more. And certainly not to kiss Molly. That was a bit frightening, the thought of kissing her. Something deep and powerful said he might catch a glimpse of paradise if he kissed her, and he didn't need paradise. Not that kind. He'd find his in Montana when this case was over.

Two days ago, while researching the stolen money, he thought he'd stumbled upon a clue as to who the father of Molly's baby was. Karleen had mentioned a man had asked Molly to marry him. Then he'd learned the man had left town well over a year ago and hadn't been back. No woman could be pregnant that long.

It was perplexing. Molly wasn't friendly, and two people had to be friendly for a woman to get in the family way. Unless someone had forced himself on her. He'd toyed with that idea, but couldn't quite accept it. Molly was as ornery as she was stubborn. She'd have shot any man who got close to her. Or clubbed him, or stabbed him, whatever it took.

Not that a woman even as obstinate as Molly couldn't be overpowered, but there would have been evidence of that. She was a fighter and would have pointed out the man, seen him punished for his wrongdoing, no matter how embarrassing it may have been on her part. She was ashamed of her condition, he understood that— but moreover, Molly Thorson was deep down trembling in her socks, scared, which told him she'd had something to do with getting into the predicament she was in.

He'd been cautious with his questions, letting them flow naturally into conversations that wouldn't raise any suspicion as he'd questioned Karleen. He'd asked if Molly had been gone for any length of time. Karleen had sworn Molly hadn't—she'd never consider leaving Ivy and her alone. Ultimately, he had no reason to believe anything Karleen told him wasn't true, but Molly had to have been gone long enough to get in her condition.

Carter shook his head and used the movement to check for traffic as he crossed Huron's main street, and then headed down a road that led to some of the more stately homes.

His undercover work told him no one knew about Molly's condition—yet. He'd been careful there, too, just weaved in tiny bits and pieces into discussions with customers and other folks in town. One man had claimed to have courted Molly, but soon admitted he'd lied. Carter probably shouldn't have threatened the man as he had, but he wouldn't have anyone spreading rumors about her. Molly didn't deserve to be persecuted, not by the law and not by the people of Huron.

No different than little Ivy. Indian or not, she was one smart little girl who deserved to be in school just like every other kid in town.

A soft spot formed in his heart and he let it be. Even smiled at it. He still didn't know how Ivy had convinced him to have a tea party with her and her dolls, but he had. He'd sat right there on the floor next to her little table and pretended to drink tea while talking to the painted-face toys as if they were real people. There wasn't a Pinkerton man out there—not one that knew him—who would have believed it. Carter hadn't believed it himself, but Ivy's joy had been worth it. That's when this idea came to mind, while talking with Ivy and her dolls. The child had no one to play with, and he was set on changing that.

He would miss her during the day, since she was practically glued to his heels when not doing her school lessons, but lessons were what she needed. He'd never attended school outside the classes at the orphanages. After leaving New York, he never slowed down long enough to do much more than stand outside, wondering what all those kids were learning inside a school building every now and again.

Things would be different for Ivy. She would go to school. He'd see to it.

Carter stopped, glanced up at the big brick home his mission had carried him to, and before he could think much more about it, he raised a hand and knocked on the door.

When Mrs. Rudolf answered the door he pulled up his most charming smile. Today was Saturday, the day of the woman's garden party with the wives of the city council members. He was going to take advantage of that, as well as the crush the older woman had on him. She'd been at the mercantile every day since her cups had arrived, and always insisted he wait on her. The role he was playing was a bit hellish at times.

"Good day, Mrs. Rudolf," he greeted, removing his hat. "I just wanted to stop by, make sure those new teacups were working out for you today."

"Why, Mr. Buchanan," she said, blushing brightly and batting her eyelashes, "how kind of you. Do come in, let me introduce you to everyone."

"I'd be obliged," he said, stepping over the threshold.

It worked, and by the time Carter left the Rudolf home, Ivy had a place in the school. Every woman at the party personally promised they'd see that Ivy would be welcomed. At that, he'd insisted she be treated just like every other child. No special attention, just included. That's how it should be.

As long as he was out and about, Carter stopped

by the railroad headquarters, to meet with Wilcox. The man was due an update. They hadn't met since the day Wilcox apologized to Molly about the broken cup, and he would soon know Carter was out and about today. Wilcox's wife had been at the garden party.

As it was Saturday, Wilcox was the only one in the office space above the depot, and they spent an hour or more going over details they both already knew. Carter gave him the five-dollar bill from his pocket. They hashed out possibilities, but no conclusions were found. Carter was about to leave when Wilcox said something that snagged more of his attention than it should have.

"Why is he coming out here?" Carter asked, referring to James J. Fredrickson, part owner of the Chicago and Northwestern Railroad.

"He'll just make a brief stop," Wilcox said, "on his way to Wyoming, to the railhead there. But I know he'll want to talk with you during his layover here."

Carter nodded. That was to be expected, yet his instincts were ticking. "Is there trouble there? At the railhead?"

"Just James's son."

"Robert Fredrickson," Carter said, recalling the name. "He was on the train last year."

"Yeah," Wilcox agreed, frowning. "You can't

be thinking he had anything to do with the robbery? His father hands him over money like he used to hand him candy. He'd have no reason to steal it."

"I'm not thinking that," Carter lied. For he was tossing the idea around. "I was just recalling the names from the passenger list. Remembering that's where I'd heard it. What kind of trouble is the kid in?"

"Actually, I'm just assuming it's trouble, and he's not a kid anymore. Has to be twenty-five or twenty-six." Wilcox's head shake showed disgust. "James has let his son try a hand at every job the C&NW has to offer. Sent him here once, to be my assistant. Within a few months, I told James it was either me or Robbie."

"Why?"

"He had the whole town hating the railroad, and he has a real knack for stirring up trouble," Wilcox said. "Matter of fact, the last time he rolled through, I wouldn't let him get off the train."

Carter lifted a brow.

"He was in his private car," Wilcox explained. "Had no reason to take a hotel room. Besides, it was full up then, too."

An eerie sensation was tickling Carter's spine. He wasn't sure why. Could be because the entire town was talking about that woman with all her kids still at the hotel—the man who'd ordered her claimed he hadn't. That's how the gossip went. Then again, it could be because the detective vibes inside him were kicking like Sampson penned up too long.

"Let me know when Fredrickson arrives," Carter said as he rose from his chair, needing time to ponder.

"I will," Wilcox answered.

He accompanied Carter down the stairs, making small talk along the way, and it wasn't until they stepped into the bright sunlight that Carter felt inclined to answer. The man had mentioned Molly.

"The Thorson sisters are just fine," Carter answered through clenched teeth.

"It would be beneficial to you if you could convince Molly to give up that store while you're here. You seem to have created quite a rapport with them."

"Just doing my job," Carter said, disguising things he couldn't describe leaping to life inside him. "As a Pinkerton operative," he added. "That's who I work for. Not the railroad."

"I know," Wilcox said. "But I do have the authority to reward you for going above and beyond your duties."

Carter fought the urge to shove the man against the wall and clearly explain that everyone, including the railroad, better stay away from the Thorson sisters. A company that large was persistent, could afford to be. In the end, when they turned dirty, Molly wouldn't stand a chance. He'd just learned that it wasn't the town that didn't want Ivy going to school. It was the railroad. And it didn't have a thing to do with Ivy's heritage, just the mere fact they wanted things as difficult as possible for Molly and her family.

"I'll remember that," Carter finally said, showing no emotion as he walked away.

The other person in town who knew Carter was a Pinkerton man was the telegraph agent, so he stopped there next. Nothing new had arrived for him, and he explained messages could still be sent to the mercantile. He sent one telegraph asking exactly who at the Chicago and Northwestern Railroad had hired the Pinkerton agency to investigate the robbery—a year after it had occurred. He'd need all the information he could get to see this thing through now, not just in finding the robber but in stopping the railroad from harassing Molly.

When he arrived home, Ivy was having a tea party in the soddy, and Karleen was sitting behind the counter in the store, reading a book.

"Slow afternoon?" Carter asked, glancing into the farthest corners.

"Yes," Karleen answered without looking up.

"You weren't here. As soon as word got out, the queue slowed."

The girl was too smart for her age, but she was still likable. Accepting her mockery, he offered a bit of his own, "Are you going to put that one back on the shelf when you're done reading it? Sell it as new?"

"Of course," she answered. "You're welcome to do the same. I've told you that before." Whispering, she added, "Molly won't ever know."

"Where is Molly?" That had been his first question, and he'd held off asking for as long as possible.

"Upstairs. She said she had too much sun in the garden today."

Concern zipped up his spine, and he sought to quell it by rearranging a pair of the ugliest shoes imaginable on a shelf. "That doesn't sound like Molly."

Karleen looked at him over the top of the book. "Nothing has sounded like Molly for months now."

Every shelf and display table was organized and clean, as always—the girls were meticulous about that—so he moved to the counter. "Have you checked on her?"

"She's not a baby," Karleen answered, returning to her book.

"No, she's not, but too much sun can be dangerous." He'd go check on her himself, but couldn't. Anything other than the kitchen was off-limits to him. He'd agreed to that the first day. "I'll keep an eye on things here, you run upstairs and make sure she's all right."

Karleen huffed out a breath. She did enjoy her books, and spent plenty of time between the pages of one every day. He, too, enjoyed reading, even if it was just the dictionary one of the nuns gave him years ago, but there was a place and a time.

"It'll only take you a minute," he said, in a tone that demonstrated how serious he was.

She set the book down and marched past him, glaring the entire way, giving him a particularly nasty look over her shoulder as she passed through the doorway.

Carter grinned and held it until she was well out of sight. Agitated, mainly because he shouldn't be this concerned over Molly, Carter took a moment to check the cash drawer. There weren't any new or unusual bills, and the diversion didn't work.

If Molly was ill, they'd have to fetch the doctor. He'd swear the man to secrecy. There wasn't any other choice. The day would come though when even the doctor's secrecy wouldn't work. Carter was used to hiding things, it was part of his job, but usually when the truth came out, the fact he was a Pinkerton agent explained it all. That wouldn't work this time.

Footsteps on the porch had him glancing up. A cowboy strolled in, all smiles and swank, and there wasn't a single thing Carter liked about what he saw.

"Afternoon," the newcomer said, glancing around. "Had me a cinnamon roll here a few months back, served up by a cute little blonde. Thought I'd have me another one."

Carter's frustration hit a boiling point, and he rounded the counter, one hand hovering over the gun strapped to his hip. "How many months ago?"

"You're new here," the man said.

Carter kept moving forward. "How many months ago?"

The other man drooped slightly, took a step backward. "Two."

"And before that?" Carter asked, backing the man across the room.

"Never. I just started out at the Triple J two months ago."

"We're all out of cinnamon rolls," Carter said directly.

The stranger nodded, then spun and shot out the door.

Carter let out a growl. He'd never been so obsessed that he questioned every person he encountered. When he turned around, Karleen stood in the doorway. "How is she?" he asked, keeping his tone even. He could hope Karleen hadn't just witnessed his behavior, but that would be useless, about as useless as her not picking up how concerned he was about Molly.

"Sleeping." Eyeing him, Karleen walked behind the counter, picked up her book again.

"Are you sure?"

"Yes."

"In the middle of the afternoon?"

"What's wrong with that?"

"Nothing, but it's not like Molly." Frustrated, Carter glanced toward the doorway. His gut feeling just wouldn't let this one go.

"Go check for yourself," Karleen said. "First door on the left."

After he looked out the front door, made sure no one was coming down the road or lurking about, he crossed the store, telling Karleen, "I'll be right back."

He took the stairs two at a time. Molly was sleeping, lying on her side with her head on a pillow. Quietly, he backed out of the room, pulling the door closed.

"Satisfied?" Karleen asked when he entered the store minutes later.

He nodded, a touch startled by the heat in his cheeks. These women were driving him mad.

He'd just chased away a customer, and before that he'd irritated the railroad enough to increase their stance against Molly. His being here was putting the sisters in more danger than his protection was offering.

"So where did you go this afternoon?" Karleen asked, setting her book on the counter.

"I'll tell you at supper." He'd almost forgotten about his accomplishment today. The meeting with Wilcox had caused the thrill to die. "It's a surprise," he added, mainly because of the curiosity on her face.

"Do you do this all the time, Carter?"

"Do what?"

"Get so involved with the people you work for?"

A chill creeped around the top of his spine.

"Don't get me wrong, we like you. You've been great for business, but…"

Carter moved to the window, gazing through the glass without looking at anything. Taught to do so, as part of his job, he was used to jumping in, taking control of the situation, but he usually didn't get this involved. Actually never had, and he wasn't overly sure why he was this time. "But what?" he asked.

"Well, you remind me of my father."

"I've never been anyone's father, Karleen, and I don't intend to be."

"Ever?" she asked. "Don't you want a family? A wife to live on that ranch in Montana with you? A son to inherit it?"

"Nope."

"Why not?"

Over the years he'd came up with a thousand reasons why he liked being alone, and he turned around, figuring one would form before he opened his mouth, but it didn't. Not because of Karleen, but because of Molly, who was standing in the doorway. Of their own accord his eyes went to her stomach. He could never be a father because he didn't have the faintest idea as to how to be one, and unlike the Pinkerton agency, there was no manual to teach him how. Besides, being a Pinkerton man wasn't the safest job. He knew what it was like to grow up without parents, he didn't want that kind of responsibility—that of leaving others in his wake.

Truth was, the only child he'd ever met that he hadn't minded was Ivy. The one growing in Molly's belly might be all right, too. She had a way of making kids behave, Ivy was proof of that.

But he wouldn't be around to meet her baby. Most likely he would be in Montana by then. Not liking the notion of that, Carter pulled his eyes off her bump, but they had their own agenda and moved upward, where they caught Molly's gaze.

Only for a moment, though, because she spun around and disappeared.

Molly had never known simply breathing could be so hard. Air wouldn't catch in her lungs, and when little snippets did, they burnt, making her huff them out, and her very being trembled like she'd never known.

She'd been right in imagining Carter had a way of knowing her secrets. It was impossible, and there was no way he could know, yet he did.

Turning, Molly paced the length of her room on wobbly legs, only to once more stop at the window that overlooked the barn.

He knew she was pregnant. His eyes had said so.

How?

Molly crossed her arms, hugging herself as if that could protect her. She'd had a bad feeling about Carter Buchanan from the beginning, since the moment she realized he was the cowboy on the palomino.

He had to leave, that's all there was to it.

Now.

Before he told someone.

"You are awake."

Molly didn't turn around or reply, just wished Karleen would leave, give her time to think.

Carter was so stubborn she was going to need a plan. Just telling him wouldn't work—she'd tried.

Karleen didn't leave, either; instead she asked, "Were you downstairs a few minutes ago? I thought I heard someone on the stairs."

Instead of answering, Molly asked, "Where's Carter going?" He'd gone into the barn a short time ago and was now leading Sampson out the door, saddled. The sight tore at something raw inside her.

"He said he was going to take a ride after he was finally convinced you were sleeping," Karleen said. "He didn't believe me, had to check for himself. He didn't wake you, did he?"

Molly had heard Karleen, and moments later, Carter, open her door. Each time she'd kept her eyes closed, pretending to be asleep. Her nap had been over some time ago, but she hadn't been ready to face anyone. If she were smart, she'd have remained in her room rather than following him down the stairs. Then she wouldn't have heard the conversation between him and her sister.

But she wasn't smart. She'd followed, and stood there, waiting, wanting to know his answer. When he'd turned, his eyes had instantly gone to her belly, and that had been the moment she'd known he knew. Even before he'd glanced up.

Swallowing before her throat plugged, Molly

turned away from the window. Carter was out of sight. She'd watched until he was, not so unlike that first day, except then she'd been dreaming of the palomino.

"No, he didn't wake me. Maybe he's leaving." She walked to the door, head up, acting as if she'd be happy if that's what he was doing. It was exactly what she wanted. "Found a different job, or heading for Montana."

"He's not leaving," Karleen insisted, following her down the stairs.

"How do you know that?"

"Because that wouldn't be Carter."

Molly didn't slow when they reached the bottom. Keeping up her momentum, she marched her way down the hall and into the store. "How do you know? He's only been here a few days. You can't know what he will or won't do."

"Yes, I can. Carter will give us plenty of advance warning long before he leaves." Karleen opened the cash drawer. "You know it, too. You're just too grumpy to admit it."

It was a challenge to keep from glaring at her sister. If Karleen was as old as she tried to act, this would all be so much easier. Molly could just leave and put Karleen in charge of the store. She'd claim she'd met someone, and go someplace to have her baby. Then, in a few years, she could return and pretend her husband had died.

It was a good plan, but Karleen and Ivy were too young to be left behind, and Molly could never abandon her sisters. Not to mention that Karleen was too smart for that. She'd never believe such a tale.

Molly walked to the door and grabbed the handle, which wouldn't budge. "Why is the door locked?"

"Because I closed the store. We haven't had any customers all afternoon, and it's almost time for supper." Holding up a few bills, Karleen asked, "Do you want to hide this tonight, or do you want me to?"

Molly had no idea what she wanted, nor did she care who hid the money. "You can, I'll start supper."

"Just like that?"

"Just like what?" Molly asked.

"No argument?"

"I never argue over cooking supper."

"No, I mean my decision to close early?" Karleen stepped from behind the counter, blocking Molly's path to the kitchen.

"We've done it before," she said.

"Yes, we have," Karleen agreed. "But not for months. Carter told me to lock up early."

Molly should be irritated by that. He had no right, but the fight was slipping out of her.

"There's no use keeping the doors open when there aren't any customers."

"Glory be," Karleen said, reaching out and wrapping both arms around Molly's shoulders. "I do believe my sister still is in there somewhere."

The hug felt good, too good to ignore, and Molly returned it with one just as solid. "I'm sorry," she said while they were still arm in arm. The apology was real, she was sorry for so many things. "I guess the workload has been getting to me lately." Knowing just how hard her sister worked, too, she added, "Getting to both of us."

"And Carter has lightened it," Karleen said. "For both of us."

Molly remained silent. He had done a lot of work lately, but that hadn't made things easier. She was still pregnant. The railroad still wanted the store.

They parted, but Karleen kept one arm looped around Molly's shoulders. "Now if I can just get you to wear some of your old clothes."

"I like my dresses," Molly lied. "They are much more comfortable than—" she waved a hand at the tight waist and fitted bodice of Karleen's lavender dress "—all those buttons and stays."

"I don't doubt that," Karleen said, "but they make you look so frumpy. Like you stuck your head through an old sheet hanging on the line and then threw an apron over it."

The two of them used to giggle and laugh a lot, several times a day no matter how bleak things had looked, and Molly didn't realize until this very moment how much she missed it. Her laughter died as abruptly as it had formed, leaving her overly weepy inside. "I love you," she whispered.

"I love you, too," Karleen said, still smiling brightly. "And always will, no matter how frumpy you look." Her sister spun around then, grabbing both of Molly's upper arms. "Do you want to know a secret?"

No, she had enough to last a lifetime. But trying her best to wear a smile, she nodded.

"I hope Carter never leaves."

Ice crystals formed in Molly's veins. She no longer worried about Carter's interest in her sister, but hadn't spent much time worrying about the opposite. "Karleen, you—" she had to swallow "—you aren't..."

"Falling in love with him?"

The massive smile on Karleen's face was like a butcher knife, yet Molly managed to nod, though she was bleeding to death. She couldn't handle one more twist of fate.

"No." Karleen laughed extra loud. "But I

do like him. He reminds me so much of Papa. Which is why I hope he stays."

A small amount of relief had Molly's blood flowing as it should, her heart back to beating regularly.

"Surely you've noticed how organized he is, not to mention how authoritative. He's rearranged the store and he has all the things men are looking for right where they can see them instead of having us point them out. He makes everyone pay full price no matter how much complaining they do—and they don't complain to him. Why, he even had Mr. Wilcox guarantee our shipments will arrive on time. Papa hadn't even managed that. If anyone can, Carter will be the one to stop the railroad from putting us out of business." Karleen spun around and walked to a cupboard where she hid the money, now somewhat crumpled, inside an extra pitcher.

When her sister turned back around, she sighed dreamily. "Think about it, Molly. With Carter running the mercantile, we can have a life of leisure. The kind we used to know." Walking forward, still smiling, eyes somewhat glassy, Karleen continued, "You can go riding again, I can read until I'm blurry-eyed and we will both have time to try our hand at courting."

The baby chose that moment to move, making Molly freeze. Karleen had stopped walking, and she too looked starched stiff, as if she'd said something she hadn't meant to. Molly willed herself to breathe, not let anything show. Neither the baby, nor just how naive and young Karleen still was.

Lifting her chin slightly, Molly forced a smile to reappear, and because she truly wanted to know, she asked, "Is there someone you want to have court you?"

Karleen's sigh wasn't audible, but Molly saw it. "Not right now," her sister said. "I promised you I wouldn't think seriously about marriage until I'm eighteen, and I'll keep that promise," Karleen said resolutely. "Because it takes both of us to keep this place running."

The weight on Molly's shoulders increased tenfold.

"But, when I am eighteen, and Carter has this place running as well as Papa had it…" Karleen paused as a grin returned to her face. "I will take J.T. more seriously."

A year from now things would be worse. The railroad might own the store. Once her condition was revealed, the entire town would shun them—including J.T. and his entire family. Therefore supporting the hope in her sister's eyes was impossible.

"J.T. Walters is just a boy," Molly snapped.

"Neither of you have any idea as to the responsibility marriage brings."

Karleen frowned. "And you do?"

"Of course I do." Molly stomped across the room, but not so far she didn't hear her sister mumble. "What did you say?"

"Nothing."

"Yes, you did."

"I said it's no wonder you don't have any friends left. You can't be happy about anything," Karleen answered. "Just yesterday J.T. told me to tell you hello from Emma, but I didn't because I knew it would make you mad. Just like everything else."

The door slammed as Karleen left the house, but it was the amount of guilt rising inside Molly that made her flinch. Emma Smith, now Walters since she'd married J.T.'s older brother, Ralph, had been her best friend for years. They'd never argued, not once in all the years they'd known each other, until two months ago, when Emma had burst into the store, joyously proclaiming she was pregnant. The very day Molly had owned up to herself that she, too, was pregnant.

Seeing the shine, the excitement, in her friend's eyes had been more than she could take right then. Emma's ploy had worked. Molly's hadn't.

It had been in this very kitchen, just a few

days before her wedding, that Emma had told Molly about it. How she and Ralph had already been together. Emma said Ralph kept putting off the wedding, and she couldn't wait any longer, so she'd packed a picnic lunch and when Ralph became amorous, she encouraged him instead of stopping him. Afterward Ralph had agreed they should get married immediately.

On that day, and several others, Molly had thought her friend had been foolish, but the night of Emma's wedding, for some irrational reason, all she could think about was how it had worked. How Ralph had changed his mind.

Chapter Six

Molly spent the next hour or more moving slowly, cooking, for no matter how miserable she was, her family still needed to eat. The meal was ready and the table set when she walked out the back door in search of her sisters.

They were across the yard, picking daisies from a cluster near the barn.

She'd almost arrived at their side when Carter rode in. Her entire being somersaulted and Molly had to admit it wasn't a bad feeling he gave her. Furthermore, she'd known he'd be back, that he hadn't truly left.

"Hi, Carter," Ivy yelled as the palomino walked closer.

"Hello, Miss Ivy, Miss Karleen, Miss Molly," he greeted, full of smiles and grace as usual, while nodding at each one of them as if they were almost royalty.

Ivy giggled, and Molly had to confess the sound was musical. Everything Karleen had said about Carter was true. He was organized and authoritative, but her sister had missed a few things. He was also charming, way too charming, and handsome. Undoubtedly handsome.

"You're silly," Ivy said.

Molly cringed, half afraid she'd said her thoughts aloud.

"And you're pretty," Carter replied, climbing carefully out of the saddle.

His movements triggered alarm inside Molly, and she examined him more carefully. He was holding his side with one hand, which had her fearing he'd been thrown. She was about to step closer when Ivy spoke again.

"Not as pretty as Karleen, or Molly. No one's as pretty as Molly."

Carter's gaze had locked on hers and it didn't move, not even to glance at Ivy as he answered, "Well, Ivy, I reckon there is no one as pretty as Molly."

If there would have been air in her lungs, Molly would have spoken, then again, maybe not. She couldn't imagine what she would have said.

"Molly," Ivy said, "do you remember the dresses Mama sewed us? Me, you and Karleen?"

The only way to get past the haze swirling in her mind was to pull her gaze off Carter, so Molly did that.

Karleen had already knelt down in front of their little sister and was asking, "Do you remember those dresses? It was a long time ago."

Molly had been thinking the same thing. It had been more than three years. They'd been the last identical dresses Mother had made for the three of them.

Ivy's long braids bobbed as she nodded her head. "They were blue, a pretty blue, like Molly's eyes. And we all three looked alike. Like real sisters."

Karleen had looked up, but Molly's heart was already tumbling. "We are real sisters, Ivy. You, me and Karleen. We're family."

"I know," Ivy said. "But it was fun to look alike, wasn't it?" She looked to Karleen for reassurance.

Karleen pulled Ivy into a hug. "Yes, it was."

Molly had to walk past Carter to get to Ivy, and she didn't let it stop her. She knelt down beside both sisters. "You know what? There's some pretty green-and-white-striped cotton in the store. Enough for dresses. How about I make one for you and one for Karleen?"

"And you?"

Molly didn't have the heart to say no, but at

the same time, she didn't want to get Ivy's hopes up. "I'll see if there's enough material for three, but I know for certain there's enough for two."

"You are going to need a new dress, Ivy," Carter said.

Molly glanced up, only to discover he'd crouched down, too, was right beside her, and she pressed her toes harder into the earth to keep from wobbling.

"Why will I need a new dress, Carter?" Ivy asked.

"I'll tell you at supper," he whispered with a wink. "It's a surprise."

He shifted slightly, still holding his side, and once she got over how wonderful he always smelled, Molly wondered again if he was hurt. The smile on his face didn't show pain, but he was very good at masking things.

"Right now, I have another surprise for you," he said.

The hint of excitement in his voice had Molly holding her breath. Surprises, the good kind, hadn't been overly abundant lately and she couldn't deny the shine on Ivy's face.

"You do?" her little sister asked, nearly trembling with glee.

"I do," he said, unbuttoning his vest.

"What is it?" Ivy danced from foot to foot. "What is it?"

"Just a minute," he said. "Let me find it."

"I love surprises, Carter, I truly do," Ivy insisted.

Molly shared a quick glance with Karleen, reading her sister's mind. They were both getting caught up in Ivy's enthusiasm. Her middle sister, though, was also saying I told you, which made Molly glance away. Her gaze went back to Carter who was unbuttoning his shirt now. She tried to look away, but her common sense wasn't listening, and then a little head popped out the opening.

"It's a puppy, Carter!" Ivy squealed. "You got a puppy in your shirt."

"That I do, Miss Ivy."

When the entire animal—a wiggling bundle of yellow fur with long gangly legs—was extracted from his shirt, Molly couldn't help but wonder how it had all fit in there. How she hadn't noticed it.

"Where'd you get him, Carter?" Ivy asked, laughing as the puppy licked her face.

"At a farm up the road," he said. "He'll make a good watchdog. His mother is."

"Were you out at Mr. Ratcliff's place?" Karleen asked, laughing as the puppy licked her face, too.

"That's why he needed nails," Carter said. "He was building a new doghouse. Did a good job of it, too, and insisted I take a pup for showing him how to season those nails."

"It's a Labrador, then," Karleen said. "They make excellent pets."

Molly glanced at her sister.

"I read it in a book," Karleen explained with a very logical look.

"I believe that," Carter said, chuckling.

Last year at this time, even six months ago, Molly would have laughed too. But not now. Her world was already topsy-turvy, and Carter made it more so. She stood instead. Which Carter noticed and took her arm, to assist her. She stepped back as soon as possible, out of his reach.

"I've always wanted a dog." Ivy, hugging the pup, spun in a circle, filling the air with glee.

"Me, too," Karleen said. "We haven't had one for a long time."

Not since Duke. Even their father had shed a tear when the dog had died. Molly couldn't help but glance toward Carter, wondering if there'd ever been a time when he'd cried.

"I've always wanted a dog, too," he said, ruffling Ivy's hair instead of the dog's.

"If you rode all the way to the Ratcliff place," Karleen said, "you rode to the end of our land, Carter."

"I did?" he asked, buttoning his shirt.

Ivy set the puppy down, laughing as it ran

around her legs, which is where Molly told her eyes to stay. She'd tried hard not to wonder when Carter would button his shirt, and tried even harder to keep her eyes off him. A strange sensation was happening inside her, almost as though that dark and gloomy spot within—the one that had been frozen for so long—was thawing, and she was smart enough to know it was because of Carter. He, with his puppy and open shirt, had her thinking differently about men.

"Yes, you did," Karleen said. "Our land goes for several miles. If we sold some the store wouldn't have to earn as much to pay the taxes. But since the railroad is the only buyer, we aren't selling. Are we, Molly?"

Selling the land wasn't an option, never had been, and that was just enough to snap Molly out of her stupor.

"Supper is ready," she said, turning about. There wasn't a man on earth she'd ever completely trust again. And puppies were nothing but a lot of work.

"I wouldn't sell it either," Carter said earnestly. "It's good land."

Molly was walking toward the house and kept right on going as if she hadn't heard him. As usual. Carter held in a sigh and glanced at the younger sisters.

He hadn't meant to adopt a dog, but Owen

Ratcliff was a persistent man. The part about always wanting one was true, but he'd figured on waiting until he got to Montana, got settled on some good land. About as much as the Thorson sisters own. He'd known they owned the acreage around the mercantile, but hadn't expected it went as far as it did.

"Aren't you coming, Carter?" Ivy asked.

He tore his eyes off the horizon. All three Thorson sisters had started walking toward the house, and they'd all turned around and were looking back at him. They were pretty, standing there with the sun shining down on them, but his eyes only wanted to settle on one. Not the one wearing a stylish purple dress, or the one letting the puppy chew on one long black braid and grinning from ear to ear, but the prettiest. There truly wasn't anyone prettier than Molly Thorson. Even dressed in a large, ugly, gray dress.

"I have to put Sampson up." His throat felt as rusty as Owen Ratcliff's nails had been. "You three go ahead."

"Well, hurry," Karleen said. "We'll wait, but not too long."

Carter did hurry, truly didn't want them waiting on him, and though the meal wasn't any different from all the others they'd shared with him the past week, this one tasted better, and he wasn't exactly sure why.

He'd done some thinking while riding, about a lot of things. Very little of it had been about the money. He was thinking differently, acting differently, and it wasn't just the role he was playing. Truth was, he was enjoying this assignment. Not all of it: he still didn't have a suspect as to who stole the money. But coming home—that was a word he'd never used much before, but found himself thinking it often enough—and sharing meals as he was with the sisters was something he'd never experienced before, and it suited him. Although he questioned why and if it should.

"I swear, Carter, that pup was the best surprise ever," Karleen said. "Listen to that." The puppy was chasing its tail, spinning in circles until it rolled across the floor. "The pitter-patter of little feet," she continued. "A baby in the Thorson house, who would have ever imagined that?"

There had been several times over the past few days he'd wanted to tell Karleen to be quiet, and one was right now. All her reading left her believing she knew much more than she did. Some things you only learn through life. Like how stupid it was to bring a puppy home. He should have thought about how it would affect Molly—who was staring at her plate. The fingers holding her fork had turned white.

"Whose puppy is it, Carter?" Ivy asked. "I mean, is it yours, or is it ours?"

"Well…" Carter set his fork down. He couldn't very well take the pup back. Ivy would be crushed. "How about if we share it for now? While you're gone, I'll take care of him, and while I'm gone, you can take care of him."

Ivy nodded, but then said, "I don't go anywhere, Carter, 'cept church on Sundays."

"Well…" he said again, drawing the word out. Then he realized it was his opportunity to change the subject. "The puppy wasn't my surprise. Not my original surprise."

All three sisters were looking at him again, intently. "Remember I said you were going to need a new dress, Ivy?"

She nodded. Karleen frowned, and Molly stared. No expression. Just stared.

He had to gulp, not so unlike a man heading to the gallows. The smart thing would have been to consult her on this, too. The pup had upset her, and this might too. He wasn't used to asking for permission, but might want to remember it in the future—the near future, while he was here.

Picking up his fork, he scooped up some potatoes, and right before popping them in his mouth, he said, "Every schoolgirl needs a new dress."

"School?"

"Carter."

"Mr. Buchanan."

He knew exactly who said what, but chose to explain it once, to all three of them. Not used to explaining himself, he took a shot at it in one breath. "I went to Mrs. Rudolf's garden party today, and talked to the wives of the town council, explained how many states have set laws that all children must attend school, and by them not allowing Ivy to go, they could be breaking the law."

"Not in the Dakota Territory," Molly said.

"She knows, she tried that one last year," Karleen offered.

"Me? I get to go to school like all the other kids?"

Though he wasn't afraid to fight—never had been—he did know how to pick his battles, and when. He turned to Ivy. "Yes, you get to go to school. Starting Monday."

"You are a miracle worker, Carter," Karleen said. And when Molly called him Mr. Buchanan again, the younger sister reached over and laid a hand on Molly's arm. "Not now." She gestured her head toward Ivy, who was beaming as bright as the North Star. "Please."

"Is it a deal, Ivy?" he asked, keeping one eye on Molly. "I'll watch him while you're gone, and you watch him while I'm gone?"

"It's a deal, Carter," Ivy said. "It's a deal."

Thoughtful for a moment, she asked, "Are you going to church with us tomorrow?"

There was a slight trembling in his fingers. He hadn't gone to church for a long time and not even the Thorson sisters could change that. "Why?"

"'Cause then we'd both be gone." Ivy glanced straight across the table, to where Molly sat. "Or would you watch him for us, Molly?"

Karleen was across from him, and before Molly answered, the younger sister said, "Whose turn is it while you're both here?"

Deeply wondering why Molly didn't go to church with Karleen and Ivy—that seemed remarkably odd—Carter remained silent.

It was Ivy who asked, "Why?"

"Because he just piddled," Karleen said.

Sure enough, the pup was standing in a puddle, looking up at them with eyes so bewildered even Molly laughed.

"I'll clean it up and take him outside," Ivy said. "I'm done eating." She glanced toward Molly. "May I be excused?"

Molly nodded, but her smile faded as soon as Ivy left the table.

Once Ivy was outside, Karleen said, "You made her day, Carter." She sighed heavily. "If we were a rich family, in a fancy house in a big city, we'd have a glass of wine to celebrate the occasion."

Molly dropped her fork and Carter froze. She'd gone as white as she had in the barn the other day, right before fainting. He waited, watched, and when it was apparent she wasn't going to topple, he asked Karleen, "Is that something else you've read about?"

"Of course," she answered notably. "But I have tasted wine."

"When?" Carter turned to Molly, noting her wide eyes as well as the fact she'd asked the question the precise moment he had.

"At a wedding last spring," Karleen said, giving Molly a somewhat snooty look. "Ralph and Emma Walters's. Afton Smith is Emma's father and he had gallons of cherry wine at the wedding. Everyone tried it."

It wasn't his place to admonish the girl, but he couldn't refrain from doing precisely that. "You're too young to be drinking wine."

"It was just a small amount," she justified. "It tasted a lot like cherry jelly. Both J.T. and I had some."

Carter hadn't felt this type of anger ever. It was almost laced with fear. "You were drinking wine with a boy?" He turned to Molly. "And where were you when this wine tasting was happening?"

Her face turned crimson, and recognizing the snap in her eyes—she was about to go off on a rant—he grabbed her wrist. Without taking his eyes off Molly, Carter said, "Karleen, you can clean up the kitchen, Molly and I need to talk."

When Molly parted her lips, he squeezed her wrist a bit more forcefully, kicking the chair out from beneath him. She had to know what could have happened if Karleen and J.T. drank too much wine. Together. He pulled Molly from her chair, not hard enough to hurt her, but firm enough she knew he meant business.

Once he'd marched her into the hallway, she tried to break his hold. "I have nothing to say to you, Mr. Buchanan. Other than leave."

"Too bad."

"Let me loose. I have things to speak with my sister about."

Carter didn't bother answering, just kept moving forward. If he was to respond, he'd tell her it was too late for talking. She was proof of that. That too—her condition—angered him as it hadn't before. He led her through the store, to the far side where the storeroom was located. It was the farthest he could get from the kitchen, and from Karleen, who loved to eavesdrop. Most kids her age probably did. He had. But that didn't mean it was right, and he didn't want Karleen listening now.

"Where were you while your sister was drinking wine with a boy? On the dance floor?" His anger was growing. "Or you were you off drinking wine with someone, too?"

He'd let her loose, but when she raised a hand, as if to strike him, he caught her wrist again and used it to pull her forward, challenged her as much with his glare as his hold. "What were you doing at that wedding?"

She was breathing hard, and heavily. So was he.

"I wasn't at that wedding," she retorted.

"Why not?" Before she could answer, he added, "Where were you?"

Her faded blue eyes had turned stormy enough lightning could have flashed in them. "I was here. At home."

"With whom?"

She wobbled slightly, and he sensed how hard she fought to maintain control. He was too. His thoughts were no longer centered on Karleen and J.T. drinking wine. Notions of what Molly had been doing were flashing across his mind as bright as the lightning in her eyes. Her will might be one of the strongest he'd encountered, and he respected that, but he wanted answers. Now.

"With whom?" he repeated.

"No one," she snapped.

He didn't believe that, and wasn't going to

let her off that easily. "You were here, at home, alone?"

"Yes, I was."

"Why?"

Her tongue slid out to lick her lips as she swallowed and Carter had the urge to kiss her again, which made him madder. He was a Pinkerton operative, trained to interrogate people, not think about kissing them. "Why?" he barked about as loud as Ratcliff's old mother dog.

After she drew in a staggering deep breath, and then let it out slowly, which caressed his neck due to their proximity, Molly said, "Because the freight arrived as we were preparing to go. I couldn't leave it outside, so I sent Karleen and Ivy to the wedding and hauled it in myself."

"Why didn't you just have the driver unload it for you? Carry it in?"

A sneer formed. "He already had unloaded it," she said. "In front of the barn. As usual."

"The barn?" he scoffed. "That's over a hundred yards from the store."

"I know how far it is, Carter," she affirmed. "But that's how it is when the railroad is trying to take something away. They make it as difficult as possible for those trying to hold on."

The tears that trickled out of the corners of her eyes deflated a good portion of his anger and he let her arm loose, took a step back. "They leave your freight in front of the barn?"

"Yes." She spun around and he could tell she was wiping her eyes. "No matter what the weather, what time of day it is, they pile it in front of the barn."

There was no doubt she was telling the truth—about the railroad and the freight. He'd be talking to Ted Wilcox again, first thing in the morning, but right now he still had questions to ask her. "And it took you all night to carry it in?"

"Most of it. By the time I was done, the wedding was over. I could hear the dance music and…"

Her back was still to him, but he could tell she'd covered her mouth with one hand. She was shaking too, from tip to toe. He stepped forward, laid his hands on her shoulders.

"I didn't know she drank any of that stupid wine, Carter," she said softly. "I swear, until tonight I didn't know." Her shoulders trembled harder as she buried her face in both hands.

His anger had dissolved into compassion. "I believe you, Molly," he whispered. Carter could have carried on, made her tell him more, but the want to do that was gone. She'd been through enough for one day. Enough for a lifetime, but it wasn't over for her, far from it, and that tugged at something inside him, very near his heart.

He eased her around and tucked her head under his chin, let her cry a bit. It wasn't something he'd ever done before, held a woman as she cried, but it felt right. It also gave him time to contemplate what he'd learned. Though it didn't help as much as he'd hoped. It was impossible to think about anything besides her. How comforting her was uniquely satisfying, rewarding even.

Wrapping his arms more firmly around her, he swayed her tenderly and placed a tiny kiss on her hair.

After a while, when her crying slowed, he said, "When J.T. comes to the store, I'll be the one waiting on him, not Karleen."

Molly's chin bumped his chest as she nodded, even while saying, "She'll hate you for that."

"I know," he answered.

Molly lifted her head then, and even with tears still glistening on her long lashes, she cracked a tiny smile. The desire that sprang up inside him rocked Carter. He'd never desired someone so badly.

Seconds before he gave in to it, the impact of what he had just learned hit him. "When was this wedding?"

She bowed her head and took a step back. "March."

"Five months ago?"

There was no need for her to answer, the time

line fit. At least from what he knew of pregnancies it did. Which had nothing to do with why he was here, nothing to do with apprehending robbers or finding stolen money. Not exactly sure what to do, Carter turned and left her standing there. His anger was returning, and by the time he entered the kitchen, it was about as strong as it had been when he'd dragged Molly from the room.

"You're not my father, Carter," Karleen said from where she stood at the sink.

She'd been listening, no doubt, heard his comment about J.T. coming to the store. "I never claimed to be," he said, heading straight for the door.

"Then don't tell me what to do." Chin up, with a snooty little glare, she continued, "I'm doing the dishes because Molly cooked. I'm part owner here and do my fair share in every way. Including waiting on customers."

Arguing with a child was useless, but telling her the truth was necessary. "I'm not your father, Karleen," he said. "But I'll turn you over my knee and paddle your backside as if I am if you don't start acting your age." He wasn't overly sure that's what fathers did, but he'd heard it said often enough and it sounded fitting.

Without waiting for her response, he strode out the door.

Getting away from the Thorson sisters was not easy. Ivy was in the soddy, having a tea party with her dolls and the pup, who was asleep on the floor despite the bonnet on his head.

"Carter," she said as he walked in. "Does it cost money to have a dog?"

He sat down on the bed. "I suspect not. It'll just eat scraps and such." In desperate need of some solitude, he said, "It's probably hungry right now. You should go get something for him before Karleen throws it all out."

Ivy stood, but instead of gathering up the dog, she walked across the room and stopped right in front of him. Chin up, in a way that reminded him of Molly, she said, "Thank you for the puppy, and for letting me go to school."

Before he had a chance to answer, she bounded forward and flung both arms around his neck. As if it was as natural as the sun rising, he hugged her in return. It didn't seem odd at all, and actually caused a tender, unique warmth to swirl in his chest.

"I sure do like you, Carter."

His throat grew thick as he answered, "I sure do like you, too, Ivy."

She stepped away then and skipped across the floor to the dog. He did like her, and her sisters. Outside of Sampson, he never thought too much about liking someone—person or animal—because it just couldn't be. There were people he befriended, respected, such as Allan Pinkerton and a few other agents, but the last person he'd liked had been Amelia.

Picking up the puppy, Ivy asked, "Can he sleep in my room?"

Carter figured he'd already caused enough turmoil bringing the dog home, but saying no to those big eyes was next to impossible. As a compromise, he said, "Only if it's all right with Molly."

Pausing for a moment, Ivy bit her bottom lip before she nodded. "I'll bring him back if she says no."

Molly must have said yes, for Ivy didn't return that night, and regardless of a sleepless night, Carter was up early the next morning. When he noticed the little girl outside with the puppy, indicating the rest of the household must be up too, he shouted across the yard, "The chores are done. If I'm not back when you leave for church, just put the puppy in the soddy."

Ivy waved and Carter headed up the road. A sleepless night gives a man plenty of time to think, and he'd done that. Pondered all sorts of things.

Freight would never be left outside the Thorsons' barn ever again. He'd make sure of that, and as soon as he apprehended the robber and solved this case, he'd head out. It had taken twenty-some-odd years to figure out who he was. A cowboy working his way to Montana was as close as it came. A man who needed no one, and never wanted anyone to need him.

Chapter Seven

Molly sat behind the counter, working on a green-and-white-striped dress for Ivy. She'd started it last night, after Carter had left her in the store, where Ivy had found her. It had been an excuse then, when the child asked what she was doing, moments before asking if the puppy could stay in the house. Which it had, crying most of the night. Babies did that, so it hadn't bothered Molly, just reminded her of yet another thing she had to prepare for. Like the sewing did. The baby would need clothes, too, so she'd tucked an extra length of the material in her room to create infant gowns and diapers while everyone else was sleeping.

Sucking on a finger she'd pricked, Molly glanced up when footsteps sounded on the porch. Sunday mornings were slow, but an open store gave her an excuse not to attend church. She just couldn't bring herself to sit in a pew listening to lessons in her condition, though she probably needed it more than ever.

It was Carter who walked through the door, and her insides did several things all at once. How could she like and dislike him at the same time? There was so much to like, and so much to be frightened of, which is where the dislike came from—or something akin to it, for not liking Carter was as hard as liking him was easy.

"Slow morning?" he asked.

She nodded.

"Do you sell enough it's worth not going to church?" he asked, straightening the hideous white shoes from the peddler. She'd been swindled, and had learned from it.

"We need every sale we can get," she answered.

This morning, when she'd crawled from bed, she'd feared facing him, after letting him hold her the way she had, but when he'd never appeared at breakfast, she was more fearful that he'd left. It was all so confusing, and exhausting.

"Is that for Ivy?" he asked, nodding toward the material in her hands.

"Yes."

"She'll like school, and be good at it."

Staying mad at him was impossible, too. What he'd done for Ivy is what she'd been trying to accomplish for two years, and had her fingers crossed it would go well for her little sister. Ivy did deserve to go to school, and wanted it so badly. Therefore, Molly had to say, "Thank you, Carter, for convincing them to let Ivy go to school."

A slight shimmer glowed across his suntanned cheeks, which only increased his handsomeness. One more thing she thought about too much last night.

"The puppy isn't in the soddy," he said. "Have you seen him?"

She gestured toward a box near the door to the hallway. The pup had fallen asleep as soon as Ivy set him down and hadn't stirred since. Exhausted after being up most of the night no doubt.

Her mind was spinning, searching for something to say. It was maddening, how she didn't want Carter to leave when he was near, yet she did want him gone, as far away as possible. It made no sense. The two couldn't happen at the same time.

There was more to it—him being here. In the short time he'd been living in the soddy a sense of security had blanketed her, one she'd missed since their father had died, and wanted to hold on to even while knowing she couldn't.

He moved, and suddenly frightened he would leave, she blurted, "I can't believe you had that puppy inside your shirt and we didn't notice. It's practically half grown."

Stopping near the box, he knelt down, ran a single hand gently over the ball of fluff. "Sometimes we don't see things unless we know what we are looking for."

The hair on her arms stood on end, sending a shiver all the way up to her shoulders, and Molly pricked her finger again, drawing significant blood this time.

"He'll make a good guard dog," he said. "I could tell that right away."

The air left her lungs. Maybe he hadn't been referring to the baby. Perhaps he didn't know about it, either. He's never said anything, she just assumed he knew. Her mind took off again, started thinking about all the things she didn't know about him. Those thoughts had kept her up most of the night, and she removed her injured finger from her mouth. "How old are you, Carter?"

Leaving the puppy sleeping, he walked to the counter, leaned against it as he had that first day. "I figure around twenty-seven."

"You figure?" She shook her head, baffled. "You don't know?"

"Nope."

"How can that be?"

"My folks died on the voyage from Ireland

to America. I think I was about five, but I don't know for sure." He took his hat off, set it on the counter and ran a hand through his straight black hair. "Over the years, people guessed my approximate age, and when I averaged it all out, I estimate by now I'm about twenty-seven."

"So you don't even know when your birthday is?"

"Don't have a clue."

Sincerely touched by his openness, his willingness to share such information with her, she whispered, "I'm sorry, Carter."

"For what?"

She shrugged, not really sure why melancholy was settling in so deep, as if she was hurting for him. Then again, it could be her own foolishness, how she'd felt so sorry for herself when no one had remembered her own birthday last March. "Your parents, your birthday."

"Thanks, but it's not necessary," he said. "It was a long time ago, I don't remember much about it."

He was smiling, not sorrowful in the least, which increased her compassion while brightening her mood. He had the uncanny ability to do that, flip-flop a person and their thinking. Taking advantage of the opportunity to simply converse, she questioned, "Ireland? Buchanan doesn't sound Irish to me."

"It's not," he said. "My grandfather was from Scotland. But he married an Irish girl, and so'd my father. I'm mostly Irish." He pointed to his dark hair. "Black Irish."

She grinned. His black hair was only a small portion of what made him so strikingly fine to look at. "We have a touch of Irish in our blood, too. From our mother. Father was Swedish, full blood. He was big, with blond curly hair and the deepest voice you'd ever hear. He could tell stories, too. Grand ones that had everyone laughing."

"Even you?"

"Oh, yes. I remember laughing so hard my face hurt, my stomach, too." She ran a hand over the countertop, as if the wood her father had polished to a shine still held a touch of him. "No one could tell a story like my father." Memories, as strong as they were, of laughter filling the house, faded as she thought of what Carter had told her.

"Who raised you?" she asked, "After your parents died."

"No one really."

"How can that be?"

"When the boat arrived in New York, there were several of us whose parents had died. Plenty of children had died, too. Babies, the youngest of the young. The lot of us without kin were taken to an orphanage, and…" He twirled his hat around as he grew thoughtful for a moment. "I didn't take to life at the orphanage very well, so I left."

"Where'd you go?"

"The streets."

"Of New York?" She'd heard of such things, children living in the streets, but had never met someone who'd lived such a life. "What did you eat? Where did you sleep?" she asked, all of a sudden full of questions.

"I managed," he said as if he'd had no hardships. "Until I was old enough to jump a train."

"How old were you then? Where'd you go? Were you by yourself?"

"About twelve or so," he answered, grinning slightly as if amused by her onslaught of questions. "Two other boys and I made it as far as Ohio before we were discovered."

"Were they older than you?"

"No, we were roughly the same age."

Molly had a slew of more questions, but sensed a change happening in Carter, so she told him, "I was born in Ohio. We moved here from there when I was six."

"Really?"

She nodded.

"Well, we didn't hang around there long. Made our way to Chicago." He picked up his hat, then nodded toward the dog. "I better take him out. He'll probably have to go as soon as he wakes up."

There was so much more she wanted to know, but his features had turned hard, almost brooding. Unable to stop herself, she said, "There are cinnamon rolls in the warming oven, if you're hungry."

He'd already gathered up the pup, and gave a single nod. "Obliged."

Molly watched as he made his way through the doorway toward the kitchen, and thought about following, but keeping her distance was what she needed to do right now. Mainly because there wasn't a single part of her that disliked Carter Buchanan. Whether he knew about her baby or not.

Two hours later, after her sisters had returned home from church full of anecdotes proving they'd listened to Pastor Jenkins's sermon, Molly left Karleen in charge of the store and followed Ivy out the kitchen door. She had changed out of her Sunday dress and was on the hunt for the puppy, and Molly carried a glass of water for Carter.

With the help of Sampson, he'd dragged several dead trees from the bank of the stream that ran through the pasture and was now chopping them into logs to split for firewood—she'd witnessed his activities out the store's window.

Thoughts of his childhood had settled deep in her mind, and though it didn't ease the burden she still carried, it did offer hope. For herself, that is, and the baby. Carter was living proof people could face adversity and come out ahead. He had, living in the streets, and she would, too.

The sun was hot and Carter had removed his shirt, which was hanging over a fence post. It wasn't the shirt that had Molly slowing her footsteps. Bare skin glistening, covered with sweat, showed just what a strapping man a boy from the streets of New York had grown into, and Molly's breath caught at the sight and her heart turned a touch frantic. She'd hoped to come out here and strike up another conversation with him, but that didn't seem like a good plan now.

"You're not going to weed your garden in this heat."

There were times, like right now, when Molly felt as if she was on a teeter-totter, bouncing up and down and all she could do was hold on and hope she didn't flip off. Gnawing on her bottom lip, she lifted her gaze slowly until it met his.

His blue eyes were bright, but his gaze was stern. Carter was not only fit, he was a hard man who commanded respect and didn't tolerate disobedience. Which could be one of the things that rattled as well as annoyed her. She'd bowed once, given in to what she thought a man wanted, thinking it would change her life, and she would never do that again. Not because it had failed—it had changed her life—but because it had been wrong from the beginning.

Keeping that in mind, she stepped forward, handed Carter the glass of water. "Not right now." She waited until he was drinking before adding, "But I will later."

He finished emptying the glass and handed it back to her. "Not in this heat you won't. I'll hoe it for you."

It was hard to say what provoked her more. How he could keep his tone even and slow even while irritated, or having him think he could tell her what to do. He couldn't, and she certainly didn't need him to think he could. She didn't need him to cut wood, either, or to mollify customers or complete the list of other chores he'd so readily taken upon himself. "I've worked in the garden on days just as hot as this many times. Hotter even."

He'd settled one of those subtle gazes on her. It wasn't harsh or frightful, just direct, and it made the list of chores he'd already accomplished spin inside her head. She did appreciate all he'd done, and couldn't deny that—she had wondered about wood for winter. The shed had been full when their father died, and that wood had carried them through the past two winters, but it was almost gone now. Therefore she couldn't bring herself to defy Carter—not while he was seeing to their very welfare.

Molly nodded toward the dead trees that were gray and branchless yet so huge in girth that the thought of cutting through them was overwhelming. "There's a crosscut saw in the barn. That's what my father used to use."

That understated stare remained on her for a few moments, then with a slight grin he nodded toward the fence post and the large saw balanced against it. "It's dull," he said.

"The file is in the house." She quickly explained, "It rusts when left in the barn."

"You know that from experience?" he asked, taking a hefty swing at the log with the ax.

Splinters shot into the air, and she waited until they landed before answering. "No, I know that from my father. All his tools are in a wooden box in the supply room."

Carter took another swing at the massive log. Several, actually, hoping she'd go back into the house and leave him to the work that had to be done. Filling the woodshed was just one more chore he needed to complete before he could leave. Along with cutting the hay field. He'd hire a thrashing crew for that, but someone would have to oversee the workers, make sure they didn't take advantage of the sisters.

Preparing for winter wasn't something he'd worried overly much about before, but he'd participated in such activities while being undercover, and since he'd be doing it in the future—once he was settled on his own place— getting things done here so the sisters would be set when the snow came was good practice.

"You don't have to do this, Carter."

"Do what?" he asked, never slowing the swing of the ax.

"Chop wood."

"How else is the shed gonna get full?" He moved down the tree, having separated another foot-long section he'd later split to fit in the cookstove.

"I could hire someone," she said.

Planting the blade in the barkless tree, he rested a hand on the end of the handle. "I think you've noticed there aren't too many men looking for work in Huron. The railroad keeps them busy." The C&NW boasted a never-ending supply of jobs, which was good for the town, but left those in need of help shorthanded. He'd known that before coming to town, and that had been the reason he was practically guaranteed a job at the mercantile. Yet knowing the sisters would be on their own again when he left exasperated Carter. They'd be set for this winter, but what about next year or the year after? As self-reliant as they were, they didn't have the strength to get the hard work done, or, because of the railroad, the funds to hire it out.

"Plenty of men travel through," Molly said stubbornly. "Like you. Looking for work to get them to their next stop."

Having her depend on another man stirred something dark inside him. "Strangers shouldn't be trusted," he said, plucking out the ax again.

"Like you?"

That stung, but he ignored it. He'd never planned for the future before, not like this, and he was still struggling with the part of him that said he had to. "Go back inside, Molly, I've got work to do."

She crossed her arms. "You don't have to get grumpy. I was just trying to be nice."

If he'd been in a better mood, he might have grinned. Molly trying to be nice took a considerable amount of effort on her part. "Thank you," he said, acknowledging her attempt. "Now go back inside."

"No."

Lord, she was exasperating, and had the uncanny ability to rile him like no other. Truth was, Wilcox had started it, poking at Carter's temper by telling him all the help he was giving the Thorson sisters wasn't necessary to catch the robber. The man had been downright offensive when it came to Ivy going to school. Had the gall to say Carter was taking this case too far, sticking his nose in things he didn't need to be concerned about. At that point, he'd wanted to flatten Wilcox's nose, but he hadn't. Only because he never let anyone know what he was thinking. Ever. A kid on the street learns that early on— though he had flattened a few noses since then. A Pinkerton man was allowed to do that every now and again. That was another part of the job he never minded.

"I said no," she declared with a contemptuous edge.

He was already about as sour as last week's milk, and her snippy attitude was only adding to it. Taking her over his knee and paddling her backside wasn't a bad idea, but he doubted it would stop the urge to kiss her that was pestering him good and strong again.

She spun around and headed toward the barn. If he had half a mind, he'd let her go, but that was his trouble lately—he only had half a mind. Evidently the intelligent side had quit working, so he dropped the ax and took pursuit, having no doubt she was out to defy him.

Sure enough, that was her plan. He found her pulling the hoe from the rack. "I told you, it's too hot to work in the garden right now." The sweat pouring down his back should tell her that.

"It's my garden."

"I don't care whose garden it is." He wrenched the hoe out of her hand. "You're not working in this sun."

He foiled her attempt to snatch the hoe from his hold with one quick step. Glaring, she asked, "What does it matter to you?"

Carter couldn't rightly say why it mattered so much to him, but it did, and that was about as comforting as getting bucked off a horse and landing next to a den of snakes. Rattlesnakes. He hated those critters. Never imagined one would ever grow on him, but stranger things had happened. Like how this woman had grown on him. He'd been trying to escape that truth, but couldn't any longer. All three Thorson sisters had grown on him, and the odd thing was, they weren't as scary and hazardous as he'd once imagined. Women and kids, that is.

Molly Thorson, on the other hand, was dangerous, he had to admit that, but in a completely different way. This itch to kiss her was getting treacherous in its own right, too. The attraction he felt toward her amplified as she stood there staring at him as though he was a notorious scoundrel. He was a scoundrel, all right, and was damn close to showing her.

Carter swung around and hung the hoe back in its place. "Get in the house, Molly."

"Don't talk to me like that. I'm not a child."

He thought about ignoring her, but that was akin to disregarding the speed of a flash flood. You couldn't outrun them, either. "Then quit acting like one."

"I'm not acting like one, you are."

He'd compared their little standoffs to that before, which was ironic considering it had been a long time since he'd been a kid.

"Give me the hoe, Carter," she insisted while trying to dislodge the handle he still held, though the end of the tool was hooked on the rack.

He refused to relinquish his hold, which had her tugging harder while pushing at his chest with her other hand.

"I mean it, Carter."

Her words were sharp enough to blister and despite all else, he once again wanted to grin. He didn't. Instead he stuck to his original reasoning. "It's hot out there." An authentic pang let loose inside him then. "Do you want to faint again?"

"I'm not going to faint again."

"How do you know?"

"I just know."

Her eyes were snapping like flames. Things were flaring hot and fast inside him, too, though Carter wouldn't necessarily say it was his temper. He and Molly were in the corner of the barn, with little space between them, or for that matter, around them, and their miniature scuffle was stirring up enough dust to have little motes dancing in the sunlight sneaking between the wooden planks. She was so fascinatingly beautiful. Those sparking eyes, which had turned a much darker blue in the dim light, the delicate brows above them, and her mouth with lips that suggested they were as fragile as butterfly wings, even while pinched tightly together.

The gentle fragrance that always accompanied her was teasing his senses, too. She smelled like flowers, sunshine and cinnamon all rolled into one.

With a stomp of one foot, she demanded, "Give me the hoe, Carter." Tugging on the handle harder, she continued, "It's none of your concern whether I work in the garden or not. It's my garden and it's my hoe, and I'll do what I want, when I want. None of it is any of your business. Matter of fact, nothing around here is any of your business."

"Is that so?"

"Yes, that's so."

Exasperating, that's what Molly Thorson was. Downright exasperating and so adorable when she had her dander up, he could hardly take it anymore. *Hardly* wasn't the word. He'd reached his limit. Grabbing both her shoulders, he planted his lips against hers.

Carter wasn't completely a stranger to kissing a woman. There were one or two he sought out on occasion back in Chicago. Brothel women. At a time when he'd wanted a homecoming of sorts, after a long assignment. But that wasn't how he kissed Molly. Her lips were too soft and tender for hot, rough kisses. They needed gentle coaxing to come to life beneath his. So that's what he did, until, all petal-soft and warm, they parted slightly, and her breath mingled with his. The sensation was like none other. It warmed his blood and shot a thrill clear to his boots.

He tilted his head, to taste her more fully, and when her shoulders slackened, his arms slid around to her back, pulled her closer.

Her body slid against his, from chest to hips, as she wrapped her arms around his waist and returned his kiss with lips that met his over and over again. His blood let loose, throbbed hard and fast throughout his body. She was by far the sweetest treat he'd ever tasted, and when the tip of her tongue met his, he opened his mouth, capturing hers to fully explore and savor.

The connection was just shy of soul-shattering, and he cradled her face with both hands, held her as the kiss deepened, expanded until it consumed him fully. It was as if the kiss was a journey—he was remembering and forgetting things at the same time, mere flashes that all merge into one destination. Molly.

Breathless, Carter pulled back, thrilled and, he had to confess, a bit unsure. He let her loose and stepped away. Montana was his destination. His future.

Molly covered her mouth with one hand and the fear he saw flash across her face all but gutted him. She spun then, and ran, leaving him standing in the barn, the heel that he was. He'd done a lot of things in his life, but this one he may never be able to forgive himself. Molly was in a precarious position, and the last thing she needed was him taking advantage of her.

She was precious and fragile, too, and he had no idea how to treat a woman like that.

With fury now directed at himself, Carter left the barn and returned to the trees he'd hauled in. There he put his anger to good use. He let it swing the ax, chop the wood into logs he then split and stacked inside the woodshed. This he knew how to do.

The sun was hot, the air in his lungs hotter and heavier than ever, but Carter didn't slow, nor did he let his mind wander, until Ivy brought him out lunch a short time later, which he ate. The child chatted—something about her new dress and naming the dog Bear or Bob or Tom. Carter wasn't actually listening, so he truly didn't know what names she said, but nodded an approval. His eyes and mind were on the house. While at the railroad this morning, he'd learned the woman with all those kids had left the hotel, which meant there were several rooms available.

He really should go rent one.

Chapter Eight

Hiding in her room degrading herself hadn't done any more good today than it had for the past five months, so Molly left the bedroom with its walls that seemed overly suffocating, came downstairs, prepared lunch and then sent Karleen off to read a book. The store was slow, only a trickle of customers needed minimal things, and Molly sewed in between waiting on them. And thought.

Oh, yes, she thought.

She'd made a huge mistake five months ago, but today it seemed larger. Not because of her condition, but because of Carter. She'd spoiled her chances of ever having a life that might include a husband, a man she could build a future with—and sadly, kissing Carter had given her a glimpse of how wonderful that might have been.

For those few moments, being in his arms, she'd forgotten how dismal the world seemed. There, kissing him, everything had been beautiful, wonderful. She'd found happiness. Inside, where it really mattered. Where it came from.

It had been a long time, so she was a bit surprised she remembered how it felt to be happy, but she had, and she'd have given everything to have stayed right there, in Carter's arms. She would still be there if he hadn't pulled away, and looked at her with such shock on his face.

That's what had gotten to her. Carter rarely let his emotions show, but he hadn't been able to veil his reaction when he'd broken away from their kiss.

Molly buried her face in the green-and-white-striped material. Carter had been disgusted, utterly revolted by her and her behavior. She'd been shocked, too, by how she'd reacted to him. After what had happened with Robbie, she'd never imagined getting close enough to touch another man, let alone kiss one.

Kissing Carter had been so different. So wonderful and so right, she didn't regret it. She'd wanted him to kiss her for a while now, but had refused to acknowledge it. Even to herself.

She didn't want to admit it now, either. Because she didn't want to admit she was that kind of woman. For months she'd claimed to herself that what had happened with Robbie should never have happened. That it would never happen again. But her reaction to Carter suggested otherwise.

The attraction she felt toward Carter the past few days went against everything she proclaimed to hate. Watching him swing the ax, chop away at the wood, had made her want to have him hold her. Kiss her. No good could come of it, but that didn't stop her from wanting, and wishing once again that things were different.

The baby moved, but Molly wasn't surprised by the tiny flutter. The little life inside her seemed to know just when she needed to be comforted. She'd grown used to the reassurance the baby provided, but ultimately she should be the one doing the reassuring. That was a parent's job. And she was the only parent this little person would ever have.

Molly pulled the material away from her face and started stitching again while trying to stop the memories, but they came forward anyway.

It had been cold and gloomy that morning, but so had most of the days before it. March was like that, unpredictable. Anything from a blizzard to summer heat wasn't out of the ordinary. Nuisances, that's what that day had brought. Random dilemmas that had pitched her in all directions.

The first one of the day had been the chimney.

After months of nonstop fires, creosote had built up in the flue, and smoke had filled the house as soon as she'd started a fire in the big parlor stove that heated the store. Karleen had panicked, claiming the place was on fire, and when Molly had assured her it wasn't, Karleen started complaining about the smell, how all their party dresses would be ruined.

Molly had been more worried about the merchandise then, and said so. She'd also known what needed to be done, just had been unsure how to do it. Eventually she'd climbed onto the roof and dropped the chimney sweep down, knocking the crusty buildup off the inner walls of the chimney. After that she'd had to clean out the stovepipes. Karleen had helped, though she was busy with customers, whose main gripe had been the fact there weren't any cinnamon rolls being sold that day.

She'd just got everything cleaned up, including herself, when Ivy, who'd honestly been trying to help, announced she'd accidentally left the barn door open. Molly had left then to go retrieve the milk cows, which were miles away, and she got thoroughly drenched by the rain that had started to fall shortly after she left the house. Things hadn't gotten any better upon her return, and in hindsight—if she'd had the opportunity to relive that day—she'd never have opened the store, just gone to help her friend prepare for her wedding.

That had been the plan. She was supposed to be at Emma's by noon, to help with the preparations, but at noon, she'd been trudging through mud up to her ankles, leading two stubborn cows home to where a plethora of other minor disasters had happened. Little things really, but major that day. A mouse in the storage room, which had caused Karleen to uproot crates and boxes, a customer whose order hadn't arrived—nothing new in that—and a meal Ivy tried to cook for all of them burnt so badly Molly had thought the house was on fire when she left the barn after securing the cows in their stalls.

To make matters worse, Karleen was fit to be tied. Emma had sent her brother J.T. down to ask where Molly was numerous times throughout the day, which had Karleen claiming Molly was just trying to keep her from dancing with J.T. at the wedding celebration.

She hadn't been. The thought of dancing, of enjoying the evening, had been the only thing that had kept her sane. They'd needed the joy of a wedding. That very day had marked the second anniversary of their parents' death.

Eventually, once everything was cleaned up and the last customer out the door, she'd finally hung the closed sign in the window and they'd all dressed for the wedding. It had been then, when they'd walked out the front door, ready to attend the festivities, that Molly had never felt so thwarted in her life. It was her birthday—that hadn't mattered much until later, when she was all alone—her best friend's wedding—which she'd missed—but the final blow had been what she'd discovered sitting in front of the barn. Boxes and barrels and crates and bags. All the freight that hadn't arrived over the past month.

Unable to stand the tears on her sisters' faces, she'd sent them to the church, claiming she'd have everything put away in time to join them at the hotel for the dance. She'd known she'd never make it, and while carrying in load after load, the burden inside her had grown heavier than the freight. That's when it had all hit her, had her crying that it was her birthday, and no one had remembered. That her parents had been gone two years and she'd never see them again. Ever. She'd hated the railroad more than ever that evening, found herself wishing they'd just come take over the store, rid her of all the responsibilities that had fallen upon her and had her drowning with no hope of surfacing.

Through blinding tears, as she'd made yet another trek to the barn, she'd seen a vision. A man hoisting a heavy load and heading in her direction. She'd thought she was seeing things.

Robbie had been gone from Huron for months, and she'd doubted she'd ever see him again. He'd sought her out the year before because his father was part owner of the railroad and Robbie tried to convince her to sell the mercantile to them. He'd wanted one other thing, too.

She'd remembered all that, and in hindsight wondered what she had been thinking that night. He'd said hello as they passed, him heading for the store with his load, her trudging toward the barn for another armful. On the next trip he'd commented how pretty her dress was, and the one after that, he'd wished her a happy birthday.

After the last box was inside the store, they'd walked back to the barn to get a few bags of feed out of the rain that had started to fall again. That's when Robbie had offered her a taste of Afton Smith's wine. She'd refused, but when he'd insisted on toasting her birthday, she'd complied, taking a single drink from the large bottle he had.

One sip led to another—for it had tasted like cherry jelly, as Karleen had said—and soon the two of them were sitting in the hay, sharing what seemed to be a never-ending supply of wine. She hadn't laughed in so long, and Robbie had been so comical, telling her about all the places he'd been the previous year, how much she'd enjoy seeing them. That's when it had happened, when she'd wondered whether she could learn to love Robbie, maybe even enough to sell out.

It hadn't worked. She'd ended hating herself and Robbie.

A premonition of sorts chased away the memories midthought and Molly glanced toward the doorway before the thud of heels sounded. Another forewarning had her climbing off the stool and standing so that the counter completely concealed her stomach before Mrs. Rudolf appeared in the open doorway.

"Hello, Molly," the woman greeted, glancing in all directions.

A sour taste filled Molly's mouth. It was obvious the older woman was looking for Carter. Every woman who entered the mercantile, which was quite regularly these days, wanted him to wait on them. Bitterness grew inside her, making it almost impossible to answer, but not doing so would be bad for business. "Hello, Mrs. Rudolf."

Making her way slowly across the store, both because she was searching the farthest corners and her size didn't allow her to move quickly, the woman finally arrived at the counter. "Oh, are you making yourself a new dress?"

"No," Molly answered. "This is for Ivy." Her insides churned then, wondering if that's why the woman was here. To say the town council had changed their minds.

"For her first day of school?"

The smile on the woman's face could be deceiving. It was hard to know if she was happy for the child or happy to bring bad news. Mrs. Rudolf was capable of both, or either.

"Yes," Molly replied somewhat hesitantly.

"I'm so happy the town council listened to us this time." Leaning across the counter, Mrs. Rudolf whispered, "Husbands do listen to their wives, you know. As they should. Poor Mrs. Wilcox was very concerned her husband wouldn't agree, but he did once he heard we were all insistent upon this."

A shower of shame had Molly bowing her head. "Thank you, Mrs. Rudolf. I sincerely can't fully express my gratitude for the opportunity this is giving Ivy. She's beyond excited."

"As she should be," Mrs. Rudolf agreed kindly. "But Carter—Mr. Buchanan—is who you need to thank. He made us see the railroad should have no control over who attends school."

Molly couldn't come up with a reply, not before the woman spoke again.

"Where is he? Mr. Buchanan, that is?"

"I was outside, earning the salary Molly pays me for being a hired hand, but had to come wait on you, Mrs. Rudolf. You're one of my favorite people."

Molly went so stiff a cramp tore up the back

of one calf. Not only due to Carter's overly pacifying tone, but by the way the other woman lit up as if she'd just stepped into the sun.

"Oh, Mr. Buchanan," Mrs. Rudolf cooed. "You are a charmer."

That was putting it lightly, Molly thought, barely managing to keep from voicing it. He'd put his shirt on, had tucked it in as well, but his face still held the sheen of sweat from the work he'd been completing outside. Unfortunately, it made him all the more handsome and likable. Not what Molly needed right now. Nor was remembering how warm and hard his skin had felt beneath her fingertips.

"What can I help you with today?" He stepped closer, fashioned a frown to grace his lips. "Your replacement cup hasn't arrived yet."

"I know," Mrs. Rudolf assured. Casting a fleeting glance toward Molly, she added, "There's no rush on that, dear. I'm getting along fine with just the five."

Molly nodded, unable to do a whole lot more. Carter had moved to the counter, now stood within touching distance, and that had warm fuzzy things bursting inside her again. He was looking at her, too, and there was none of the disgust she'd seen in the barn. Instead, his eyes were bright, clear, and once again glimmered with that mysterious hint of mischief they always held. Her cheeks heated up and Molly had to bow her head.

"It's too bad, dear, that you aren't sewing a new dress for yourself," Mrs. Rudolf said. "You're such a pretty girl, and this material would look stunning on you."

Before Molly came up with an excuse, Carter said, "It would look stunning on you, too, Mrs. Rudolf. Perhaps you'd like to buy some." He took a few steps toward the materials table.

"I'm not a fan of stripes," the woman said.

Considering Mrs. Rudolf's size, that was a good thing in Molly's mind, and although she held in the thought, the sparkle in Carter's eyes said he knew what she was thinking, or close to, anyway.

"How about this one, then?" he asked, holding up a bolt of white cotton covered with large pink roses.

Molly bit her lips together. He looked almost silly, holding the colorful cloth below his chin, but the expression he tossed her way said she'd better not laugh.

His grin said he was teasing, and Molly covered her mouth, to make sure a giggle didn't escape. Carter flashed another look, saying he knew she was laughing inside, and he was too. It reminded Molly of how she and Karleen used to communicate, simply by glancing at each other.

They hadn't done that for a while now, not in the fun playful way she and Carter were doing right now.

Once in his salesman role, Carter couldn't be beat. Molly had seen it before, and today it didn't grate on her nerves; instead, his antics had jolliness creeping about inside her until she was enjoying them as much as Mrs. Rudolf. The older woman eventually bought the fabric, the entire bolt, thread and buttons to match, and a pair of the ugly white shoes Carter had convinced her were the height of fashion on the East Coast.

He was standing behind the counter next to Molly, wrapping the purchase in paper while she took Mrs. Rudolf's money, and Molly wanted to ask him how he did it. Go from a cowboy or hired hand to a salesman in the blink of an eye.

Opening the drawer to provide change, Molly stalled. A new five-dollar bill sat atop the others. It hadn't been there earlier, and no one had bought anything of significant cost this morning, not while she'd been in the store anyway.

Beneath the five she found the correct change and bid Mrs. Rudolf farewell. While Carter carried the woman's packages to the door, Molly pulled out the receipt book from the shelf and scanned the day's entries. Other than the few minor ones she'd penned, there weren't any.

After marking down Mrs. Rudolf's purchases,

Molly left the book on the counter and marched to the doorway. "Karleen," she shouted down the hall, knowing her sister was in the parlor, reading a book.

"What's wrong?" Carter asked.

She met him at the counter the same time Karleen appeared in the doorway. "What?"

"I've told you before," Molly said. "You have to mark down every sale."

"I do," Karleen answered.

"No, you don't," Molly argued. Pointing to the book, she said, "You didn't mark anything down today."

"That's because I didn't sell anything," Karleen insisted.

"What's wrong?" Carter asked again. This time he reached across the counter, laid a hand upon the one she had on the receipt book.

It took a moment for her to maintain her composure. His touch, though wonderful, wasn't nearly as off balancing as the concern on his face. Carter did let things show. She just had to know what she was looking for, as he'd remarked earlier.

"Have you made a sale today?" she asked, her voice softer than she'd intended.

"No," he said. "I've barely been in the store today. Only came in when I saw Mrs. Rudolf."

She wanted to ask why he'd come in then, but that could wait.

"Why?" he asked.

Using her free hand, she reached in the cash drawer, pulled out the five-dollar bill. "Because of this," she said. "It wasn't here when I put the money in this morning. I haven't sold anything worth five dollars today."

"Another mysterious five-dollar sale?" Karleen asked, moving closer to inspect the bill.

"What do you mean, Karleen?" Carter asked, edging around her and the end of the counter to stand next to Molly. He couldn't see the serial numbers, but in truth, didn't need to.

"This is the third time it's happened," Karleen said. "And each time I get blamed for not marking down a sale."

"Money doesn't just appear out of thin air," Molly said.

"May I?" Carter asked, nodding to the bill.

Molly handed it to him. The serial numbers were a match. "Five-dollar bills have shown up three times?" he asked, already knowing the answer. "When?" He knew that too, but needed to get the conversation flowing, especially while Karleen was still here. Her interest was waning, that was apparent by how she glanced toward the hallway, thinking of the book she'd been reading no doubt.

It was Molly who answered. "Yes, once in May, and then once just last week. It was a new bill, like this one back in May, but an older one last week. We didn't have a sale for that amount in May, but last week I truly thought it was an addition mistake or a sale not recorded."

"So the bills have just shown up?" he asked, choosing not to mention he'd switched out the new one for an old one last week. Overall that held no bearing. "No one's handed them to you?"

"No. I mean yes, they've just appeared," Molly said, pressing two fingers against her temple. "I'd remember a sale that large."

"I would, too," Karleen answered with an exasperated sigh. "And I'd write them down. Can I leave now?"

"Yes," he answered, handing the bill back to Molly. It wasn't until Karleen was gone he realized she hadn't been asking his permission. Molly was still gazing at the bill as if it was a great mystery, so he chose not to apologize for overstepping when it came to her sister. Besides, his mind was working too fast. At one time he'd thought Molly was involved with the stolen money, but that idea was now ludicrous. "So these bills have just randomly appeared," he said, needing to get her talking.

"Yes." She lifted her gaze and her pale eyes were full of worry. "That's scary, Carter. If someone can sneak bills into the drawer, they could be sneaking them out as well."

He had the undeniable urge to pull her into his arms and give her a reassuring hug. When Mrs. Rudolf had entered the store, he'd considered staying put, chopping wood, but afraid the woman was here to say the council had changed their mind about Ivy going to school, he'd grabbed his shirt and jogged across the yard. He'd arrived in time to hear they hadn't. Then, too, he'd considered not entering the store, unsure how Molly would react to him, but he'd been too curious. He wanted to know if she hated him or not.

It appeared not, so he followed his instincts now and eased one arm around her shoulders. Peering up at him, the tiny smile she displayed wobbled as she sagged slightly.

Few things in Carter's life had been impossible, not when he'd set his mind to it, but not reacting to Molly was just that—impossible— and more. It was akin to telling tomorrow not to come, and he knew he had to accept the inevitable and go from there. Just where it would lead was a mystery. Cupping her shoulder, holding her tighter to his side, he asked, "Has any money come up missing?"

She shook her head. "No." Staring at the bill,

she whispered, "I have a bad feeling about this, Carter."

He took the bill, laid it on the counter and then twisted her about, folded both his arms around her. Holding her tight, he kissed the top of her hair, which smelled as wonderful as the rest of her. "We'll figure it out," he whispered. "We'll figure it out."

For the first time in all the years he'd been a Pinkerton agent, he wanted to tell someone everything. Who he was, what he was doing, even more about his childhood and how those memories kept popping up lately. But he couldn't. He couldn't tell Molly any of that, so he just held her instead. Taking as much comfort from the embrace as he gave.

She was the one to end the hug. When she struggled slightly, pushed at his chest, he had to loosen his hold. He let his fingers slide down her arms to catch both her hands as she took a single step backward. Worry still filled her eyes, but there was more in them now. Shame perhaps.

That he wouldn't tolerate. "You have nothing to be ashamed of, Molly."

She hung her head, shaking it as a somewhat bitter groan sounded.

There was a limit people could endure, and he knew she was close to hers. He also didn't know what he could do about it. This was a role he'd never played, but, in all honesty, it was one he wanted to master. The idea of easing her burdens—not chores or duties, but the ones she secretly carried—enticed him. A primitive instinct he'd never experienced before told him it would be more rewarding than solving any case had ever been.

She refused to budge when he pulled on her hands, so he stepped closer and used one hand, still holding hers, to lift her chin, making her look at him. Feelings had never overwhelmed him, not for many, many years anyway, yet they were about to right now. He'd changed since arriving in Huron, and the intuition that he'd counted on over the years said there was more to come—if he was brave enough to face it.

He was.

"I'm sorry, Molly. I should never have kissed you in the barn." He shrugged, partly because he really wasn't sorrowful for the action, just for her reaction. "I lost my head for a moment. You're so pretty, and I've wanted to kiss you for some time now."

She closed her eyes, whispered, "It's not your fault. I wanted you to kiss me."

Excitement she might want him to do it again was working its way through his system, and Carter drew in a deep breath, trying to quell it for the moment.

"But I know it was wrong," she whispered.

The disdain in her voice was akin to being doused with a bucket of cold water, but he wasn't going to give up that easily. Not on her. Not when he was convinced she wasn't referring to the kiss they'd shared. "What was so wrong about it?"

Tears formed in her eyes, welled against her bottom lashes. "You don't know me, Carter. You don't know the things I've done."

He let go of her hands to cup her face and wipe away the tears with his thumbs. "You don't know the things I've done, either, Molly." He brushed her forehead with his lips, taking a moment to get the gravel out of his throat. "But I tell you what, I promise not to hold yours against you, if you promise not to hold mine against me."

Carter had never promised anyone anything, and had never believed he would, but right now, the way she was looking up at him with complete wonder in her eyes, he wanted to promise her the moon and the stars and the sun and the rain and everything else miraculous and unexplainable on this earth.

"I'll promise you something else, too," he said while his mind was still chasing rainbows. "I'll find out where those bills are coming from." Seconds ticked by, and when she still hadn't spoken, he added, "I don't want you to worry about them. I don't want you to worry about anything."

"Carter—"

"Let me help you, Molly."

A tiny sob sounded and Carter set his lips to hers, held them there, barely touching hers until a little sigh escaped her mouth, mingling with the one he let out. "Just promise me you won't worry about those bills. We'll work on the other one later."

Still gazing at him, she frowned slightly. "What other one?"

"That you won't hold what I've done against me."

She grinned slightly. "I highly doubt you've done anything that could be held against you, Carter."

"Really?" he asked, enjoying the touch of happiness that had sparked in her eyes.

"Yes, really."

Her grin increased, so did his.

"Then don't hold this against me, either." His lips caught hers swiftly, without him making any effort whatsoever. The idea of doing this, kissing her whenever the urge appeared, was more than appealing to him. Something he could definitely learn to live with.

Carter didn't want to, but ended the kiss when his ears alerted him to the fact they'd soon not be alone. "You go back to your sewing, I'll wait on this customer," he said, their lips still so close his brushed hers as he spoke.

"What?" She turned her head toward the door, their noses colliding in the process.

Chuckling, he spun her about by the shoulders. "I heard a horse. Go sit down."

She scrambled to the nearby stool, cheeks red, and picked up her sewing. Carter was closing the cash drawer, the new five-dollar bill hidden inside, when the pastor walked through the door. The man settled a longing gaze at Molly before turning an even, steady stare toward him.

"Pastor Jenkins." Carter figured he probably should have attempted to sound pleasant, but he hadn't like the way the man looked at Molly since arriving, and after kissing her, he liked it even less.

"Mr. Buchanan," the man replied. "Molly." His gaze returned to her. "We missed you in church again this morning."

There'd been a time, a few hours or so one day, when Carter had wondered if the pastor was the father of Molly's baby, but he'd changed his mind. He did still wonder if the man knew about it, or at least suspected it. There was something there, inside the man's mind. Carter saw it again as the pastor waited for her to answer. Which was highly unlikely. She was extremely skittish around the preacher.

"You do realize how hard Molly works to take care of her sisters, Pastor." He didn't want to alienate the man, since he might know something, so Carter continued, "I myself asked her this morning about not being able to attend church, but as she said, they need every sale they can get."

Jenkins's expression held understanding. "I do realize that, Mr. Buchanan, it's just that Molly is sorely missed at church, by many people. She was an integral part of our congregation for years, up until a few months ago."

Carter wasn't impressed with how the man spoke as if Molly wasn't even in the room. "I'm sure things will change soon, and she'll once again have more time for such things."

"Do you?"

That was a definite challenge in the man's words, so Carter replied with, "Don't you?" When the man didn't supply an answer, Carter flipped the conversation with a very straightforward question. "Have you received any new bills in the collection plate recently?"

The man frowned. "New bills?"

"Yes, crisp, newly minted, haven't been in circulation long."

Clearly intrigued, Pastor Jenkins stepped forward. "No, I can't say we have. Why?"

"Just a mystery we're trying to solve," Carter

said. "I'd appreciate it if you wouldn't mention it to anyone." He moved along the counter, closer to the stool she sat upon. "So would Molly." A bit of curiosity here and there that could leak around might be enough to make whoever had the money nervous, attempt to move it. "We can't say more than that. But, please do keep your eyes open, let us know if you see any."

The pastor passed a cagey gaze between him and Molly before he nodded. "I will."

Karleen appeared just then and Carter had to admit her timing was impeccable. Molly's hands were trembling and he wanted her out of here.

"Here's your cinnamon roll, Pastor Jenkins," Karleen said, setting a paper-wrapped roll on the counter. "I heard your voice. Ivy and I both shared how wonderful your sermon was with Molly."

"Thank you, Karleen." The pastor handed over a coin for the roll before he turned to Molly again. "The congregation was abuzz with Ivy's news."

"We have Carter to thank for that," Karleen said.

"Yes, you said that this morning," Pastor Jenkins answered.

Carter chose that moment to make their escape. "Karleen, watch the store. I have wood to chop and Molly needs to have Ivy try on her new dress."

Molly finally looked up from her sewing and he smiled reassuringly at the relief in her eyes. Taking her elbow, he helped her off the stool, and as they walked past the younger sister, he said, "Write down all sales."

"I do," she groaned.

He hadn't said it just to irritate her, he'd said it to see Molly smile, and it had worked.

Chapter Nine

Carter wouldn't say that what he and Molly had was friendship, but since Sunday they had formed a kind of amity. She didn't appear as high-strung or nervous and smiled more often, and he resigned to refrain from kissing her again. Which was hell. Plain and simple.

It wasn't as if they were ever alone, so though the temptation was there, the opportunity really wasn't. That helped. As did teasing her until she blushed, and the chatty conversations that consumed meal times. School agreed with Ivy and she sang nonstop like a lark on a sunny morning. That pleased Molly, and therefore it pleased him, too. This new role he was playing—or living, for that's what he was doing—was one of the easiest he'd ever acquired, but it hadn't made him forget his original one. The reason he was here.

No other new bills had shown up, but he had gotten a telegram from headquarters, telling him Eli Greer was the man who had hired the Pinkerton agency to investigate the robbery. Greer owned seventy percent of the railroad, while James Fredrickson owned thirty. Fredrickson was due to arrive tomorrow night, late, which is when they'd meet.

Greer, it seemed, had hired the agency only after a second shipment of money had come up missing. That was new information, and Allan Pinkerton, who'd sent the message, informed Carter it had happened at the railhead in Wyoming a few weeks ago. A suspect had recently been identified and would soon be interrogated. The results would be sent as soon as possible. Carter wondered if that was why Fredrickson was on his way to Wyoming, and planned on asking the man point-blank.

He hadn't told Wilcox about the other bill that had surfaced, and couldn't exactly say why, other than that Wilcox had irritated him again by once more suggesting when they'd met earlier this week that there was a reward if Carter could convince Molly to sell out.

That would not happen. He'd buy the store himself first. There was more than enough money in his bank account.

The slam of the screen door had him glancing up from stacking wood in the shed, and the smile that formed on his lips had become a regular happening—another thing he didn't mind.

Molly and Ivy walked down the steps. He moved into the sunlight, waiting and watching as they came closer, and chuckled at how the puppy nipped at the hem of Ivy's skirt flying around her shins.

"Hi, Carter," she greeted him.

"Hello. Did you have a good day?" They were still halfway across the yard, so he had to shout.

"Yes," she returned just as loud. "I don't go back now until Monday. We don't have school on Saturday or Sunday."

If someone had said making one child this happy would have felt this good, he'd have thought them crazy. Maybe he was the crazy one. Either way, he waited until they stopped in front of him before he asked, "Is that so?"

"Yep," Ivy said proudly. "We just have school Monday through Friday. And today is Friday."

He shook his head and created a mock frown. "I don't know, Molly, maybe Ivy is too smart for school."

Making Ivy happy may have been crazy, but hearing Molly's musical laugh was utterly captivating. Like nothing he'd ever heard.

"You may be right, Carter," she said, forming her own pretend frown and glancing at the child.

Ivy wasn't to be had. Giggling herself, she proclaimed, "You two are just teasing me." A flash of worry tugged at her tiny brows as she then asked, "Right?"

"Yes, we are," Molly assured.

"I thought so," the girl answered. "Here, Carter." She held out a plate. "Molly made cookies for my after-school snack, and she said I could share them with you."

Wonders never ceased to amaze him—all the new feelings that popped up inside him—and he knelt down. "Thank you. They look good enough to eat."

Ivy giggled. "We have milk, too," she said, gesturing toward Molly.

He hadn't noticed the two glasses she held. "I'll get us a log to sit on," he said, standing a stump on end and gesturing for them to set the cookies and milk on it.

Within minutes he had a long log, which he and Molly sat upon, and a smaller one for Ivy and her puppy beside the makeshift table. While they ate the cookies, including the dog that ate a fair share, Ivy explained she needed a new tablet. "I've already filled up my other one. Miss Denny says I have excellent penmanship."

"Is that so?" Carter asked. He was interested in what the child had to say, but sitting next to Molly was stealing his attention.

"Yes. And guess what else, Carter?" Ivy didn't wait for his response. "Next month we are going to have a recital. All the parents will get to come and listen to us. You can come too, and Molly and Karleen." After pausing for a brief moment, she added, "I don't think Bear can come. Dogs aren't allowed at school. He'll have to stay home, don't you think?"

Carter wasn't thinking about the dog. Molly had gone as stiff as the log they were sitting on. "Yes, Bear will have to stay home," he said. "Right now you should take him for a run. He's been locked up in the house most of the day."

The child was soon gone, as was the dog, and he reached over, took Molly's hand. "Are you all right?"

She sighed, nodded and glanced his way all at the same time, yet he knew she wasn't. In a month her pregnancy might not be concealable. He understood that, and for all the things he had come to understand, he had no idea what to do about it. Standing, he guided her to her feet beside him. "Let's take a walk."

"Where to?"

He shrugged. "Does it matter?"

A tiny grin formed as she answered, "No."

They walked around the woodshed and then he set a pace for the tree-lined creek that ran through the pasture. All the while Carter was unable to come up with anything to say. He'd never been self-conscious before, but found himself being just that lately. In several ways, and he'd started to let things show; he just couldn't help it at times. Mainly it occurred when a male customer entered the store and thought about taking advantage of a woman owner. For the most part Carter was able to keep things fairly hidden. One look was all it usually took to cause the men to back off, but Carter couldn't help but wonder what would happen if it came out in front of Molly, or even the girls.

It was what made him a Pinkerton man. Allan had told him so. Said it was his fiery Irish blood. Carter wasn't sure it was his blood, but his past. That fight for justice that had kept him alive since the boat ride from Ireland. It scared him a bit, too. Not that he couldn't control his anger—he'd been doing that for years—but how Molly might act if she ever discovered the real him. He'd never been ashamed of being a Pinkerton man. It had transformed his life and for that he was grateful, but this time he was regretting when the time would come for him to reveal his true identity.

He couldn't help but wonder if Molly would think of him—as many did Pinkerton agents—as little more than a trained thug.

Truth was, if he hadn't left New York, or if

Allan hadn't found him in that alley in Chicago, that's exactly what he might have become—a thug. Or maybe he still was, on the inside, and that's why the job had fit him so well. He hadn't pondered any of this before, but being around the sisters had him doing so, and wondering whether he should be protecting them from *him*. The least he should do was tell Molly who he was, what he was doing here. Keeping it from her felt dishonest, and he didn't appreciate that. The other thing he didn't appreciate was knowing that when he told her, this friendship they'd formed would vanish.

They'd arrived at the water, and searching for a way to break the silence, or maybe the heaviness inside him, Carter said, "I should come fishing here someday, catch us a few fish for supper."

"Do you like fish?" she asked.

He'd never been too particular about what he ate. A result of having gone hungry for days on end at times. "Sure, do you?"

"Yes." Moving closer to the stream, she picked up a pebble and threw it into the slow current, making rings that gradually disappeared. "My father loved fish, and he loved fishing. He'd sit on that big rock—" she pointed downstream "—near that wide bend, said there was a pool there the fish liked to gather in."

"I'll remember that," he said, stepping up behind her.

Molly closed her eyes and wished with all her might that Carter would put his arms around her—while at the same time wishing she wasn't wishing that. It had been that way all week. It hurt, too, that she couldn't reveal how she felt, but she didn't have either the wit or the strength to tell him everything that had to be said. Once it was said, this would all be over, the precarious relationship that had formed between them. *Relationship* might not be the right word, but she didn't know how else to describe it.

Carter's hands, strong and firm, settled on her shoulders and he gently spun her around, or maybe she turned freely on her own, sighing at the wondrous sensations his simple touch created.

"Molly." His expression was sober, his voice laced with quiet sincerity. "I'm not too sure what's happening here, but I've come to care about you and your sisters, more than I thought possible."

A large lump formed in her throat. She was a ruined woman, and the pain of that had her forcing back tears. What she wouldn't give to have met Carter a year ago. Even six months ago. Not willing to grow any weaker, to end up a sobbing mess, she lifted her chin a notch.

A peculiar twinkle appeared in his eyes. "Even Karleen. She has an appeal about her."

Molly tensed.

"Kind of like the kid sister I never wanted."

She tried not to smile.

"You know what I mean," he said secretively. "The kind you gotta love because it's illegal to kill them."

Completely understanding—for that was exactly how she felt about Karleen at times—Molly cracked a grin. "We've come to care about you, too, Carter."

His smile faded as he lifted a hand, cupped one of her cheeks so tenderly she almost swayed. In another world, where she hadn't destroyed all chances of happiness, she could have been the one person that mattered most to Carter. She wasn't being boastful or conceited, or even dreaming—she saw it in his eyes, and that wounded her more than anything else had so far in her miserable life.

"I'm here, Molly," he said as softly as before. "For whatever you need. And your sisters."

She shook her head, tried to make light of his seriousness. "What more could we need, Carter? You've fixed the barn and fence, got rid of the hornets, filled the woodshed…" Her throat was burning, making her stop, and her eyes were stinging. Sentimental tears, that's what they were. Because he'd helped them in so many ways, and certainly not because she was in love with him and could never tell him, could never act upon that love. She hadn't come upon that declaration easily. Loving him. It had taken days.

Days of watching him, contemplating all she knew about life and herself. She'd even denied it, thought it was little more than her emotions being out of whack, but in the end it was true. She loved him. And that was just one more thing she couldn't do anything about.

A crazy, wild thought flashed across her mind, and before she could stop herself, she blurted out, "When are you going to Montana?"

He frowned slightly, caught off guard by her question as much as she was. "I don't know. Not for a while."

"Why?" The crazy thought was growing, as was a bit of hope.

If Carter noticed her impatience, he pretended not to. "Because I have things to finish here. Your woodshed's only half full. Your hay field needs to be swathed." He was eyeing her keenly now. "Besides that, I don't know where in Montana I'm going. I have to scout out land for sale. That alone could take a year or more."

The small amount of optimism inside her crashed somewhere around her ankles. What he said was true. A man might be able to just leave, but a pregnant woman with two little sisters couldn't, not without somewhere to go.

Once again, as if he knew her deepest thoughts, he said, "You have so much here, Molly, more than a lot of people will ever have."

Unable to meet his gaze, she kept her eyes downcast, but nodded so he'd know she heard him. Understood. Her parents had worked hard to achieve all they had, and she couldn't just walk away from that.

A nod didn't seem to satisfy Carter, he forced her chin up with one knuckle, and what Molly witnessed in his eyes had her heart stopping and starting again with such force she gasped.

Without a word, Carter's lips met hers, so gentle and tender she had to grab his arms to stay upright. It was what she wanted, what she craved, but a moment later, it wasn't enough. She needed him so badly, in ways she didn't understand but couldn't contain, either.

Arching her neck, she grasped Carter's face and parted her lips, begging his to do the same. He didn't disappoint her, and while they kissed, a somewhat frantic storm of lips and tongues, Molly stretched onto her toes, felt the immense power that radiated off his body.

Every sense was heightened, became a part of their turbulent connection, and she gloried in the delicious pleasure racing across her breasts as Carter held her tighter.

Moments later, he let out a low growl as he tore his lips from hers and looked down at her briefly. She held her breath, looking up at him, still holding his face with both hands, still silently begging for more.

The next instant his mouth was on hers again, hot and demanding, and the kiss grew more demanding, more fulfilling.

When he shifted, started to lower her to the ground, Molly went willingly, pulling him downward without breaking their connection. Once on the grass, stretched out beside him, she closed her eyes when one of his hands cupped her breast, making it throb with joyous pleasure.

He was still kissing her, too, long and sensual unions that were broken up by short, hot ones that provided her with the perfect amount of air to keep the kisses going, and growing.

It wasn't until after he'd teased her sensitive nipples to the point they were aching in an almost wicked fashion that an ounce of sense had her grabbing his hand. It had been inching lower, and though a part of her mind told her it didn't matter, that he already knew what he'd feel, she just couldn't face it.

She settled his hand back on her breast, held it there as she willed for a whit of composure.

Carter had stopped kissing her, but was nuzzling the side of her face, placing tiny pecks along her hairline, and when she opened her eyes, he stopped and searched out her gaze instead.

The smile on his face filled her heart, and she couldn't help but grin in return.

"You," he whispered, kissing her brows, "are the most beautiful woman I've ever seen. And you grow more beautiful every day."

She tried to shake her head, but his words stopped her.

"Inside and out," he added, with such sweet affection a sigh filled her lungs.

Even with all that had happened, who she was and what she'd done, lying beside Carter, with his hand still cupping one breast, she felt utterly cherished. Holding on to that sensation with all she had, Molly rolled her head, pressed her temple to his.

He shifted slightly, and with the arm beneath her neck, he encouraged her to rest her head upon his shoulder.

She did so and buried her nose in his shirt collar. "You always smell so good," she whispered.

"Aw, Molly," he said somewhat huskily. "What am I going to do with you?"

"I don't know," she whispered, and then giggled, untroubled for the moment. He'd done it again. Erased all the worries she constantly carried, and this time she relished how wonderful that was.

Carter broke the tranquil silence a few minutes later when he said, "I knew a little girl at one of the orphanages I was in, who wanted to be adopted so badly she cried herself to sleep every night."

Intrigued, and slightly proud he was comfortable enough to share his past, Molly ran a fingertip over the buttons of his shirt. "Did you want that, too? To be adopted."

He covered her hand with his, held it still in the center of his chest. "No."

"Why not?"

His other hand was running up and down her arm while keeping her cradled against his side. "I was too old, already set in my ways."

She giggled at that. "How old were you?"

"About ten."

Lifting her head to see his face, she asked, "Did the little girl get adopted?"

"No." He moved just enough to kiss her forehead. "She died."

Saddened at his loss, she tucked her head beneath his chin. "I'm sorry, Carter."

"It was a long time ago," he said.

Sensing much more than he let out, she asked, "You loved her, didn't you?"

"I was only twelve when she died."

"So?" Molly argued. "Children can love."

He was quiet for a moment before he answered, "Yes, they can. I do know I felt sorry for her."

A sudden, searing fear shot over Molly. "Is that why you're helping me? Us? Because you feel sorry for us?"

Scrambling to sit up, becoming overtaken by the thought, she had to forcefully fight against Carter's hold. When he finally relinquished her, she was breathing hard.

He was still prone on his back, and snagged the back of her neck. "Would it be so awful if I was?"

Torn between wanting to escape and having him hold her again, Molly shook her head. "I don't want your pity, Carter."

"Pity?" He was pulling her toward him. "Do you really think what I feel for you is pity?"

Not sure how to answer, Molly chewed on her bottom lip. His fingers, wrapped around the curve of her neck, were sending tiny shivers down her spine, as was the glint in his eyes.

"If so," he whispered against her lips, "I'm not doing a very good job."

It wasn't as if his kiss caught her unaware, she'd known it was coming, still, she was somewhat taken aback by how completely soul-shattering it was. When it ended, Molly slumped against his chest, and stayed there as his hands roamed up and down her back, soothing her all over again.

This time, when she sat up, it was to ask him more about his childhood. "Do you still know some of the people from the orphanages?"

He tucked his hands behind his head and stared up at the leaves creating a canopy over them. "No," he finally said, thoughtfully. "I suspect if I saw Sam or Malcolm I might recognize them, but I wouldn't know them."

"Are those the two you ran away with? Sam and Malcolm? Ended up in Ohio?"

"Yep."

She pondered a few things herself before tentatively asking, "Do you think we'd have met, you and I, if we'd both have stayed in Ohio?"

Smiling, he removed one hand from beneath his head and threaded his fingers between hers. "I think if we were destined to meet, we would have. Whether here or in Ohio."

"You believe in destiny?" she asked, a bit surprised.

"Of course. Everyone does." His gaze grew serious. "Destiny is our dreams coming true, Molly. Sometimes it's dreams we didn't even know we had."

That seemed rather profound coming from a man as practical and sensible as Carter. "And your destiny is Montana?" she asked.

The silence that followed had her heart ticking away the seconds as persistently as a newly wound clock, and when Carter planted his heels on the ground, arched his back and bounded to his feet in one swift movement, she remained seated. He held his hand out to her, but she shook her head, she wasn't ready to get up, not until she heard his answer.

He appeared taller and broader, and for a moment, she wondered if this was how Ivy saw him, and fully understood how the child had taken to him so quickly. He was like a towering giant, reaching down to offer assistance.

His hand was still there, and even though he hadn't answered her question, Molly laid her fingers in his palm. While she rose, he asked, "What's your dream, Molly?"

Having been stuck in the past for so long, she couldn't answer, but still hoping he'd provide one, she offered the truth. "I've so many regrets, wishing I could change things, I can't say I have a dream."

He ran a single finger down the side of her face. "That's not right, Molly. A person always has to have dreams."

Her insides atremble, she had to close her eyes for a moment. "Have you always had them?"

"Yes. I'd have never gotten out of that first orphanage without dreaming of how better things could be."

Molly couldn't discredit his belief, nor did she want to be this hopeless, but the truth was, very little could compare to what was in her future. The joy, the blessing of having a child should be one of the greatest ever, but hers was greatly overshadowed by how her condition came to be. She'd allowed it to happen, and nothing could ever change that. "What if they can't?" she asked. "Can't ever get better."

"Everything can always get better, Molly."

She knew the opposite. Was living proof. And she didn't need to drag him down with her. Dredging up what she hoped resembled a smile, she said, "I better get back to the store. I shouldn't have left Karleen alone this long."

Carter frowned and his features turned hard. His hand slid from the side of her face to grasp her chin firmly. "I won't let anyone hurt you, Molly, or Ivy, or Karleen."

Ironically, she did know that, and that he wouldn't be here forever. She couldn't ask him to stay, to right her wrongs, to give up his dreams. The things that made him who he was. A truly remarkable man. "Thank you, Carter. For all you have done. It's made a world of difference." She broke from his hold then, started walking away.

"I'll take you to Montana," he said from behind her. "You and Ivy and Karleen, if that's what you want."

The struggle within her was fierce. Half an hour ago that had been exactly what she'd wanted him to say. She even contemplated it for a moment, as she stood, staring toward the big house with its storefront and the outbuildings surrounding it. She did have more than many people had, and she wouldn't give it up, or more so, wouldn't make her sisters give it up. "Thank you, but no. That's your dream, Carter, and I don't expect you to share it with me."

Chapter Ten

Carter was already in a foul mood, had been since yesterday when Molly had left him alone at the creek bed, and standing here listening to Wilcox prattle on about his wife was making it worse by the second. He was impatient too, wanted to get this meeting with Fredrickson over. Molly had been avoiding him all day, and although he had expected that from the Molly he'd first met, he didn't expect it from the one he now knew. Nor did he like it.

"Women are fickle creatures," Wilcox said. "What pleased them yesterday won't please them today."

Carter scowled at the man's back, half contemplating what he'd said. There was a lot to learn about women and such. It wasn't something he'd ever needed before, but Wilcox's bitter tone didn't suggest his lessons would be worth listening to. Therefore, Carter didn't listen. When it came to Molly, he needed the right advice.

Looking out the second-story window, he peered down the tracks. It was already well past midnight. "You're sure his train's coming in tonight?"

"Yes, it'll be along soon," Wilcox said. "It's running off the schedule, just a few cars and Fredrickson's private coach, so it can only roll while the tracks are free."

Carter left the window as the man took to prattling again, this time about rail schedules. Taking a seat on a chair in front of the mahogany desk, Carter tilted his hat to shield his face from the wall lanterns lighting the office. As soon as his lids closed, a picture formed.

Molly.

He'd become quite obsessed with her, had grown committed to helping her, too, which was proving to be rather difficult. She didn't want his help. Truth was, he had no idea what she did want.

When she'd asked about Montana, he'd thought it was because she wanted him to take her there, but when he had told her he would, she'd said no. What was a man to think about that? Other than it had been a stupid offer. He had nothing in Montana. No place to live, no way to make a living. And a woman needed both. A house and an income. That's what it took to raise a family. A street orphan understood that deeper than most. He also couldn't let her give up all she had. Land. The mercantile. Friends and family. No one in their right mind would do that.

Molly was confused, he understood that. And scared. He still believed there was more behind her fear. Being unwed and pregnant was enough, but there was more, and solving that mystery was becoming first and foremost. That's where he was at. Unsure. And it didn't settle well with him.

"There it is," Wilcox said with a portion of relief.

Carter rose from his chair and followed the other man out of the office, ready to get this night over with. He and Wilcox were on the platform when the train approached. There was no whistle blowing, just the chug of the engine and the hiss of the brakes.

Fredrickson soon stepped down beside them. A short man, moderately pudgy around the middle, and hosting a long handlebar mustache that curled beyond his cheeks due to a good portion of wax. The man was shifty too, and it was clear to Carter that his superior size intimidated the smaller man. Carter didn't mind that in the least. He'd used his size to intimidate before and would use it again.

"Mr. Buchanan, I presume," Fredrickson said rather pompously.

Carter gave an indifferent nod and shook the man's hand. An instant dislike had already formed inside him, and the man's squishy, damp hand confirmed his initial impression was on target.

As soon as the pleasantries were over, they headed for the depot and the stairs to Wilcox's office. The sooner he got this over with, the sooner he'd be home. Not that he'd see Molly tonight, it was too late for any chance encounters, and he'd never trespass into her home uninvited. He'd come to appreciate being there though, knowing he was on hand to protect all three sisters if anything disruptive happened.

"So what kind of trouble is Robbie in this time?" Wilcox asked as they walked through the big double doors.

"You know how women love my boy," Fredrickson chortled. "Appears he forgot his papa's advice, got a woman claiming she's carrying his baby." Harsh laughter echoed off the empty space as the man looked over his shoulder, gave a knowing nod.

"A man's got to stick with whores or at least married women, no one cares when they come up pregnant."

Carter was not only disgusted, his disposition

hit about the darkest point it had ever been. The urge to throttle someone hadn't been this strong in many years. A kid in the streets sees plenty of things, and one of those is the mistreatment of women. Though Carter would never claim to have been taught how to treat a woman properly, he did know how not to treat them, and he'd like to teach Fredrickson and his son about that. Firsthand. With his fists. Until they learned that every woman, no matter who she was, deserved respect.

"What are you going to do about it?" Wilcox asked.

Fredrickson, huffing as he climbed the last of the stairs, chortled again. "She won't be a problem, and I've got a job my boy's gonna love."

Once in the office, Carter took a seat. However, the desire to solve this case was waning fast and furiously. He held no empathy for crude men, and the only thing keeping him in the room was the fact Fredrickson hadn't hired him. If he had, Carter would have quit on the spot. No, that wasn't quite true. He'd have quit on the spot if Molly wasn't somehow involved. She was. His intuition said that, so he stayed, and willed his temper to remain hidden.

Planting his round frame in the leather chair behind the desk, Fredrickson started firing questions. Carter answered woodenly, undisturbed that the man wanted far more than he provided. The pompous fool even attempted to demand redundant details. Considering the mood Carter was in, Fredrickson's attitude was no match. He did, in a self-indulgent way, enjoy the way color rose up on the jowls that hung over his crisp collar and spread across his jaw.

Carter's determination never to let his temper show hadn't changed—not here on the job, anyway. Back home, however, it was a different story. Karleen had told him at supper he was acting about as grumpy as Molly, who hadn't come downstairs for dinner. She'd spent most of the day up in her room.

"I have a feeling, Mr. Buchanan, you aren't telling me everything you know," Fredrickson said, drawing Carter's attention back to the meeting.

"Then the feeling's mutual." Carter tipped his hat back, just to level his gaze on the man. "I'm waiting for you to tell me about the second robbery."

The man bristled and tugged his sparkling gold vest down to cover his protruding stomach. "That has nothing to do with this one."

"How do you know?"

"I just do."

"How?"

Backed into a corner, Fredrickson switched

gears. "That's what I'd like to know, how *you* know about the latest robbery."

Carter lifted a brow to accompany the insolent stare he gave the man. "It's my job."

The tension in the room increased and Carter waited it out. He had all night. It was Fredrickson who had a train to catch. It was about that moment, while waiting for the man to reply, that Carter understood why he never let his temper show. It irritated his opponents more than fisticuffs did. He'd spent enough time fighting as a kid, and was glad when he finally learned it took more skill to win without ever throwing a punch. And that the majority of men never learned from having their face bashed, they just got meaner.

Once again focusing on the man across the room, he now wondered if it was time to change that habit, too.

It wouldn't be a fair fight, but he'd feel a whole lot better after breaking Fredrickson's nose. That was about the only thing that would change, though, so Carter stayed in his chair. The utter disrespect the man had displayed while speaking of his son still had every muscle in his neck tense. He couldn't help but think of Molly, the insolence she may soon encounter, and how he needed to make sure that didn't happen.

"I suspect it is your job," Fredrickson drawled. "But not the one you were hired to do. I suggest you quit worrying about that robbery and solve this one."

"I'm not worried about it," Carter assured. "Just curious why the connection between the two hasn't been revealed."

"There is no connection." Fredrickson narrowed his eyes as he leaned forward, planted his hands on the desk. "I wasn't the one who hired you, but I'd gladly be the one to fire you."

"And I'd gladly let you do it," Carter answered, meaning it. "But we both know that's not going to happen."

Fredrickson's entire face turned as red as the lit end of a cigar. "I'll be back in two weeks and will expect this case to be solved by then."

"You can expect all you want." Carter stood. "This case will be solved when the robber is delivered to Chicago." He left the office too infuriated to care if he'd offended the owner, or part owner, of the railroad. The man's attitude had taxed his tolerance. Anyone with such low regard for women didn't deserve any more of his time. He'd solve the case because he'd given his word to the Pinkerton agency, and more important, to Molly. He'd said he'd find out how those bills got in her cash drawer and he would.

The full moon thinned out the darkness of night, and Carter walked home slowly. The desire to get the case centered in his mind was there, it just wasn't working overly well for him. Molly took up more space mentally. He hadn't purposefully put her before the case, it had merely happened that way. She needed him. The railroad didn't. A frustrated sigh left his lungs. The Pinkerton agency was counting on him, and he'd fulfill the commitment.

All these years he'd imagined he'd put his past behind him, but now he knew by becoming a Pinkerton man he'd just moved it to the next level. All this undercover work was simply covering up who he really was. An orphan. A loner. He wasn't so sure that was what he wanted anymore.

He was cutting across the yard in front of the mercantile when a deep intuition kicked in, shattering his thoughts and clearing his thinking at the same time.

Quickening his steps, knowing someone was behind the house, Carter arrived at the corner. Silently, he flattened his back against the wall while drawing his pistol. After taking a moment to listen to the quiet that revealed little more than crickets and frogs, he eased his head around the corner. The strain burning his shoulders instantly slackened, washed over his body and he holstered his gun. The light shining under the outhouse door said it was just one of the sisters.

He let out a sigh, but it didn't help much. He was still strung tight.

Carter made his way to the soddy, glancing toward the smaller building several times, and he left his door open so he could make sure whoever it was got back into the house safely. It was a bit odd, he'd never seen one of them use the facilities after dark, and had assumed they had little chamber pots for such things. After lighting a lamp, he moved to the doorway to wait.

A click sounded, followed by the creak of the door hinges, and his heart tumbled inside his chest when he recognized Molly carefully stepping out of the tiny building. She carried the lantern with one hand, a small bundle in the other. An appreciative sigh, one he'd grown accustomed to, begged to be released.

Her hair was in a single long braid, flipped over one shoulder and hanging almost to her waist, and her nightgown was almost as big as her gray dresses, and she was as beautiful as ever, illuminated by the soft glow of the moon.

Carter considered not saying a word, just watching her walk past, but that idea faded as quickly as it formed.

Stepping out of the soddy, he searched his mind for an appropriate greeting. When nothing formed, he whispered loud enough for her to hear, the one thing he wanted to know. "Are you mad at me?"

It all happened at once. Her startled gasp. The lantern going one direction. The bundle another. And her crumpling to the ground. Carter ran, cursing himself the few steps it took for him to arrive at her side.

"Molly." Crouching beside her, he helped her sit up and cupped her face. "I didn't mean to scare you."

Twisting against his hold, she whispered, "The lantern."

Carter stretched, righted the lamp so it sat on the ground. "The flame went out. It's fine." He also grabbed the bundle, which appeared to be another nightgown. After setting it down, he rubbed her cheek. "I didn't mean to scare you."

She dropped her head so low her chin almost touched her chest.

Unsure what else to say, he whispered, "I'm sorry, Molly."

She shook her head. "It wasn't you. I tripped over my gown."

Taking her arms, he offered, "I'll help you up." Her slim shoulders drooped even more and she made no attempt to stand. "Molly?"

"I'm bleeding, Carter," she whispered.

"You are? Where?" He scanned her arms.

"Did you skin your elbows when you fell? Your knees?"

"No," she said despondently.

A shiver was spiraling his spine, and it increased when he noticed the tears on her cheeks. Still crouched beside her, his knees grew weak as an unthinkable thought occurred. "Where are you hurt, Molly?"

The panic worming a path through his system was confirmed when she covered her face with both hands.

He cursed himself again, and tried to pretend he wasn't about as afraid as he'd ever been. Scooping her up, he carried her into the soddy, laid her down on his bed. "How long?"

"All day," she groaned.

He spun from the bed, took a step, but had no idea why, so he turned back. "Why didn't you say something? Tell someone?"

"Who?"

Raking a hand through his hair, he admitted, "I don't know. Karleen?"

Molly glared at him for a moment, then her face collapsed like she had, and the tears started trickling from her eyes again. "I'm scared, Carter."

Kneeling, he laid a hand on her forehead. "I know you are, sweetheart." His mental abilities had returned, thankfully. "But there's no need to be. I'll be right back."

She grabbed his arm. "Where are you going?"

"To get the doctor."

Her nails dug into his skin. "No."

"I have to, Molly." He kissed her brow. There was no way to ease her fears, other than to promise, "Don't worry, I'll swear him to secrecy."

"No, Carter, I—"

"Molly," he interrupted sternly. "You need a doctor, and I'm going to go get him. I'll be right back."

He didn't really know if she agreed or not. He was already out the door, wondering if he should run or take Sampson. Figuring he'd need the animal if Dr. Henderson wasn't home, Carter ran for the barn. He didn't take time to do more than open the stall door before swinging onto the horse, then rode out of the barn as if hell was nipping at Sampson's heels.

Berating himself for not checking on her when she hadn't shown up for supper, Carter almost rode past the street the doc's house was on, and without a bridle, it was all he could do to convince Sampson to make a sharp right.

A moment later, Carter slid off the horse's back and cleared the little fence separating the house from the street. When his knocks went unanswered, he leaped off the porch and ran to the barn behind.

Empty. Carter was as close to full-blown panic as he'd ever been, when someone shouted.

"You there—are you looking for the doctor?"

For the briefest of moments Carter wondered if the buggy had appeared out of thin air. It hadn't been there a moment before, nor had he heard the clip-clop of the horse pulling the rig to a rolling stop.

"Is that you, Mr. Buchanan?"

"Yes!" Carter rushed past the horse so fast it tossed its head at the wind he created. "It's an emergency."

"It always is at this time of night," the doctor said. "Was just out to Bob Fisher's. His wife thought the baby was coming, but it was a false alarm."

"It's Molly Thorson," Carter said, vaulting into the buggy, knowing full well Sampson would find his way home.

"Molly? She hasn't been sick a day in her life," the doctor said. "What's wrong?"

Grabbing the reins out of the other man's hands, Carter answered, "I'll tell you along the way."

He might never remember exactly what he said, but knew he'd gotten the message across when the doctor, holding on to the brace rails with both hands, declared, "I'll never have a chance to tell anyone if you kill us both before we get there."

Carter had no intention of killing either of them, but he did stiffen against the terrible storm of emotions Molly had planted inside him. The seeds had been sowed about the first time he saw her, and right now, they'd become a raging blizzard he wasn't quite sure how to contain.

Looking small and scared, she was still in his bed when he hurried through the door, and she kept her gaze averted from the doctor going to the washstand in the corner. The same one he used each morning. A crushing pressure Carter couldn't have explained if he had to squeezed his chest from the inside. He knelt next to the bed, took one of her hands in both of his.

"You shouldn't have—"

"Shh," he stopped her hushed protest. "There's nothing to worry about. You don't need to explain anything, just let him help you."

Her eyes were paler than ever and full of what Carter had to call dread.

"So, Molly," the doctor said, splashing in the water. "Have you been dizzy, light-headed, fainted?"

She closed her eyes, and Carter answered for her. "Yes."

Snatching the towel from where it hung on the

wall hook, Dr. Henderson asked, "How else have you been feeling? Happy one minute, cranky the next?"

"Yes," Carter answered without giving her the chance. He also lifted a brow when the doctor frowned.

"What about swelling?" the man asked. "Your feet or other places?"

Carter couldn't say on that—other than her stomach—and turned to Molly. Despite her paleness, her cheeks were tinged pink.

"What about cramping? Or pain?"

Carter was staring at her, waiting to hear her answer. Which didn't appear to be about to come out, not with the way she was gnawing on her bottom lip.

The doctor spoke again. "Mr. Buchanan, I need you to leave us alone."

"No," Carter answered.

"I've heard of you men. Never met one, but heard of them, and how they don't take no for an answer." The doctor stood at the foot of the bed, eyed him squarely. "I don't take no for an answer, either."

Carter was about to protest when the doctor added, "I'm sure Molly will be more comfortable with you outside."

The trepidation in Molly's eyes chilled him in ways winter weather never had, yet the way she glanced toward the open doorway told him he had to go, wait outside. "I'll be on the other side of the door," he told her. "I'll hear if you call."

She gave a tiny nod, and seeing her so meek and mild only added to how fragile she was right now, and that tore at him. Not caring that Dr. Henderson still stood near the bed, watching their every move, Carter kissed Molly. Full on the lips. "You don't have to explain anything to him," he said again, hoping she understood he was referring to how she'd become pregnant.

Once she nodded, Carter stood slowly and faced the doctor. "I'll be right outside the door."

"I don't doubt that."

Carter left then, though it was extremely difficult. Molly needed someone, and he wanted that someone to be him. Before the door closed behind him, the good doctor said, "Put my horse in the barn, would you, Carter?"

Carter whirled about, but discovered nothing to stare at except the firmly closed door. After an indiscernible amount of time, which felt like hours but was probably only minutes, he moved, and went to put the doctor's horse and buggy in the barn—only because he didn't want anyone to see it in the yard.

Molly didn't know what to expect and was embarrassed by how thoroughly Dr. Henderson examined her. He didn't say a lot, not concerning her condition, but did ask about Karleen and Ivy, and shared his enthusiasm that the girl had been allowed to go to school. Relishing talking about anything except the reason he was here, she found the capacity to explain Carter was to thank for Ivy's education.

"I'd heard that," the doctor said, covering her with the sheet and blanket.

She pulled the covers up to her chin, grateful to be completely covered again, and kept her gaze on her hands where they'd naturally gone to rest upon her stomach.

"I'm going to let Mr. Buchanan in now—that way I won't have to repeat myself. Is that all right?"

"Yes," Molly said. Dr. Henderson had frowned several times during the examination and she wanted Carter by her side when she heard the doctor's findings. He entered immediately and her heart somersaulted. So did the baby—at least it felt that way. Without a single word, Carter rushed to her side.

She lifted a hand and blinked at the tears forming when he took it, kissed it, then knelt beside the bed. He was so very handsome, so strong and solid, and genuine. Beyond all good sense, she wondered how she'd ever manage when he left.

"Are you all right?" he asked.

Unsure how to answer, Molly glanced toward Dr. Henderson.

The man was replacing his instruments in his black leather bag. "A little bleeding isn't unusual during pregnancy," he said. "Everything seems fine, so that leads me to believe it's nothing to worry about this time, either. Just to be on the safe side, I'd like Molly to rest for a day or two."

Relief was flowing over her, and that set a few tears free. Yet if word got out she was bed-bound, rumors could spread. In her case, it wouldn't be rumors.

Dr. Henderson seemed to understand her plight. "You don't need to stay in bed," he said, picking up his suit coat. "But take it easy. No heavy lifting or long walks."

"I'll see she rests, follows your orders," Carter said.

Molly was unprepared for how devoted Carter sounded, how deeply his sincere gaze penetrated. Yes, she'd admitted her attraction to him, even fathomed she'd fallen in love with him, but she had no right to ask him to take care of her, especially not while she was carrying another man's baby.

"I must admit, I was a little surprised," Dr. Henderson said.

Molly wasn't sure which increased her frown,

the doctor's words or the way Carter snapped his head to stare at the other man.

"You're several months along, Molly," the doctor continued. "I'd say the baby will make an entrance in December."

She'd already calculated that herself, as well as how long it might be before the world knew.

"I'll need to see you again, tomorrow, and again in a couple of days." Dr. Henderson moved to the door and waggled a finger at her. "I'll need to see you regularly thereafter. A first pregnancy isn't the time to disregard your health."

Molly flinched at his frown. She wouldn't say she'd been disregarding anything, and once again held her breath, waiting for him to ask who the father was. It had to be coming, and when that got out, life promised to be impossible. It was the one thing she had been able not to concentrate on. She didn't want to now, either.

Carter gave her hand a gentle squeeze as he stood. "Thank you, Doctor," he said, crossing the room to shake the man's hand. He also dug in his pocket. Molly should protest she'd pay her own bills, but decided to wait and tell him that after the doctor left.

He followed the man out the door, and she let out a long, heavy sigh. Relief now flowed into disgrace. If only she'd known more. If she'd had someone she could have asked, then she'd have known the bleeding wasn't life threatening. It hadn't been that bad, and she'd been telling herself since noticing it this morning there was nothing to worry about. It hadn't been until she saw Carter after leaving the outhouse her true fears had burst open. The tiny life already meant so much to her, and she'd feared her behavior had brought this on. How she'd wished things were different, that she wasn't pregnant. She didn't wish that, not entirely.

It was as if she was stuck in the middle of a very rickety bridge and didn't know which way to go. She couldn't leave town, abandon the only home her sisters had ever known, but she couldn't stay either.

She wanted the baby with all her heart, but she didn't want her child to be surrounded by humiliation—or worse. Both choices left her feeling extremely selfish and somewhat terrorized.

Flipping back the covers, she eased her legs over the edge. She would take it easy, do nothing to cause harm to the baby, and she'd make a decision soon, figure out which direction she'd have to go to get off the bridge she was on.

About to stand, Molly paused when the door opened.

"What are you doing?" Carter asked.

He moved like lightning, starting in one spot

and landing in another in little more than a bright flash.

She pushed off the bed. "I'm going to the house."

"No, you're not."

He lifted her into his arms again and laid her back down on the bed, then gently tucked the blanket around her. Molly considered protesting, just getting up, but the doctor's warning wouldn't let her, or maybe it was Carter's attention. Mood swings. Dr. Henderson had mentioned them. She buried the back of her head in the pillow, suddenly exhausted. The doctor said that was normal, too.

"You heard the doctor," Carter said. "You can't walk all the way to the house, up the stairs."

"I have to," she said, smothering a yawn.

He took off his hat and his gun belt, setting them both on the table. "No, you don't. You can sleep right where you're at."

She shook her head while her eyes closed of their own accord. "No, I can't."

The mattress shifted beneath her, and she opened one eye, too tired to lift both lids at the same time. Carter was sitting on the edge and after kicking off his boots, he lay down beside her. She shouldn't like it, shouldn't want it.

"Yes, you can," he said, scooting closer.

The intimacy practically stole her breath.

"And I'm going to lie right here to make sure you do."

She had to attempt some type of protest. "But the girls. They can't—"

"They won't. I'll wake you long before sunrise. Make sure you're in your bed before they wake up." He snaked an arm beneath her neck.

The tears that gathered weren't in her eyes, but in her throat. Being held by him erupted a desperation of feelings, of needing, and of irrefutable comfort.

With his other hand he dowsed the lamp, and then folded that arm around her, too. "Go to sleep, Molly. You're safe."

Safe. That she knew. It was everything else she had to worry about. Molly closed her eyes, wanting to block the surplus of warnings that were sure to come, but all that happened was a great sense of respite. She was still trying to convince herself she couldn't sleep in Carter's bed, snuggled next to him, breathing in his wonderful spicy scent, when that was exactly what she did—and fell into a deep, restful sleep.

She didn't realize how deep her slumber was until he was saying her name, waking her gently. When she stirred, tugged her heavy lids open, he whispered, "It's almost daybreak. I'm going to carry you into the house."

Her tongue was thick, didn't want to work,

wouldn't form the word *no*, or tell him she could walk. A grumble deep in her throat was all that came out.

"Shh," he said, lifting her off the bed. "We don't want to wake the girls."

That she did agree with, and wrapped her arms around his neck.

Chapter Eleven

Molly barely remembered the trip into the house, how Carter settled her into her bed and then disappeared. She actually wondered if she had dreamed it all, until she opened her eyes and saw Karleen standing next to her bed.

"Ivy and I are leaving for church now. Carter is minding the store. He said you were still sick most of the night. That you spent a considerable amount of time in the outhouse."

Heat flushed into Molly's cheeks.

"I brought you some tea and toast." Her sister gestured to the bedside table. "That should help. Carter said to tell you to stay put. I'll come check on you when we get home."

Molly waited until Karleen closed the door before letting out a groan and pressing one palm against her forehead. Carter hadn't been surprised about her pregnancy. He had already known, as she'd feared. A heavy but cleansing sigh left her chest. In reality, having him know was more of a comfort than anything.

Her gaze went to the door, and more than curiosity had her wondering if she'd still feel this way when she saw him again.

There wasn't a lot she'd be able to do about it either way, and she'd have to face it, now or later. She flipped back the covers, smiled at the thought of Carter tucking her beneath them and crawled out of bed.

She was dressed and had just finished making her bed when a soft knock sounded on her door. Several emotions jostled inside her, strong enough that she had to take a deep breath before she started to cross the room. The door opened before she arrived, and she stopped, stood in the center of the rug covering the open space.

"Good morning, Molly."

Air going in and out collided inside her lungs. "Good morning, Dr. Henderson."

"Don't worry. I waited until the girls left for church."

She nodded, though in many ways she felt more exposed than she had last night.

A man well past middle age, Dr. Henderson probably understood his patients beyond their medical conditions. His passion for helping others and his perceptions of how to best see to the needs of all kinds of people had never waned in all the years she'd known him, and didn't now.

"I won't need to examine you completely again, just check things and ask a few questions." He gestured toward the bed. "Why don't you sit down."

Molly sat, needed to, and folded her hands in her lap to prevent him from seeing how they trembled.

He set his bag on the table and while digging in its depths, he asked, "How did you sleep?"

"Fine, thank you," she replied.

Assembling his stethoscope, he nodded toward her. "Unbutton the top few buttons of your dress, please. I need to take a listen."

She did, and forced herself to relax when he set the cold metal against her skin. "How's the bleeding? Has is stopped?"

"Mostly." Having used the chamber pot under the bed just moments ago she was able to answer.

"Bright red or dark?"

"Dark, I guess."

He nodded and she waited, wondering what difference, if any, it made.

"Good, that's good." He waved a hand. "Lie back, I want to listen to the baby."

Molly followed his directions, and held her breath to keep from flinching when he unfastened one button over her stomach for the end of his stethoscope. He moved the instrument around a little bit and then grew very still, listening. She didn't dare breathe until he straightened and started dismantling the listening device.

"Everything sounds good," he said, taking her hand. Once she was sitting up, he turned to replace the stethoscope in his bag. "You can button up. Do you feel the baby move?"

She fastened her dress, the buttons at her waist and neck. "Yes. More often lately."

"How does it feel?"

"Wonderful." Swallowing the lump in her throat, she bowed her head.

"That's how it should feel, Molly. Wonderful. It's quite a miracle."

"I know," she whispered. Not being able to freely cherish and express the sensations, the love she already felt, was so incredibly disappointing and grew more so each day.

He'd picked up his bag, now stood before her with sincerity filling his wise and wrinkled face. "I understand you and Carter need to keep this a secret a bit longer. You don't have to worry I'll disclose anything, but don't let the situation prohibit you from experiencing the joy of becoming a mother. That's part of a healthy pregnancy."

Molly was listening, but her mind was stuck. She needed to keep it a secret. Carter didn't.

Other than for her. Yet the doctor sounded as if he thought the baby was both hers and Carter's.

"I still want you to go slow. Sit a lot. Let others do things, especially for the next few days. I'll be by to see you soon."

She'd been nodding, mainly to let him know she'd heard his instructions, but lifted her head now. His visits would arouse suspicion.

"Don't fret, Molly. No one will know why I'm here."

His smile was gentle and sincere as he turned and crossed the room, but once at the door, with the knob securely in his hand, he paused. Glancing over his shoulder, he frowned slightly. "I have to tell you what I told Carter. You won't be able to keep this hidden much longer. He needs to complete his business soon."

Dr. Henderson was long gone, and Molly was somewhat frozen where she sat on the bed, staring at the closed door.

Carter's business was to earn enough money to make it to Montana.

Nettled at herself for being selfish again, she finally rose and walked to the door. Of course that was Carter's business. He'd said it from the first day he'd arrived. She was the one who kept forgetting it.

Carter was in the store, sweeping the floor near the front entrance, and the sight turned her into little more than a grin with a body behind it. He looked as handsome as ever, but the broom didn't fit him. His movements were stiff and rather awkward, and she hadn't wanted to laugh out loud so badly in years.

"I can do that," she finally said.

He spun, smiled. "No, you can't." Using the handle, he pointed toward the stool behind the counter. "You can sit down and watch me. Tell me what I'm doing wrong."

"Wrong?" She moved to the stool. Not because she was tired, but because that's what he wanted her to do, and doing what he wanted felt right. "You aren't doing anything wrong."

"I'm sure I am. I've never used one of these before."

"A broom?"

"Yes. A broom."

She could no longer stifle a giggle. "It shows."

His expression flashed distress, but she knew he was teasing and laughed again.

"So tell me, what am I doing wrong?"

"Well, to start with, you should sweep in one direction." Her heart was thudding steadily, enjoying the silly conversation as much as the rest of her. "Short strokes forward, until you have a pile, not back and forth."

"Aw, that makes sense," he said, following her instructions.

"You've really never used a broom before?"

"Not that I can remember," he answered, now sweeping the small amount of dirt out the open doorway.

Molly refrained from saying he'd now have to sweep the porch; she'd do it later. He put the broom in the storage room and then walked around the counter, all the way over to where she sat. His expression had become more sober, and she bit her bottom lip.

"How are you feeling?"

"Fine."

He lifted a brow.

"The doctor said everything is fine."

Carter touched her cheek, rubbed the side of her face with his fingertips. "He told me that, too."

"You don't believe him?"

"I want to," Carter admitted, though in all honesty he was having a hard time believing a whole lot of anything. Including how utterly lovely she was this morning. Her cheeks were flushed an adorable shade of pink and her pale blue eyes were glistening with slivers of silver. He did want to believe everything was fine, including her health, but there was still an instinct inside him that warned of danger or troubles ahead.

"Thank you, Carter, for—for helping me last night."

All she'd been through swirled in his mind— and what might have happened if he hadn't been there. He leaned down, kissed her forehead. "You're welcome."

Their gazes locked as he lifted his head and once again, Carter grew unsure. He'd done that a lot lately, and although he was almost getting used to it, he wasn't fond of the feeling.

"Has it been slow this morning?" she asked.

He took a step back and leaned against the shelf lining the wall behind him. "Yep, not a single customer."

"It's Sunday."

He nodded. "Karleen made cinnamon rolls before she left. Do you want one?"

"No, thank you. I'm fine."

He nodded again, feeling like a man with two left hands who didn't know how to use either of them. While she'd slept last night, cradled in his arms, he'd lain awake, pondering all the complexities of life, especially those he'd never wondered about before. Like holding someone as they slept. He'd never done that, and instinctively he knew the marvel at doing so wasn't something he'd forget anytime soon. Perhaps ever.

Carter had also admitted, while holding her in the quiet darkness of night, that he wasn't exactly sure what he felt for Molly. He liked her, he cared about her and worried about her, but there was something else there, too. It went deeper and he couldn't explain what it was. Not even what it felt like. He'd wondered, there in the bed, whether it might be love, but he couldn't fathom that's what he felt. How could he? He'd never experienced love, didn't know how it happened or when or why, or even if. Especially if. If love could ever happen to him. He didn't know what it was, so if it did happen, how would he know?

There were things he did know, and questions he did want to ask her, which were tumbling forward now faster than dried-up tumbleweeds rolling across the flat plains he'd seen down in Kansas. He tried, but was unable to catch one as it rolled across his tongue.

"Who's the father of your baby?"

The way her expression fell had his very soul plummeting deep inside him, yet, unlike her, he didn't let it show. The question was out and he wanted to know the answer.

"No one," she whispered. "No—"

"That's impossible," he interrupted.

Sighing wearily, she said, "I was going to say no one that matters."

"That, too, is a bit impossible." He saw her features tighten and held in the ragged sigh snagging somewhere between his lungs and his throat. There wasn't anything he could do without knowing, so he asked again, "Who is it, Molly?"

She had one hand on her stomach as she stared across the room, out the open doorway. "Just someone I used to know."

Regarding the several meanings that could have, he asked, "Did he die?"

"No." There was little emotion in her tone. "But he's gone. Left town several months ago."

"Do you want me to go find him?" The question surprised him. Her, too, it appeared, when she turned, looked up at him astonished.

"No, Carter." She was still unemotional, almost detached, which was so unlike her.

"Is he married?"

"No." There was a bit of dignity behind her answer.

"Did he ask you to marry him?"

Fidgeting, she didn't answer right away, and when she did speak, it included a desolate gaze that stung him.

"He wanted me to abandon my sisters." Waving a hand about, she added, "To sell out and leave everything behind."

Carter shook his head, regretful that there was a man out there that incredibly stupid and, at the same time, thankful the man had been—whoever he was—as foolish as they come.

"I couldn't do that."

"He shouldn't have asked you to," Carter answered, distracted slightly by the antagonism simmering inside him.

A miniature grin wobbled as it filtered across her lips, but then she bowed her head. "That was over a year ago."

"How can that be?" he asked, referring to her condition.

She propped an elbow on the counter and rested her chin in her palm. "Some days I don't even know, Carter."

He didn't like how lost she sounded, how alone and hopeless she appeared, and wanted to go to her, but he had nothing to offer. There was also his training, it had kicked in, and he knew if he touched her now, made any movement, she might clam up. Remaining silent and still, he waited.

Her sigh hung in the air, and then, just about when he thought she wasn't going to say anything, she started, "One evening last spring, on a day when the world was against me, he appeared. I don't know why I didn't tell him to leave, other than I was tired. So tired of everything. He started talking about all the places he'd been, and the thought of having such freedom fascinated me. The more he talked, the more I could imagine myself in a different life. Selling all this, moving away." She shrugged. "I thought I saw something in him I could love, but…"

Carter could imagine the seduction. She'd been dealt a rough hand when her parents died, leaving her with two younger sisters to care for, a mercantile to keep open and the railroad breathing down her neck. A man could easily have swayed her, wooed her with tales of beautiful countrysides and bustling cities. He knew what was on the other side though, of both the landscapes and the towns boasting prosperity, and had no doubt the other man knew too.

"But?"

"It wasn't there," she whispered. "What I thought I saw."

"What happened…afterward?" he asked, not wanting to know the intimate details. They just might be more than he could tolerate.

"I realized my mistake. That people don't change. That no one is going to swoop in and transform my life into a fairy tale of happily ever after like the stories Karleen reads."

If there was one thing Carter could have told her, it would have been that she was wrong. People do change. He had. Not just recently, but years ago when he understood this was his only chance at life and it was up to him to redirect it.

He'd forgotten that, in a credulous sort of way, but remembered it now, and hoped it wasn't too late.

Carter didn't say any of that because voices sounded outside the doorway. Four men bustled their way through the door and he moved to the end of the counter, where his gun belt lay on the shelf beneath the cash drawer. The pup he'd explained would someday be a good watchdog was still sleeping soundly in the box Ivy had placed near a front window before she'd left for church, and it didn't offer so much as a wiggle. He'd have to start it on a training regimen soon.

The men were of varying ages, perhaps a ten-year span of early manhood to Carter's own age, and they looked enough alike to be brothers, all big with sand-colored hair and homespun cotton clothes. Farm boys, he'd guess, unsophisticated and branching out of their natural habitat.

"How do," the first one said, definitely the oldest.

Silently acknowledging his perceptions were still in order, weren't completely buried inside the new grounds that had emerged inside him recently, Carter returned the man's greeting with a nod.

"Hear tell you can sell us some supplies to take on the train. Vittles and such," the man said with a clear and strong German brogue.

"We're heading to the railhead," another one offered. The youngest of the bunch, by the looks of the pimples covering his cheeks and chin. "But what Ma packed us done ran out."

It was one of the middle ones Carter was keeping an eye on. The man was eyeing Molly, and had even pushed back the brim of his hat to get a better look.

The notion of tossing all four out on their backsides flashed in Carter's mind, but another thought was just as strong, that of Molly seeing him do such a thing. She'd be appalled. Perhaps frightened, and he couldn't do that to her on top of everything else.

She'd climbed off her stool and her hand settled in the center of his back when she paused beside him. "I'll see what we have in the kitchen as far as bread goes while you show them the canned goods," she said softly.

Carter walked beside her as far as the doorway to the living quarters, keeping himself between her and the men, and let his eyes tell them how careful they better step.

"We aren't here to cause trouble," the oldest one said.

With as few words as possible, which weren't many, Carter directed them toward the items they might want. The four men conversed quietly, adding up the costs while comparing it to what they each dug out of their pockets.

Instincts were good things, and Carter liked his. Right now they told him these men weren't looking for jobs at the railhead, but that they were on a mission. Another place and time, he might have been curious enough to learn what it was; right now, he just wanted them gone.

Molly returned with several loaves of bread, and Carter caught her elbow, silently encouraging her to stay behind him as he loaded everything into two boxes and then took the money the men counted out right down to the last penny.

The men offered their thanks and bid farewell as two of them picked up the boxes and they all headed out the door.

"They're just customers," Molly said, walking up beside him after the last one stepped off the porch.

There had been plenty of customers during his time here, but none like that, a whole group of men at once, and he wasn't impressed. Not by her nonchalance either.

"How often do you get groups like that?" he asked, straightening out the few crumpled bills.

"Regularly enough. All sorts of people travel through on the trains."

He was about ready to riddle her with cautionary words as he opened the cash drawer, but his spine turned as hard as a rifle barrel. Lying right on top was a new five-dollar bill. Karleen had told him the money was in the cupboard this morning while she'd been baking, and he'd retrieved it, counted it and put it in the drawer. There had not been a five-dollar bill amongst the cash then. He'd been the only one in the store all morning, other than Molly, and this was the first time he'd opened the drawer.

"Where did that come from?" she asked.

"I don't know." There was no need, but he scanned the serial numbers, confirmed them.

"Carter, it's not you, is it? Slipping bills into the cash drawer."

That goaded him. "No," he snapped. Then frustrated he'd made her jump, he asked more calmly, "I wasn't here in May, when the first one showed up, was I?"

"No."

"Then it's not me. Why would you think it was?"

She shrugged. "Because you've done everything else."

"What?"

Her gaze was apologetic, and her lips quivered slightly. "You've done everything else. The chores, the repairs, took care of customers, and—" she shrugged again and shook her head "—I guess it wouldn't surprise me if you were putting money in the cash drawer too, just so we could keep the doors open."

That was closer to the truth than she knew. He had thought about it, and there was still that niggling thought about buying the store just so the railroad would have to deal with him firsthand.

Carter put the money from the German men in the drawer and closed it before he turned to face her and took hold of both her hands. Her fingers trembled beneath his and he clutched them a bit firmer. "Come here."

Her smile was tender and a bit secretive. "I am here," she whispered.

"No," he said, taking a step forward and guiding her hands around his back. "Come here."

While her arms tightened around his waist, his went around her shoulders to tuck her snugly against him. "Now you're here," he whispered.

He'd never known what hugs could do, never understood how deeply and profoundly they engrossed a person. Holding Molly, feeling her in his arms, was like crossing a threshold to a land full of lush valleys and open, undaunted plains that went on for miles and miles. As far as he could imagine. Carter wasn't quite prepared for what it meant, either.

Nor was he prepared for the way she lifted her face, as if offering her soft lips for him to own in some mystical way. He could re-read his dictionary from beginning to end and never discover a word to define all that was taking place inside him.

He did, however, lower his face and take her lips in a sacred communion he'd never have believed himself worthy of. The kiss stirred him all the way to his toes, both in spirit and a more earthly way that included a few parts only men had. He'd have to stop this—kissing her, holding her—for as phenomenal as it was, he was putting too much stock into it.

However, he'd give it a few more minutes. Take in a few more glimpses of those glorious landscapes littered with sunshine and sparkling creek beds full of glittering specks of gold. That's what kissing her was like, tasting a sweetness that was far more than he ever dreamed existed.

Chapter Twelve

Somehow Molly managed to stay upright when Carter ended the kiss. It may have been his arms still holding her tight, or the way she held on to him for dear life. "What's happening here?" she asked, thinking aloud and growing slightly embarrassed when he cocked a brow. She hadn't been addressing him, but was so light-headed the words had simply slipped off her tongue. The same one his had been tormenting in the most delicious way only a few minutes ago.

Disoriented, that's what she was. How else could she be pregnant and yet craving a man at the same time? Wanting to participate in the very act that had put her in this position? She didn't remember a lot about that night with Robbie, thanks to Afton Smith's wine, or perhaps because she didn't want to. There had been a fog about her that night, a blending of what was real and the dream she'd envisioned. A very specific pain was what had cleared it away, snapped her to her senses. She'd attempted to tell Robbie to stop, but by then, it had already been too late.

Regret and shame had followed, and remained.

"Molly?"

She snapped her head up, welcoming the intrusion. There were bits and pieces of that night she never wanted to remember. Carter's arms were still around her and, needing the comfort of them, she tightened her hold, laid the side of her face against his solid chest. Afraid to close her eyes, not exactly sure how far away the memories had gone, she locked her gaze on whatever was near. Which happened to be the cash drawer. "What's happening, Carter?" she asked, this time purposefully addressing him. "Where's this money coming from?"

He rocked her gently, his chin resting on the top of her head, and she might have missed how the air never left his lungs if her ear hadn't been pressed against his chest.

"I have to tell you something, Molly," he said when the air did flow again.

She attempted to lift her head, to look up at him, but he laid a hand on her other cheek, keeping her where she was. A twinge of panic raced over her, but his hold tightened, slowing it from growing. "What?" she asked.

"You can't tell anyone."

She almost caught the humor in that, considering what he knew about her, but sensed this was not a laughing matter. "I won't."

"Promise?"

A pinch devastated he didn't see the irony, she half groaned, "Carter."

He kissed the top of her head and then took her by the shoulders, spacing their bodies a few inches apart. His expression was somber and she gripped his elbows. "What is it?"

"There was a train robbery last year."

Not sure how that affected her, for such things did happen, yet knowing it did somehow involve her, she nodded. "And?"

"And these five-dollar bills that keep showing up in your cash drawer are part of the stolen money."

Quivers attacked her knees with direct force. Carter must have noticed because he guided her to the stool, helped her sit, and then wrapped his hands around her fingers, which had started shaking as well. "Stolen money? Here?"

He nodded.

"How?"

"That's why I'm here."

Dr. Henderson's parting statement echoed inside her ears. "Your business is stolen money?"

"I was hired to find the robbers."

"Not me—not us—"

"No, I don't believe you stole it."

Unsettled and confused, Molly wasn't sure that was the answer she was looking for. Shaking her head, more to clear it than anything, she asked, "Who hired you?"

"The railroad."

Instinct had her attempting to pull her hands from his, but his grip wouldn't let that happen. "You work for the railroad?" She was getting worse at choosing men instead of better. Molly closed her eyes to gain some sort of control over thoughts leaping in all directions. Yet, when she opened them, even distraught, she found his slightly devilish grin appealing.

"No, I don't work for the railroad."

"You just said—"

"I should have said I work for the agency the railroad hired to investigate the robbery."

"Oh." That did make things better. Didn't it? Shaking her head, she admitted, "I'm confused."

His chuckle surprised her, so did the way he stole a quick kiss. Stole it because if she'd known it was going to happen, she'd have participated.

"I know you're confused," he said, brushing a

fingertip over her cheek. "But you can't tell anyone why I'm here."

"Other than a train robbery and some stolen money, I don't know why you are here, Carter."

He grinned again, and then proceeded to tell her the only place money from the robbery had surfaced was here, at the mercantile. Her bewilderment grew and he explained all over again how each bill had turned up, including the one today, as mysterious as the others.

When he mentioned Karleen, Molly shook her head. "You know her. She couldn't keep a secret like that. Furthermore, if she had the amount of money you said was stolen, thousands of dollars, and if she somehow believed it was hers to spend, this place would be wall-to-wall books."

"Who else? Who else has access to the cash drawer?"

"No one," she admitted. "Just you and I."

"I think we both agree it's neither of us."

Molly nodded, although a tiny click happened somewhere in the back of her brain. "You thought it could be me, didn't you? At one time?"

"Yes, I did."

His honesty was to be commended, but it still managed to sting.

He ran a finger on the underside of her chin. "I knew you were keeping a secret."

That compounded everything. "When did you know?"

Carter clearly understood what she was asking, and he tipped her face up, kept her gaze locked with his. "When you fainted in the barn."

His other hand, which had been on her shoulder, ran down her arm, and when it settled on her stomach, the baby moved, as if it too wanted to be as close to Carter as possible. A tiny moan rolled silently in the back of her throat.

"I was checking you for injuries," he said, caressing her stomach, which was beyond intimate. "And felt this tiny little bump."

He kissed her, and this time Molly did respond. Cupped his jaw to cherish the connection as long as possible, and when it ended, his lips left hers, she asked, "What are we going to do?"

Molly wasn't exactly sure what her question was pertaining to, but felt mollified when he replied, "Whatever it takes."

They kissed again—it was completely mutual, two people giving and taking—and even outright confused by all he'd told her, Molly found that one place where nothing mattered. Lost in that wonderful world, she wasn't ready to return when his lips stopped chasing after hers.

"I hear the girls coming," he whispered.

She groaned and sighed.

He laughed and kissed her one last time.

The puppy, knowing Ivy's voice, leaped from its box, but with all four gangly legs going in opposite directions, it did more tumbling than running. Near the door, all four paws hit the floor at the same time, and with an excited bark it bounded over the threshold.

The dog's antics provided both Molly and Carter with something to laugh at, and they were still doing just that when Karleen walked through the door.

"I see you're feeling better," her sister said. "I even detect a slight glow about you."

Molly refrained from glancing at Carter, who'd moved to the stockroom and was now carrying out supplies to replenish the items their morning customers had purchased. "Because we made an excellent sale this morning."

"Oh?" Karleen asked. "To whom?"

Her sister did like to mimic some of the characters she read about, and was doing so right now as she strolled across the room, nose in the air.

"A group of men traveling through on the train," Molly answered. "Two crates full. Ask Carter if you don't believe me."

"I believe you," Karleen said. "I'm just thankful I won't have to make lunch."

"Why do you think that?" Carter asked.

Astonishment crossed Karleen's face. "I

cooked and worked in the store while she was sick yesterday. Today is my day to relax."

He placed another can on the shelf. "Your sister is still recovering, Karleen. You will make lunch, and supper." Turning, he cast a deep frown. "Unless of course it was your cooking that made her ill in the first place. In that case," he said, grabbing a can out of the crate, which he held up. "I'll cook. Beans."

Karleen huffed and Molly opened her mouth, fully prepared to say she could cook. As a matter of fact, she felt better than she had in a long time, despite everything. However, the gaze Carter sent her way had her closing her lips before uttering a word. He had the ability to do that, stop people in their tracks with a single look. She'd seen it more than once with seedy-looking customers, and she liked it. He tried to be subtle about it, and she liked that, too. How he tried to hide how protective he was, how manly and strong and tough, was amazing. She liked him being here. Watching over them so closely.

"Let me know if there is something I can help you with," he said to Karleen. "Killing a chicken or whatnot."

Karleen made a show of crossing her eyes at him before stomping from the room. "I'd probably still have to cook if I'd spent the night in the outhouse," she declared in her wake.

"Probably," Carter agreed overly loud.

Molly was still grinning, and it increased at the clanging and banging happening in the kitchen. She climbed off the stool and walked closer so Karleen wouldn't hear what she said to Carter. "I feel fine. I can cook."

He eyed her speculatively for a moment, then tapped the tip of her nose with one finger. "You will do as the doctor said. Take it easy."

Molly had to speculate if this is what it would be like to be married to him. A silly thought indeed, but a wonderful one no less, even though it could never happen. No man wanted a woman with sisters to raise, let alone a bastard child. Chasing that thought aside, she nodded toward the doorway. "Karleen does her fair share around here."

"I know she does." He set the now-empty crate on the counter. "And I know it won't hurt her to do a little bit more the next few days." Pinching her chin, he added, "Don't worry. I'll help her."

Lowering her voice even more, she asked, "Shouldn't you be looking for the robber instead of working around here?"

"I have been doing just that the entire time I've been here."

"You have?"

He nodded. "I have a list of every person who

has been in and out of this store the entire time I've been here."

"You do?" She sighed heavily for several reasons. Flustered over the money, still confused over what she should do, and now, deeply concerned Carter's time here would be shorter than she'd imagined.

"Some things take time, Molly."

"But the money hasn't come from one of our customers." With a shrug, she added, "How could it have?"

"I don't know, but I will. Sooner or later they're going to slip up."

"Who? How?"

The click of heels on the front steps stopped him from saying whatever he'd been going to, and Molly turned, took a step closer to the counter. Her habit of hiding her stomach wouldn't work for much longer; Dr. Henderson had confirmed that when he'd said Carter needed to hurry up and finish his business.

Carter had picked up the crate and was just rounding the end of the counter when Pastor Jenkins walked in. Dressed in black, as usual, the pastor paused in the doorway, staring at Molly as if she had two heads. Carter had hesitated, too. She could see that out of the corner of one eye.

"I expected to see you in bed, Molly," the man

said. "The way Karleen acted, you were practically on your deathbed."

Carter leaned back slightly and shouted over his shoulder, "It was something she ate."

The crash coming from the kitchen displayed exactly what Karleen thought about his teasing, and Molly had to grin.

Carter was grinning too, he couldn't help it. Picking on Karleen was fun, especially when she was pretending to be much older and more dramatic than she was. But the truth was, he liked watching Molly when he teased Karleen. It was as if they shared a secret. A chill snagged his humor then. He and Molly didn't need more secrets.

Pulling up the emotionless expression he'd mastered, Carter nodded to the pastor as he carried the empty crate to the storeroom. It was as if he'd become two people lately. The Carter he'd come to be the past few years, the one that held true when he was out and about, and a second one that had burst to life inside him while living with the Thorson sisters. There were bits and pieces of this new one he remembered from years ago, when life hadn't become so serious.

Whichever Carter he was right now kept one eye on the man who was approaching the counter, tossed the crate into the storeroom haphazardly and purposely strode back behind the counter to stand beside Molly.

"I'm glad you're feeling better," the man was saying when Carter arrived.

"Thank you," she replied.

The pastor glanced between the two of them, not necessarily curiously, but cautious for sure. "I was hoping to speak to the two of you," he said.

"About what?" Carter asked. Molly had swayed slightly and he took her waist, guided her the few steps to the stool and explained to the pastor while doing so, "She was ill yesterday and last night."

"Oh, well, perhaps this should wait, then."

Molly was the one to answer. "No, I'm fine, really. What is it, Pastor Jenkins?"

The way the man looked left and right had the hair on Carter's arms standing on end, but he held silent, waited.

After another glance around, the pastor reached into his coat while leaning closer to whisper, "This showed up in the collection plate this morning."

Molly gasped and Carter reached over with one hand, made sure she was securely seated before taking the five-dollar bill from the pastor with his other hand. Newly minted with serial numbers he knew well.

"Last week, before you mentioned the new

bills, I'd asked the congregation to consider making an extra donation this week. There's a widow out on Rock Creek, her husband died last year and she can no longer keep up with the taxes on her property. She'd sold everything she could just to live the past few months and is now destitute. I told her I'd try to raise enough money for train tickets for her and her three children to return to Missouri where she has family."

"Oh, my," Molly whispered. "How much more does she need?"

Carter bit the inside of his lower lip to keep the smile from creeping onto his lips. Caught up in the widow's plight, Molly had forgotten about the bill. That was so like her, and it made him a bit proud to be her acquaintance. Actually, more than a bit proud—and certainly more than an acquaintance.

"Did you see who put this in the collection plate?" he asked.

Pastor Jenkins hadn't answered Molly's question, and he was shuffling from foot to foot, making Carter wonder if the man wasn't going to answer his question, either.

"Pastor?" Carter asked, lifting a brow. The man didn't want to say something, that was apparent.

"That bill made what we collected enough for the widow and her children, but I knew I had to bring it here. To find out why you were asking about new bills like that."

Carter laid the bill on the counter and dug into his pocket, pulling out others that were old and well circulated. "I'll buy that one from you," he said, handing over several times what the bill was worth. "See that the widow gets the extra too, for meals for her and her family along the way and whatnots afterward."

Molly laid a hand on his arm, and gazed up at him with such a tender smile that Carter thought about emptying his other pocket.

"This is very generous of you, Mr. Buchanan," the pastor said. "Very generous, but tell me, what's so special about that one?"

"What are we whispering about? Oh, another new bill."

If Carter hadn't been focused on Molly, he would have heard Karleen approaching, and if he hadn't been thinking about that poor widow and her babies, he would have hid the bill. He was growing lax in his skills. Careless even. Not a good trait for a Pinkerton agent.

"Here's your cinnamon roll, Pastor Jenkins," Karleen said. "Since it appears neither Molly nor Carter were able to walk into the kitchen, where I'm slaving over a hot stove, I thought I'd better bring it to you." With an inflated sigh, Karleen spun around and trudged toward the kitchen.

Molly patted his arm. "I'm going to go help in the kitchen while you talk with Pastor Jenkins." She glanced at the other man. "The cinnamon roll is on the house today."

"Thank you," the pastor said.

Carter, as stone faced as possible, held his breath as Molly's hand brushed his back while she walked past him.

"Thank goodness," the pastor said, sounding overly relieved. "I didn't want to mention this in front of Molly."

"Mention what?"

"Who put this bill in the collection plate."

"Who?"

The pastor let out such a long sigh, Carter's spine went straight. Finally, while gushing out the last bits of air, the man mouthed, "Ivy."

Carter's jaw fell open as his shoulders slouched. "Ivy?" He straightened then, frowned. "Our Ivy?"

Whispering as if they were in a dark alley, the man leaned over the counter. "Yes, Ivy Thorson. I saw her sneak it in while everyone was leaving. No one else noticed."

That certainly explained how the one got in the cash drawer today, and the others, but still, Carter had to shake his head. "Ivy?"

Still acting as if they were on a covert mission—he was, the preacher wasn't—the other man asked, "Where'd she get it?"

"I don't know, but I will." Children were capable of just about anything, he'd never doubt that, nor did he doubt Ivy would tell him all he needed to know. "Thank you, Pastor, and I'd appreciate if you didn't tell anyone about this. Including Molly and Karleen."

"Not a word, Mr. Buchanan. You can trust me."

A chill caught Carter right at the base of his spine, and he instantly knew why. "Have you talked to Dr. Henderson today?"

The man turned the color of an apple ready to fall off a branch. Starched white collar or not, Carter was around the counter and dragging the man out the door by the back of his suit coat. Once they were several yards away from the porch, he demanded, "What did he tell you?"

"Nothing really, other than you collected him last night because Molly was ill."

Carter didn't believe that was all the man knew, and ran both hands through his hair. And cursed. Loud enough that the pastor shuddered.

"I had to go see him as soon as services were over," the pastor said nervously. "The way Karleen talked, Molly was almost dead."

"No, she wasn't," Carter growled.

"I know, the doctor said it was just a stomach ailment."

Carter experienced a brief moment of relief. "He did?"

"Yes." Lifting his gaze, the man added, "And that's when he told me."

Carter pinched at the pain in both temples with one hand. "Told you what?" He emphasized each word slowly.

"That you're a Pinkerton man."

That wasn't so bad. It would get out sooner or later. Carter huffed out the dead air in his lungs.

"And that you and Molly have been married since last spring."

He hadn't been doing a good job of not letting his reactions show, and couldn't have masked his shock if he'd been an operative for a hundred years. "What?" Some parts of last night were a blur, and this morning, he'd tried to remember exactly what he'd said to the doctor while driving his buggy through the dark streets.

"So many things make sense now. Why Molly refused my request to court her."

Carter did hide a few things on that one. Especially as he asked, "You and Molly? When?"

The pastor was shaking his head so hard his shortly cut hair was flaying. "Last year. Long before you two met. It was after that railroad man courting her left town."

He should take a moment to think, let all this information settle and contemplate his next question, but Carter was beyond that. "What railroad man?"

The pastor had gone stock-still, and Carter saw the terror in the other man's eyes. Knowing he was the cause quelled a small amount of the stunned fury inside him. "What railroad man?" he repeated, slower, calmer.

"Robert Fredrickson."

Carter's blood ran cold in his veins as the words James Fredrickson said last night stalked his memory. "Robbie Fredrickson courted Molly?"

"Mr. Buchanan," the man said, tugging at his collar. "This is probably something you need to discuss with Molly."

Stopping short of asking why, Carter said, "I just want to hear your side of the story."

"My side?"

Carter nodded.

The pastor shook his head. "There isn't a lot to tell. It was well over a year ago. I was fairly new in town and Molly had caught my eye." Blood rushed into the man's face, but he continued, "I asked around a bit, just to be sure she didn't have a regular suitor, and well, someone must have told Mr. Fredrickson because he came to the church and told me rather sternly that he was courting Molly. I can't say I ever saw proof of that. Molly's never thought too highly of the railroad, and considering how devoted she is to the store and her sisters, if she had been seeing Mr. Fredrickson, very few people would know."

Carter did agree with that. Molly worked from daybreak to sundown and that would leave little time for courting. The only reason he'd come to know her so well was because he lived here, shared meals with her. "You never saw Fredrickson here, at the mercantile?"

"Sure, but everyone knew he was trying to buy the place." Pastor Jenkins turned, stared at the store for a moment. "There were a lot of fathers who let out a sigh of relief when Robbie Fredrickson left town."

"You don't say," Carter replied.

He didn't need a further explanation, but the pastor gave one nonetheless. "Yes, Robbie considered himself a ladies' man, and I'm sure people were happy there were no unborn children left in his wake. I know I was, and I think Molly became a challenge he couldn't conquer."

Carter questioned that, but he did know one thing. On his next case, the first person he'd seek out was the town's preacher.

"So, why is a Pinkerton man in Huron?"

Considering everything the man already

knew, Carter said, "To investigate a train robbery."

"Made up of new bills?"

Carter nodded.

"Well, your secret is safe with me, as is your marriage to Molly."

This time Carter was more prepared, didn't let his shock show. He had suggested Molly's child might be his to the doctor last night, but he'd have remembered telling the man they were married. Doc Henderson must have made that one up all on his own. Something foreign and dark churned inside Carter. It was tied to one word. Marriage. That held all sorts of responsibilities. Far more than just seeing to the safety of the sisters.

"I am curious, though," Jenkins said, "who performed the ceremony. I'm the only minister for miles."

"Another Pinkerton operative," Carter replied, thinking off the top of his head. "A preacher under disguise." That was a problem with undercover work—you had to remember what you'd said yesterday so you could still pretend to be the same person tomorrow, and this fabrication might haunt him. Sensing being watched, his gaze went to the store, where Molly stood in the doorway.

Oh, yeah, this lie would haunt him.

Chapter Thirteen

Molly expected Carter to return to the store, but instead, when he was done talking with Pastor Jenkins—who waved before walking down the road—he waved, too, and walked toward the barn. She'd have followed, if Mrs. Rudolf hadn't shouted just then.

"Molly! Yoo-hoo!"

Molly returned the woman's wave, wishing she'd put on her apron. She couldn't very well run into the store, not with Mrs. Rudolf clearly expecting her to wait on the porch. Two other women were waddling just as fast up the road. Mrs. Wilke and Mrs. Phillips.

"Molly, oh, Molly," Mrs. Rudolf said, somewhat breathless upon arriving. "These white shoes made a fabulous impression at church this morning. Matilda and Jeanine each want to buy a pair, and I must have another pair, too."

"But they're identical to the ones you're wearing," Molly said, frowning slightly. The shoes didn't look as homely on Mrs. Rudolf's feet as they did on the shelf.

"I know, dear, but what if something happens to this pair?"

Molly didn't have a logical answer for that, so she just smiled. A sale was a sale.

"Is, um, Car—Mr. Buchanan here?"

The hope in Mrs. Rudolf's tone was undeniable, and unexpectedly, it tickled Molly. "He's in the barn," she answered, leading all three women into the store.

"Oh, well, you can wait on us just as well."

Molly had no doubt Mrs. Rudolf would have insisted Carter wait on her if it had just been her, but with two friends in tow she was on her best behavior.

After a considerable amount of time browsing, they each did buy shoes and material, including matching thread and buttons.

"You know, dear," Mrs. Rudolf started.

Holding her breath, waiting for what was to come, Molly forced a smile to remain on her face as she wrapped the last individual purchase in paper and tied it with a length of string.

"We meet each Wednesday morning for tea

and sewing and whatever. You should consider joining us."

Molly was stunned. Rightfully so. Before she'd come up with a reply, a voice behind her said, "That's a very generous offer, Mrs. Rudolf."

"Oh, Mr. Buchanan," the older woman cooed, batting her eyes. "How lovely to see you."

From where he stood in the doorway to the hall, he gestured toward the woman's feet. "The shoes look nice."

With a blush covering her face, Mrs. Rudolf answered, "I bought another pair. So did my friends."

"I do believe you are becoming Molly's best customer," Carter said, oozing charm.

Molly was watching all this, but unlike last week when it had irritated her, today she experienced a sense of pride. A bit more when Carter walked over to stand beside her.

"If you ladies will excuse us," he said, "Ivy has something she wants to show Molly."

Her frown deepened when he continued, "Karleen is here, and will gladly help you with any further purchases."

Karleen was frowning, too, clearly not impressed by having to take over the store.

"I'll be right back," Molly assured her sister. She then waited until Carter had led her into the kitchen to ask, "What does Ivy have?" Molly's stomach pitched then, caused by the somber look on Carter's face. "What's happened?"

"Nothing's happened," he said. "Ivy's in the soddy. Can you walk that far?"

"Of course I can walk that far," she said, increasing the speed of her steps.

Carter's hand holding her arm slowed her. "There's no rush, she's fine."

"Then why am I scared?" she asked.

"Don't be," he said. "And don't rush. The doctor said to take it slow for a day or two, remember?"

"Carter," she said, flustered.

"What?"

"Shut up."

He laughed, which only irritated her more. His eyes, back in the kitchen, had been full of worry that he couldn't hide, not from her, and she was well enough to walk to Wyoming and back.

Moments later, sitting on the bed in the soddy, the very one she'd slept in last night, Molly thought she might faint. Carter sat down beside her, looped an arm around her shoulder, but it didn't help as much as she hoped. Her head was spinning. Knowing it wouldn't stop until she had a few answers, she asked, "Ivy, where did you get this?"

"I found it."

"Where?"

"Here," her sister said, gazing back at the old traveling trunk she used to keep her toys in next to the small table-and-chair set.

The trunk was usually pushed up against the wall, but Carter had pulled it across the room so it sat right beside the bed. Right in front of her. Molly glanced his way. "It's the stolen money, isn't it?"

He nodded.

She turned back to Ivy. "Why didn't you tell me or Karleen you found it?" Tears welled in her sister's dark eyes, and Molly opened her arms. "Come here."

As Ivy climbed onto the bed, Carter scooted over, giving the child room to sit between them. That simple act touched Molly so deeply tears stung her eyes. His hand was still on her back, rubbing in a circular motion, but his other one was smoothing the hair off Ivy's face.

"You aren't in trouble, Ivy," he said gently. "Just tell Molly what you told me."

"I found it under the bed when I brought my toys out here. It was wrapped in a blanket. I asked Karleen what she would do if she found some money and she said, 'Finders keepers, losers weepers.'"

Over the child's head she noticed Carter's grin and returned it. They both knew that was exactly what Karleen would have said. After kissing Ivy's temple, Molly asked, "Why did you put some in the cash drawer?"

Wiping her nose with the back of her hand, the girl said, "Because Karleen says we all have to pay for whatever we take out of the store."

"She said she paid for her new tablet today," Carter said, still running a hand over Ivy's head. "And the material for her dress last week and a new reader, and a couple months ago it was new shoes."

"Ivy, I pay for all those things for you," Molly said.

"But you said if we have our own money we should pay."

The innocence in Ivy's iridescent eyes had guilt rolling inside Molly. She remembered the exact day she'd told Karleen that. The day she'd realized she was pregnant. "Honey, I said that because Karleen had taken a book off the shelf and spilled tea on it."

What had seemed like a disaster that day was little more than an excuse today. A reason to take her anger out on someone else.

Carter lifted Ivy off the bed and walked her to the door where he knelt down and said something. Molly didn't hear what and the scene became even blurrier as her tears increased. When Carter returned, he sat down and pulled her close. She let the tears fall freely for a few minutes. It helped, cleansed her a small amount.

"Better?" he asked.

She nodded, but as her eyes went to the trunk, she asked, "What do we do with it?" A groan filled her throat and she added, "Where else has she spent it?"

"Just here and at church today, so it's all been recovered."

"At least that's a relief." She sat up, wiped off her cheeks. "Who put it here?"

"I have yet to find that out," Carter said.

"But you have an idea?" If Molly didn't know him as well as she did, she might not have noticed how his jaw went tight. "Who?"

He shook his head. "I can't say, not right now, and I'd prefer you don't ask me."

Considering he hadn't pressed her for answers she didn't want to give, Molly agreed. "All right." Then knowing exactly what finding the money meant, she asked, "When are you leaving?"

"I don't know that either."

She'd thought her crying jag was over, but a sob hit the back of her throat. Carter turned to look at her the same time she twisted toward him. Their eyes met for a brief moment before their lips did. Desperation arose from the sob, and Molly wrapped her arms around his neck, held on for all she was worth.

They were lying on the bed, still kissing, and this time, when Carter's hand roamed to her stomach, Molly didn't try to stop it; instead she cherished his touch. His hand stroked other places, too, her breasts, her hips, her thighs. She treasured each one, wishing the material of her dress wasn't preventing even more intimate caresses, especially when Carter's kisses covered her neck, and lower, across her breasts that were throbbing as if wounded. They weren't wounded of course, simply alive in the most profound way possible. He kissed her stomach, too, which caused a tear to trickle out of the corner of one eye.

When his lips returned to hers, Molly embedded herself so deeply in their coming together she hoped to never surface, never leave this wonderful world he created around the two of them.

She had to though, return to the real world, when Carter whispered into her mouth, "Molly, we need to stop."

Shaking her head, she whimpered, and sought his lips again.

He returned her kiss, but then insisted huskily, "Yes, darling, we do."

She mumbled another protest, and he let out a groan, cupping one breast so firmly she arched into his hold.

"We have to stop before we do something we

shouldn't," he said more firmly while lifting his head too far for her to catch his lips again.

Flustered, throbbing and hot in places that weren't supposed to feel this way—at least not that she knew of—Molly slumped deeper into the bed.

Carter chuckled.

She opened one eye to peer at him with aggravation.

"You are supposed to be taking it easy, remember?"

"I am taking it easy," she pointed out. "I'm in bed."

"I know."

His overly charming smile, along with those dark blue eyes surrounded by thick lashes that told her much more than he probably wanted her to know, made a burst of happiness flow out of her in the form of a giggle.

He kissed her brow then, and she sighed, knowing she'd never felt such tenderness. "I am fine, Carter," she whispered. "The bleeding has stopped."

The hold he had her in, with both arms, tightened, and he nuzzled the side of her face, whispered in her ear, "I'm glad." A moment later, he added, "And I want to keep it that way."

She kissed his neck, right below his ear where

he smelled so wonderful, and snuggled closer, hoping he'd just hold her for a few more minutes.

Carter kept Molly in his embrace. He doubted he could have let her go right now if the building had been on fire. He'd never been so hard, so hot, so ready for a woman in all his born days. Then again, he'd never wanted something as badly as he wanted Molly. Not even food after days, weeks, of going hungry. Maybe because he didn't just need her to survive, but to live. An astonishing notion, but a true one.

When he'd been young and in a hurry, he hadn't taken time to notice a lot of things. As the years went by, he still hadn't completely seen what was happening. He'd thought he had, but he hadn't. All the while he'd been searching for where he needed to be, when in reality, he hadn't been looking for a place, he'd been looking for a person. The person. One who would love him, and one he'd love just as strongly in return.

The funny thing, in an odd way, was he'd found it while not even looking for it. He still wasn't overly confident he knew what love was, but had a good idea this was it. That was also what had him questioning his next move. He couldn't love Molly. Couldn't marry her. There was too much keeping them apart for that. Namely him. Who he was.

"What are you going to do with the money?"

Carter suppressed a sigh and rolled onto his back, but kept one arm under her neck, kept her tucked up against him. "Leave it right here," he answered. "The person who left it knows where it's at." Having a good inclination as to exactly who that was, he refused to let another sigh leave his lungs. It would take a bit more research to confirm it, but he couldn't deny the hunch that had turned his heart into a hard knot.

A heavy silence lingered before she broke it by asking, "But you're going to go find them, aren't you?"

She may have broken the silence, but not the heaviness pressing down upon him. "Yes," he said.

"When?"

Shifting, he brought them both to a sitting position, and then, when he thought she'd gained her equilibrium, or maybe when he had, he stood, helped her to her feet. "I'll let you know."

They walked to the house then, side by side, not touching and not talking, a shared but tormenting agreement neither had suggested yet both accepted.

Karleen and Ivy were at the table in the kitchen, eating lunch. After reminding them she'd cooked the meal, Karleen informed them she'd also closed the store for the lunch hour since no one had been there to take over for her.

Carter wasn't in a frame of mind to humor her, so he cast her a glare.

Karleen, reading him correctly, bowed her head and everyone ate in silence. Afterward, he suggested Molly go rest in her room, asked Ivy to see to feeding Bear and told Karleen she would clean the kitchen while he reopened the store. Surprisingly, or maybe not so, no one protested. The sisters had come to know when he was serious, and didn't question it, which only increased the churning inside him. They were all too tender and sweet to be living with the likes of him.

Later, once she was done in the kitchen, Karleen entered the store, insisting he tell her about the stolen money. Carter should be glad she'd waited until the customer had left, another man needing supplies for his train ride to the railhead, but there wasn't any gladness to be found. It seemed no one in this town could keep a secret. Except Molly.

He sighed, and cast an intolerant gaze at Karleen.

"Ivy didn't tell me. She said you told her not to." Walking toward the counter with her nose in the air, which was her usual stance when attempting to act superior, Karleen continued, "It wasn't too difficult to figure out. Newly minted bills showing up mysteriously, what else could they be but stolen?"

Carter considered remaining silent. However, living with the Thorson sisters had changed that about him, too. "You know, Karleen, being an adult isn't just about age."

She rolled her eyes.

The action bristled him, but he chose to ignore it. "I've met children who are more mature and have accepted responsibility better than people three times their age."

"I'm responsible," she insisted. "I work just as hard as Molly. Look at today."

Carter nodded. "Look at today. If you'd have been ill all night, would Molly have exaggerated your illness at church? Would she have reminded you how little help you'd been yesterday? Would she have pouted about doing a few extra chores?"

The way she bowed her head said he'd struck a chord. He walked closer, laid a hand on her shoulder. "You're still young, Karleen, and I don't expect you to behave like an adult, but I do expect you to show respect to your sisters, to customers and to me. But most important, to yourself. Adults know how to balance caring about others, along with staying true to themselves."

Remorse glistened in her eyes. "It's hard, Carter."

"Yes, it is." He kissed her forehead. "And you've had a hard time of it." Tugging her into a hug, he said, "Yes, the money is stolen, but I can't tell you more than that. Not because I don't trust you, but because if you know more than that, it could be dangerous, and I don't want any of you girls to be in danger."

She stepped back when he let her loose. "You really care about us, don't you?"

"Yes," he readily agreed. "I do."

That admission hung with Carter, partially because he wasn't sure what to do about it. If his instincts were right, when he caught the robber, he'd also be facing the father of Molly's baby. The thought gutted him. James Fredrickson was a pig, and history—that which he knew— said Robbie was worse. Yet, Molly, being Molly, had said she thought she could love Robbie, and therefore she'd want to do what was best, provide her child with a father.

Carter told Karleen he had work to see to in the barn and left. He had work to do, all right, tasks he really didn't want to complete, but putting them off wouldn't change anything.

Chapter Fourteen

⟋⟍⟋⟍⟋⟍⟍

It had taken two days to track the man down, but Carter had, in a saloon thirty miles from Huron. "Buster Freeman," he said as if they were old acquaintances, while taking a seat opposite the man at the dirty table.

"Do I know you?" Freeman asked.

With bloodshot eyes, ruddy and wrinkled skin, and smelling like something a dog would want to roll in, the man was exactly what Carter had predicted. "Yes," he lied. "We met a time or two over in Huron."

The man's smile said the few teeth he had might soon be gone. "I thought I recognized you." Hefting his smeared, empty mug, Freeman added, "I'd buy you a drink, but I'm down on my luck."

"That's why I bought you one," Carter said,

gesturing at the woman carrying two mugs. "Heard you got fired."

"It was that snot-nosed son." Freeman watched as the woman set down the mugs. "He got me fired."

"Heard that," Carter said, nodding toward the beers. "Didn't hear what happened though."

"He was rolling through town, on his way to Wyoming. Wilcox didn't want him stirring up trouble. The kid has a way of doing that." Freeman took a swallow of his beer. "Likes the women too much."

Carter sipped at his beer. Wilcox stuck to his claim Robbie never left the train last March, but J.T. said the man guarding him had said differently. And that man, Buster Freeman, had been fired last week.

"I was stationed outside his private car to make sure he didn't leave. Robbie passed me a bottle, out the window. Good stuff we can't get in these parts. We talked all evening, up until he asked me to go to the hotel, get him some clean bedsheets." Buster emptied his mug. "When I got back—I'd made sure the door was barricaded on the outside—Robbie asked me to carry them in. I did, set them on the bed, the dirty ones were already on the floor. That's where the money was, too. Wrapped in one of those bedsheets."

Carter nodded for the barkeep to bring another beer. "Money?"

"Lots of it." Glancing between the mug on its way to the table and Carter, Buster continued, "That's when I got hit in the head. I know that's what happened 'cause I had a goose egg the size of my fist the next morning. A man don't get that from just drinking. But when I woke up, Robbie was sleeping in his car. I thought maybe I'd just passed out, until I heard about the robbery up in Wyoming. That's when I told Wilcox about the money Robbie had." His beer had arrived and Buster almost downed it in one long swallow. "And what I get for it?" he then asked. "Fired. Kicked out of town with nothing but the clothes on my back."

Carter drew a breath. This trip had told him pretty much what he'd expected.

"Didn't want old man Fredrickson finding out, that's what it was," Buster said. "He's the one who didn't want Robbie getting off that train until Wyoming. Seems Robbie was sweet on a girl in Huron, can't say who, he chased all of them, but one must have been special, because Robbie said he told his papa he was going to marry her."

Every muscle in Carter had tightened. "Robbie said that?"

"Yep. He also said his father already had a

woman picked out for him to marry. His partner's daughter."

"Eli Greer?" Carter asked. This trip was proving worthwhile.

"Yep. Robbie claimed she was as homely as a hairless dog, and that he was only going to Wyoming to get enough money to leave the railroad for good. Guess that's why I was so surprised when I saw the money in that blanket. Looked like more than enough to me." Buster looked at his empty glass and shook his head sadly. "I gave that railroad the best years of my life for nothing. No one wants to hire a man my age."

Carter didn't have an answer for that, but he didn't have any more questions either, and it was getting late. He'd told the preacher and the doctor he'd be out of town for a few days, but neither man would be much protection to the sisters if real trouble happened. He gave Buster some cash, along with a couple suggestions, and left, estimating it would be past three in the morning before he got home.

It was, and Carter was practically seeing double he was so tired. Stabling Sampson, who was just as tired, Carter grinned and shook his head. Then he woke the pastor, who was bedded down on a pile of hay. As the man stumbled out the door, Carter admitted he'd passed judgment on the man too quickly when they'd first met.

He also questioned going into the house, just to check on the sisters, one in particular. Instead, he accepted what Pastor Jenkins had said, that everyone was fine, and made his way to the soddy. There he did little more than drop his gun belt and kick off his boots before falling on the bed.

A squeal and frantic flopping had Carter flying off the bed again. Landing on his feet, he was reaching for his gun when the intruder spoke.

"You startled me, Carter."

"Molly?"

"Of course it's me."

He sat down, and making out her silhouette in the darkness, took her by the shoulders. "What are you doing here?"

"Waiting for you." She kissed his cheek. "I must have fallen asleep."

The excitement of finding her here waned as fear stalled his thumping heart. "Are you ill again?"

"No. I'm fine. I just had a feeling you'd be home tonight." She'd scooted closer, was rubbing her nose against his chin.

It was the last thing he wanted, but was compelled to say, "You need to go to the house." She was kissing his neck now, making every part of his body forget how exhausted it was a few minutes ago. "Molly," he groaned.

"I'll go in a few minutes," she murmured against his skin.

He'd never worried about such things before, but did now. "I've been riding for three days. I'm sweaty and I stink."

Her giggle tickled his neck. "I'm not. I took a bath tonight." Her whispers were husky and seductive. "A long bath with lots of warm water and bubbles."

"Bubbles?" he asked, barely able to speak.

"Bubbles," she repeated as her lips lit his on fire.

Carter flipped her around, planting her amongst the disheveled blankets and angling over her, he deepened the kiss. The thought of seeing her had been stimulating, but this was beyond all. Her nightgown was soft and thin and his roaming hands said there was nothing beneath it except her, which drove his desire to immeasurable limits.

Her hands were busy, too, unbuttoning his shirt to wander inside. The connection, the feel of their skin merging, snared his breath.

Molly softly scraped her nails over the hard flesh of his chest and his sides, then she used her fingertips, and finally flattened her palms to absorb the heat. She'd missed him terribly the past few days, had started questioning her sanity while counting the hours, which had dragged on. Tonight, unable to bear much more, she'd came out here, just to lie amongst his covers, breathe in the spicy scent lingering in the air, on the bedcovers.

Now she'd attest to the fact before all in heaven and earth that Carter, the real thing, was better than all else. Her entire body hummed with the sensations his touch stirred inside her, and her very spirit, the very part of her that rarely came to life, was dancing.

His lips trailed down her neck, across the base of her throat, and driven by some elusive need, she arched, presented her breasts as his lips lowered. He kissed one, then the other, through the material of her gown, and the experience was treacherous, for it only made her want more.

When he opened his mouth, took one throbbing, beseeching nipple, Molly buried her hands in his hair and tried to keep from begging him to never stop, ever. His hand was stroking her thigh beneath her gown, and the feather-soft touch challenged the pleasure his mouth was still creating. Her heart was hammering and her breathing was little more than gasps and there was a centrifugal force fighting for all that was happening, creating a whirlpool deep inside her.

When he lifted his head slightly, the night air, cool compared to the heat of his mouth, penetrated the dampness of her gown, and a groan vibrated the back of her throat; maybe it was because he was now tending to her other breast, with the same perfect attention he'd provided the first.

His hand was between her legs, gently stroking, and a glorious heat rushed to meet each tender touch.

"Carter." His name came out in one long word, as if strung along a line, using up all the air from her lungs. He was all she could think of, and on the next breath, she repeated his name, just as extended as the first time.

"Aw, Molly." His lips were next to hers now, but his hand was creating a rhythm inside her that had her hips wanting to rise off the bed. "I missed you, Molly. I missed you."

Molly wanted to say she missed him, too, but speaking was impossible. Her fingers were still tangled in his hair, and she held on tighter. He must have understood her desperation, the frantic need she couldn't control.

"Relax, Molly, love, just relax," he whispered. "For once think of yourself, only yourself and what you want."

The driving force inside her doubled, grew too intense to manage, and she gave in, let it overpower her. Carter's hand continued to work its magic, and his lips played a fanciful game of tag between her lips and breasts. Together it had her racing toward some invisible finish line. Her thighs started to tremble as her hips propelled at the tempo he'd set.

"That's it, love," Carter whispered, "let it take you away."

She'd grown feverish, couldn't breathe, and tossed her head, unable to deny how spectacular it all was. The commotion inside her reached some sort of conclusion, a jostling shift that made her eyes fly open as her entire being burst apart in a wild spasm that sent tiny tremors, one after the other, through her body. They slowed gradually, as did her frantic breathing and her racing heart. She sank deeper and deeper into the mattress below her while the darkness of night once again absorbed the stars that had flashed before her eyes.

Exhausted, and yet elated, she said the only word she could think. "Carter."

"You are a treasure, Molly," he whispered, kissing her earlobe.

"I'm thinking it's the other way around," she said, although it took several moments to get all the words out.

He chuckled. "Go to sleep, love, I'll wake you before sunrise."

Suddenly full of energy, she flipped onto her side, wrapped an arm around his hard, broad chest and rubbed one cheek against his shoulder. Too hyper to sleep, but conceding he had to be exhausted, having ridden half the night, she whispered, "You sleep, Carter, and don't worry about me."

His sleep-encrusted moan made her smile. "I'll always worry about you, Molly," he said, somewhat groggily.

"And I'll always worry about you, Carter," she whispered.

Molly may have dozed, the security of lying next to Carter was such a sanctuary it would have been impossible not to, but she kept her promise. Crawling from the bed, she kissed his cheek, smiled at his throaty groan and then scurried across the yard before the sun announced a new day. After sneaking a peek at both Karleen and Ivy, who slumbered in their separate rooms, Molly entered hers and flopped on the bed, still not tired. Just knowing Carter was home was too thrilling.

A gentle wave floated over her body, sent a sigh out her lips and made her lids flutter shut. She was smiling, too, couldn't stop. Opening her eyes, she stared at the ceiling. She should be shocked about behaving so, but she wasn't. Nor was she embarrassed or shamed.

There was nothing embarrassing about Carter, and no shame in loving him. She just had to come up with the courage to ask him. Sighing again, she closed her eyes, now growing tired. That was her plan, to ask Carter to marry her, make an honest woman out of her. It had formed during his absence, this idyllic plan that would solve all her problems.

When Molly awoke, the sun was streaming in the window and voices sounded from the store. She completed her morning routine in record time and bounded down the steps, a bit ill at ease for having slept so late. Karleen had been so accommodating the past few days, almost as if she'd matured overnight, and Molly certainly didn't want her sister to think she was being taken advantage of.

Karleen was in the kitchen, and Molly stumbled to a stop, having assumed her sister had been in the store where there was still a conversation happening. Nothing she could make out, just voices.

"Morning," Karleen said.

"I'm sorry I overslept," Molly answered in response while glancing around to see where she should start. The kitchen was clean and smelled of cinnamon.

"It's all right," Karleen said. "I managed." Placing two rolls on a sheet of paper, she smiled. "Carter's home. The chores were done before I got up, and he's been minding the store since it opened." Folding the paper around the rolls, she added, "I have to take these in there. We've already sold a full pan."

"Here, I can do that," Molly said, hands out.

"No, I've got it." Gesturing toward the stove, Karleen said, "I saved you some eggs I scrambled. They should still be warm."

"Thank you," Molly said, but her sister had already disappeared down the hall. She did eat the eggs, which were still warm as well as fluffy and seasoned perfectly.

Molly was drying her plate, about to put it in the cupboard, when a sixth sense told her she wasn't alone. The smile creeping onto her lips also told her who'd just entered the room.

"Good morning," Carter said.

She closed the cupboard door before turning around. "Good morning."

"Sleep well?" Dressed in his usual black pants, he had on a tan shirt this morning and was freshly shaven. His hair had been washed, too. He propped one hand against the doorway arch, and his grin, a bit lopsided, was more than slightly charming.

A fascinating shudder raced through Molly. "Very," she answered. "You?"

He glanced down the hall before straightening his stance and moving forward. When he arrived at her side he leaned close and spoke into her ear, "Like I had an angel on my shoulder."

No part of his body was touching her, but specific parts of hers leaped to life as if he'd been caressing them as wonderfully as he had last night. The inner tumult was consuming, and made it difficult to come up with a witty response. She wanted the captivating chaos inside her to continue, it made her feel alive and happy. "I didn't know angels slept," she finally said, holding her breath until he let out a husky hum sound. At which point her legs grew unstable.

Carter leaned back, just enough to capture her full attention with a gaze so penetrating it had her heart clamoring for space in her throat. "Mine better," he said. "She needs her rest."

Molly couldn't swallow. The concept of being his angel had her throat locked tight, heart and all. Her mind was working, though, or maybe that, too, was her heart. Whichever one, the suggestion Carter would marry her renewed itself. She wouldn't ask him to make all the concessions, she'd go to Montana, help him create a home there. Unless he wanted to stay here. Either way, there was one thing she knew. Carter wouldn't ask her to abandon her sisters.

Courage was building inside her, and she was about to open her mouth, ask him to marry her, when he turned away.

"Coming," he said over his shoulder before glancing back to her. He flicked the end of her nose with one fingertip. "The store's been busy this morning."

She nodded, watching him walk away.

Carter entered the hall, beside himself. Literally. Side by side, he had two people walking inside him. It was impossible. He only had one body, one mind, but they, too, had become separated. It wasn't the same as being undercover, pretending to be someone else. He was still doing that, maintaining his role of store clerk as needed, a cowboy working his way to Montana. It was the other part of him that had taken on a bona fide transformation. He'd felt it coming on, like a cold that would include feverish chills and put a man in bed for days, but he still hadn't been prepared when it hit. Last night. When he found Molly in his bed.

He tugged at his collar, but, unbuttoned, it had nothing to do with the choking sensation in his throat. On the long ride home last night, he'd wrestled with all he knew, and what he had to do. That was also why this split inside him was so testing. It wanted to go against who he was.

He could handle falling in love with her. He could give up being a Pinkerton operative and going to Montana, but that wasn't all he had to contend with. At some point while riding through the darkness last night, he'd started thinking about the baby. Prior to that, he'd been so focused on himself, on Molly, he hadn't given the child as much attention as he should have.

A Pinkerton man was trained to leave no stone unturned. Molly and her baby were part of the robbery because the robber and the father of her baby were one and the same—he had no doubt on that.

He'd uncovered something else last night. The reason he'd hated the orphanages so bad. Not because they were crowded or cold or a dozen other claims he'd made against them, but because they'd tried to find him a new mother and father. He hadn't wanted that. If he couldn't have his real ones, he hadn't wanted any.

"Carter?"

He looked up to find Karleen standing in the doorway leading into the store. His mind, still at work, recalled the night she'd told him he wasn't her father, confirming everyone felt as he had.

"I need your help," she said.

"At your service," he said, once again putting on his invisible store-clerk hat.

Carter maintained that role for most of the day while working beside both Molly and Karleen. It wasn't until after Ivy returned home from school and customers trickled to one every half hour or so that he switched, explaining he had some things to see to in town.

Molly wanted to know more. All day she'd

attempted to get him alone, which he'd avoided, and he didn't offer her more now, either. Just gathered his gun belt and hat and made his way up the road. This case had intricacies most of his others never had, and since it would be his last, he wanted to know exactly how the man who'd hired him wanted him to proceed. Not Allan Pinkerton, but Eli Greer. It appeared the man had more at stake than the stolen money. His daughter's happiness. Carter had seen before how far a man would go for that.

Carter made his way to the telegraph office and the one man he'd come to trust in town. Art Sanford hadn't betrayed him. Matter of fact, the stolen money was now hidden in a safe in Art's back room. Carter wasn't ready for Wilcox to learn he'd discovered it, but in case something happened to him, he needed to know someone he trusted had access to the money and would get it to Allan Pinkerton.

There, sitting in Art's back room, Carter wrote out a long and detailed message to his superior, explaining the whereabouts of the money, and his suspicion about who stole it. He didn't mention Molly or the baby in any of it, but he did include he wouldn't travel to the railhead to detain the suspect until he was informed of what Mr. Greer wanted.

Considering the length of his message, it took

Art a while to send it. Carter read an old copy of the *New York Times* while the man clicked away at his desk. It appeared from what he read that things hadn't changed much in the city since he'd lived there all those years ago, except the police force was now run by the Irish. There was quite an inflammatory article about that. The front page held a story about a factory that had burned down. Most everything written was about the man who owned it, how and where he'd rebuild. One sentence stated most of the workers—now dead—had been orphans, therefore their names were not listed. Orphans were a never-ending commodity of the city.

Carter was glad when Art stopped clicking so he could quit reading. They conversed then about the weather and other inconsequential topics. The Pinkerton agency had a telegraph office in its building, and as long as Allan Pinkerton was nearby—which he normally was—a reply would be imminent.

When a little bell sounded and Art started writing down letters with his stubby pencil at great speed, Carter knew the reply was also lengthy. He didn't read the paper while waiting this time, but instead stared out the window at the town that was so unlike many of the big cities he'd visited. He'd simply stayed in them, never lived there. In truth, he'd never *lived* anywhere before Huron.

"Carter," Art said, handing a piece of paper over the counter as if he had no idea what was on it.

He liked that about the man, had since the beginning.

"Obliged," Carter said, taking the message. It was written in code, as they all were. Anyone who hadn't read the agency handbook wouldn't be able to make hide nor hair out of it. This one was long, too. It took up most of the page, and was from Allan himself.

It started out by thanking Carter, claiming the information might have some bearing on how Eli wanted to proceed, and ended with Mr. Pinkerton promising to send a message as soon as he'd talked with Mr. Greer.

After reading the note a second time, making sure it was embedded in his mind, Carter tore it in half, twice, then tossed it in the small woodstove in the corner and used a nearby match to set it aflame. Once the paper was reduced to ashes, he closed the door and bid farewell to Art, almost wishing the message had told him to head for Wyoming.

After what had happened last night, sleeping in the soddy was going to be a bit hellish. About like keeping his hands off Molly had been all day. He had to, though. Admitting to loving her was one thing, but marrying her, becoming a family man, was completely different. Something he just couldn't bring himself to do. Not after being alone all these years. It just wouldn't be him.

Chapter Fifteen

Molly was close to her wits' end. Carter had been home for three days and they hadn't had a minute alone. She'd tried, on numerous occasions, but fate—or, more accurately, Carter—didn't want it to happen. He was as charming as ever, to her, her sisters, the customers, but he was avoiding her.

She was scared too. More than once the past few days, Carter had mentioned Montana. Not to her, but in passing to customers and such.

Above all, Molly was mad. Carter had hired a man to help out around the place. That's what he'd said, help out around the place. They didn't need any more help, nor could she afford another employee.

Tossing back the covers, Molly climbed out of her bed. She didn't need another person to hide from, either. Buster Freeman was kindly enough, and she remembered him from around town. He'd lived in Huron as long as she had probably, but time was not on her side. People of all ages recognize a pregnant woman when they see one.

Pacing the room, she once again rehearsed exactly what she'd tell Carter when they had a moment of privacy. If he wasn't sharing the soddy with Mr. Freeman, she'd have been down there right now, telling him just what she thought of his behavior lately. He'd even had Buster build Ivy a new playhouse out of lumber he'd said he'd scavenged, but it looked brand-new to her.

Ivy adored the new building. What little girl wouldn't? It had glass windows that could be propped open, and green shutters, and miniature window boxes for flowers. Inside there was not only room for her table and chairs, there was a built-in desk and shelves. Curtains and a rug on the floor, too. Karleen had found those and installed them today. The playhouse was much cheerier than the soddy, and Molly doubted she'd be able to convince Ivy she couldn't play in it come winter, as she had the soddy.

Molly plopped down on the edge of the bed and pressed one palm against her forehead. With everything else going on, Carter has a playhouse built for Ivy. Ludicrous. That's what it was.

A whinny sounded. Molly rose, walked to the window. It had sounded like Sampson, who only whinnied when Carter was near. The palomino was in the paddock beside the barn. His golden hide looked almost yellow in the moonlight. Then the horse tossed its head and trotted to the back of the barn.

Molly left the window. Sampson's behavior told her one thing. Carter was in the barn. She collected her wrap from the foot of the bed, in case she encountered Mr. Freeman, and eased her door open, listening in case either Ivy or Karleen was still awake.

Convinced they must be sleeping, Molly scrambled down the steps. Somewhere along the hallway her heart started racing. Not from the exertion, but the excursion, the thought of being alone with Carter. She bit her lip, hiding the smile there, at the back door while peering toward the soddy, trying to see through the darkness that the door was indeed closed.

It was. She ran.

At the barn she bit her lip again, this time to quell her excitement before she opened the door just wide enough to slip in. She was still pulling the door closed behind her when Carter spoke.

"Go back to the house, Molly."

His tone stung. A joyless statement that was also unyielding. No matter how it was spoken, his command meant nothing. She wasn't going anywhere. Why should she? She had nothing to lose. Straightening her spine, lifting her chin, she went forward, marched down the wide aisle that separated the stalls from the feed and tack area, the family buggy parked so long it was dusty gray instead of black, and other odds and ends, including the large pile of hay pitched down from the loft.

"You heard me, Molly," he said from where he stood near the stall now housing Sampson.

Molly had heard him all right, both times, even with every beat of her heart echoing in her ears like drums in a marching band when the railroad hosted a summer celebration, but she kept right on walking. He was bare chested, and barefoot, wore nothing but his britches. Black, of course. Like his hair that was gleaming in the light of a lantern hung on the ladder leading to the loft.

He was squinting, frowning, trying his best to hide it, but she saw how, beneath his scowl, he was excited to see her, almost as excited as she was. She glanced away in order to keep from smirking. That wouldn't work right now. Carter had a set of rules he played by, lived by. She didn't have a book to tell her what they were, but she was learning.

Her gaze lingered on the hay pile. The pillow and blanket there, and the impression left by someone lying on them. "I thought you were sharing the soddy with Mr. Freeman," she said, still not ready to look his way.

"He snores."

Carter had moved, now stood in the corner of her vision where he was putting on his shirt. That was a sight to see, and she watched, heart thumping. He sat down next, on the bottom rung of the ladder, and pulled on one sock and a boot. As he started on the next set, she said, "Where are you going?"

"I'm taking you back to the house."

He hadn't looked up, acted as if his sock and boot took all his attention.

She let her gaze wander back to the blanket and pillow. "There's a spare room in the house, Carter. It was my parents' room."

"I'm not moving into your house, Molly."

"Well, you can't very well sleep out here."

"It's just for the night."

She grinned then. "Oh? Mr. Freeman won't snore tomorrow night?"

"Probably," Carter said.

He'd stood, and a chill shimmied its way up her spine as she met his gaze. Molly closed her eyes, flinched slightly at the thought, but still asked, "Where will you be tomorrow night?"

"Can't say for sure. Somewhere close to Wyoming, I suspect." There wasn't any glitter in his eyes now. "I'm leaving on the morning train, Molly."

An indescribable dread rose up inside her, swelling with each beat of her heart, and it threatened to overcome her. She couldn't let that happen; she had an ounce of pride left.

Somewhere.

Molly went with anger instead. That she had plenty of. And it was readily accessible. "When were you going to tell me?"

"Tomorrow."

"Right before you boarded the train?"

"Probably."

She was pacing now; there was too much energy screaming for release not to. He, on the other hand, was standing stock-still. There were a thousand things she wanted to say but couldn't decide which to spit out first.

He spoke, which didn't help at all. "You know I have a job to do."

"You have a job right here, Carter. You're supposed to be our hired hand." Things were flowing now, and she wasn't about to stop them. She even waggled a finger for emphasis. "Instead, you go hire one. You can take him with you, too. Buster Freeman. Take him on that train with you. To Wyoming or Montana or wherever you're off to. We don't need him. We don't need you, either."

"Buster isn't going anywhere."

"Well, he's not staying here." She crossed her arms, squeezed her hands in tight fists beneath her breasts. The want to make him stay was stronger than her anger, and she was fighting the impulse to run forward and throw her arms around Carter's neck. "I have *the say* in who stays and who goes around here, and he's going."

Carter sighed. He'd known this wasn't going to be easy, that's why he'd planned to say goodbye tomorrow morning, in front of her sisters so she'd have to contain herself. Right now, Molly's stomping was stirring up more dirt than a stampede, and her thin nightgown, hell, he could practically see right through it. Therefore, he kept his eyes on her face, which didn't work, either. The flickering lamplight brought out all the different shades of brown and gold in her hair and had her eyes silver-hued.

He'd have to look right through her. That he knew how to do, and it would be best. There was one bit of information he'd been willing to go to Wyoming without, with just his instincts, but having her confirm it would tie up the final loose end. Dread swirled in his stomach. She was going to hate him before the night was over.

"Buster Freeman isn't going anywhere." He

kept his tone even, his face expressionless. "I've paid him a year's salary. In advance."

She stopped, stared at him with disbelief. "A year's salary?"

He nodded. Freeman had taken his advice, cleaned up, sobered up and came to the mercantile. Other than his teeth, Carter had hardly recognized him. Buster's timing had been perfect, too. He'd appeared the day after Carter had met with him.

Molly's eyes snapped as she spewed, "With what? The stolen money?"

"No."

She pointed a hand toward the wall as if there was a window there. "It's gone. It's not in the trunk in the soddy."

"I know."

"Where is it?"

"Safe. It'll soon be with its rightful owner."

"The railroad," she snapped.

Not ready to go down that road, Carter changed the subject. "I paid Buster with my own money. He'll do all the chores you can't do right now."

Pacing again, she shook her head. "I can do anything I want to."

He couldn't deny that. "You're supposed to be taking it easy," he said. "Doctor's orders."

"For a few days, Carter. I was supposed to

take it easy for a few days, and those days are over."

They were over, all right. She was also getting closer to the time when large dresses wouldn't conceal her condition. He'd know what to do about that once he got to Wyoming, learned a few more things, but the one thing he already knew for sure was he'd made a mess of his first experience with love. He doubted he could live without her, yet knew it wouldn't kill him, mainly because of the things he couldn't live *with*. Those were what he had to focus on right now.

She'd stopped, and settled a hard stare on him. "Are you coming back?"

He'd told a lot of lies while undercover, out of necessity, but couldn't lie right now. "I don't know."

The color left her face and she started to shake, trembling like a train bridge trestle. Carter went to her, grasped her upper arms in case she went down. His touch created the opposite effect; she went iron stiff.

"Damn you, Carter Buchanan," she growled. "Damn you."

He didn't react. On the outside, that is. Inside he was a kid. Hurt.

She said it again, over and over, while pounding on his chest with both fists. He let her release the anger, take it out on him, and when she slumped against him, Carter forced his hands to stay on her arms, not fold around her.

"I was going to ask you to marry me, Carter," she mumbled.

He stiffened. Damned himself and all he knew.

"Did you hear me?" she asked.

Her head was still leaning against his chest, right above his heart that wasn't nearly as good at not responding as he'd thought. "I heard you, Molly."

She leaned back, started unbuttoning his shirt. "You can come back, Carter. After you catch the robber, you can come back."

He tried to make his body go cold, unfeeling, but it wouldn't, so he set her away from him. "Stop it, Molly."

Over the years he'd probably hurt people in various ways, but he never saw pain like what was in her eyes. He had to turn it around, make her mad again, so she'd direct the damage at him.

"What about us, Carter? What we have. What we shared the other night?"

It was the opening he needed. She was not going to be the only one to hate him. He would, too. Already did. "What about it?" he asked. "You only came to the soddy the other night so I'd sleep with you." It took all he had to remain detached. "I didn't, and I'm not going to tonight."

Her tears made his eyes burn. "That's not true. That's not why I'm here."

"It's not?" While she was shaking her head, he asked, "Isn't that what you did to Robbie Fredrickson?" The words made him want to throw up, but he had to get the truth out of her, and this was the only way. The only one he knew of.

She flew at him, and he sidestepped, but he was ready to pounce, catch her if she tripped. A disgusting type of relief flowed over him when she caught the ladder, used it to stabilize her stance.

"That's not what happened," she yelled.

"It's not?" He'd mastered the ability to look at someone and make them question themselves, and he used it now. "Robbie's not the father of your baby?"

She'd turned into stone, a chalk-white sandstone like the pyramids down in Kansas. Never in all his years of interrogating people, forcing them to tell him what he needed to know, had he felt like this. Literally sick to his stomach. It was proof, though, that he needed to protect the girls from himself. He'd never been taught how to care for others, just how to harm them.

Quiet now, her voice was barely a whisper when she asked, "How do you know that?"

The need to protect her was as strong as ever. It wasn't much, but he said, "No one else knows."

Her glare could have frozen boiling water, and that told him he'd wounded her. Deeply.

She pushed off the ladder. "I hate you." Stopping in front of him, she seethed bitterly, "Did you hear that, Carter? I. Hate. You."

"I heard you, Molly." It was what he wanted. In order for her to give Robbie a second chance, give their child a chance to know both parents, she had to hate him. His plan had been to wait until he knew more, but if he'd waited, he might not have the wherewithal to walk away a second time. This way, he just never had to return.

Unfortunately, that's what he needed to do. Never return to Huron.

Molly was gone. She'd left the barn door open, which creaked eerily in the wind.

Carter didn't see her the next morning, either, when he said goodbye to Karleen and Ivy. They, too, asked if he'd be back, and though he'd never had a hard time saying goodbye before, he found a lump in his throat. He gave them each a wink and a nod, and then left.

Wilcox was at the train station, wanting to know where Carter was going and why he hadn't met with him to give him an update. Carter said he'd learn everything he needed to know when the time came, and that he was simply going where the case took him. He then asked if James Fredrickson was still at the railhead.

He was.

Carter saw Sampson settled first, and then took his place in the passenger car. He'd thought about a sleeping berth, but sleep would only produce nightmares and he had enough of those with his eyes open. The ride was rough, long, but he couldn't say he was overly excited when the train stopped at the railhead.

The tent city that had been created was intricate, full of every kind of establishment imaginable, and recent rains had left everything wet, damp, muddy and foul. Fitting. Inside he felt so rotten a coyote would leave him behind.

Regret, recrimination, couldn't even begin to express what he felt when he thought about Molly—which was all the time—and what he'd done to her.

Besides the main track, which extended less than a mile from where the train veered onto a switchback, there were other lines laid, short ones that held private cars. It was obvious which one was James Fredrickson's. Red, with gold paint scrolling his name along the side, the car looked as pompous as the man.

Carter hadn't made his first round of the town when he came upon someone who looked vaguely familiar. Stepping closer to where the man sat on an overturned barrel near a crude forge, filing down a well-worn horseshoe, he nodded a greeting. "You and your brothers started up a business," Carter said to the oldest of the German men who'd purchased supplies at the mercantile.

"Had to," the man replied.

"Name's Carter."

The man nodded. "Reinhardt Horlacher."

"Couldn't get jobs with the railroad?" Carter asked.

Reinhardt stopped hammering with a final ping that lingered as he stared. Eventually, the big blond man must have figured Carter wasn't a foe, because he shrugged. "We didn't come to work for the railroad." His brogue, which replaced *w*'s with *v*'s, was heavy and strong, and dismal. "We came to fetch our little sister."

There had to be a thousand people trying to live in this muck and mud. "You haven't found her?"

"*Ja,* we found her."

Carter waited.

"A railroad man promised her a job." Reinhardt turned, glared toward the red-and-gold private car. "Now we need five hundred dollars to buy her back."

A month ago, Carter probably would have walked away, or never stopped to talk to the man in the first place, but now, knowing how much younger sisters meant, he said, "Have you heard of the Pinkerton agency?"

The German nodded. *"Ja."*

Holding out one hand, he said, "Carter Buchanan, Pinkerton operative." When the man hesitated, Carter pulled out a well-used calling card embossed with his name and the company logo. Eli Greer wanted both robberies solved and he didn't care who went to jail. Pinkerton's message also said to take whatever measures necessary.

Reinhardt took the card, read it and handed it back. "I have no money to hire you."

"It's not money I need, Mr. Horlacher."

Two nights later, after learning enough to make him mean and ugly, and with the help of the four Horlacher brothers taking out the men guarding Robbie Fredrickson's private car, Carter threw open the metal door. He arrived at the foot of the bed about the same time Robbie sat up.

Gun drawn, Carter cocked the trigger. "You can start talking, or you can start praying, the choice is yours. But be assured, if I don't like what I hear, neither will do you any good."

Robbie opened his mouth, and Carter recognized a shout was to follow. Before the man got the chance, he said, "No one's going to hear you. If one of your guards is still alive, he's long gone."

"Who are you?" Robbie demanded.

"A living nightmare," Carter growled. Lamps were lit, flickering shadows across the lavishly furnished car littered with liquor bottles. With a gesture of the barrel of his gun, Carter told Greta Horlacher, "Put something on and get out." She looked enough like her brothers that he had no doubt, even if his investigation hadn't said this was where they'd find her, she was Reinhardt's younger sister.

Disgust renewed itself in Carter. Greta had been on the train the night he'd met with James at Wilcox's office back in Huron. As well as a few other women the man had lured into his clutches by promising legitimate jobs. The Fredricksons, father and son, had started up a new business for the railroad, managing their own lot of soiled doves. The regulars, those that had followed the train for years, weren't impressed. Their profits had gone down to a fourth of what they had been.

Carter was disappointed, too. In the fact Robbie Fredrickson was such a pip-squeak of a man. Scrawny and whitish, and trembling so hard his black mustache was shaking, a stiff wind could give the man bruises he'd need a week to recover from. Carter smothered a sigh. He'd heard likewise, yet had hoped Robbie would be the size of the Germans. Carter was itching for a good brawl.

This little ingrate wouldn't be a fair fight.

Robbie grabbed Greta's arm as she scooted off the bed. "She's not going anywhere."

Carter didn't even bother shaking his head. "I'm not liking what I'm hearing." He fired a shot, a warning one that split a few wayward hairs on the top of Robbie's head before the bullet lodged itself in the headboard.

"Jesus!" Robbie covered his head with both hands as he ducked.

Carter kept his gun on Robbie while Greta dressed. Considering all he'd discovered the past two days, he could plant a bullet in the scoundrel and not have a whole lot of regrets afterward. The Horlacher brothers would have already done so. That's why they were outside. Carter had contemplated letting them have first crack at Robbie but, ultimately, he couldn't. It was his job. Besides, he wanted answers.

When soft squeals, those of Greta greeting her brothers, filtered into the car, Carter started pacing the length of the foot of the bed, keeping his gun on Robbie. "You couldn't spend the money from the first robbery. You hadn't realized it was made up of newly minted bills until it was too late. Why didn't you get rid of it?"

The pip-squeak cast his beady eyes around the room, suspicious. James Fredrickson was the only other person to know, and Robbie most likely was having a hard time believing his father had squealed on him.

"Why'd you hide it in Huron?" Carter pressed.

Robbie wheezed in enough air it had to have gone all the way to his ankles.

Carter stopped pacing, gun level with Fredrickson's nose. "I hope I like what I hear."

"I planned on going back for it." Robbie fretted deeper when his nervous glance proved there was still no one coming to rescue him and Carter had cocked his gun again. "Take it to Mexico or Canada. It wouldn't have mattered there. No one outside the railroad knew about it."

"Didn't you think it might be discovered under that bed?" Carter asked.

"I," Robbie started, sounding testy, "was interrupted while finding an *appropriate* hiding spot. Became a bit preoccupied by a little blonde that night."

Carter was not in the mood to hear that, nor was the bullet in his gun. It almost went off. He almost pulled the trigger. Knocking Robbie's head against the headboard was another fleeting urge, but he refrained. Barely.

"Is that who found it?" Robbie asked. "That sweet little virgin? Said it was mine?"

There were few things in this world Carter had ever truly hated. He was facing one right now. He reminded himself why he was here; therefore he didn't say a word, or blink an eye, but his hands were itching. Not just to pull the trigger, but to squeeze the ingrate's neck until his eyes bulged.

Robbie frowned deeply. "She wouldn't have known it was mine, though. No one would have."

Carter, maintaining his control, pointed out, "Your father wanted the money brought out here, to the railhead."

Proving to be as unintelligent as Carter had imagined, Robbie let his gaze flash across the room, toward a built-in wardrobe of sorts. "So someone could discover it, put an end to it. Greer was getting too worked up over it."

"That's why you stole the second strongbox, so there'd be something to find."

Robbie pressed a hand to his head as if that was enough of a penance. "Not one of my best ideas. I was drunk."

Carter was reminded of the second thing he needed to know. The one that really mattered. His life, either the one he wanted or the one fate might descend upon him, depended on Fredrickson's answer. "Where's the woman that's supposedly pregnant with your child?"

The laugh echoing in the car sounded exactly like James Fredrickson's had that night at the depot in Huron. Carter's blood turned cold.

"Which one?" Robbie asked.

Chapter Sixteen

"Wasn't that adorable?" Karleen asked, clapping loudly.

"Yes," Molly agreed. Ivy had been flawless in reciting her poem, but enjoying it wasn't possible, not with half the population of Huron crammed into the school. "Let's leave before the crowd."

"First you insist we take the buggy, which makes us late so we have to sit in the very back of the room, and now you want to leave early?" Karleen hissed. Letting out an exasperated sigh, she continued, "This the first time we've been out of the house together in months. Let's enjoy it a little bit. Mr. Freeman can handle the store."

Buster was very capable—Molly couldn't argue that, nor would she, but she would be adamant about leaving. The door was directly behind them, and with a little luck she could be seated in the buggy before too many people noticed. Her body had altered in the two weeks since Carter had left. The bump she used to have had become a bulge much more difficult to conceal. "It's hot in here," she whispered. "Besides, it's over."

"Because you're wearing a shawl, and it's not over," Karleen persisted. "There's punch and cookies, and Miss Denny said there'd be an announcement afterward."

Molly couldn't care less about any announcement, and wasn't about to walk to the front of the room for punch or cookies. The clapping stopped, and she leaned back, cast a longing glance toward the door.

"Parents, friends, family, thank you for coming today," Miss Denny, a slender woman who'd been teaching in Huron for over a decade, said. She waved a hand toward the children standing straight and proper along the front wall. "And thank you, students, for all your hard work. You did an excellent job." Clapping her hands again, the woman encouraged another round of applause by saying, "Didn't they?"

Molly shifted in her seat, ready to scoot off the edge, but Karleen grabbed her knee. Shook her head.

"Now," Miss Denny said, "Mr. Ted Wilcox

has a special announcement, and please remember to stay for refreshments afterward."

The woman gave a slight bow and moved to stand beside her students as Mr. Wilcox, with his haughty mind-set—apology or not, Molly still didn't care for the man—strolled to the front of the room.

"Good citizens of Huron," he started, hooking his hands on the lapels of his suit coat.

Molly swallowed a groan and glanced toward the door again.

"It's my pleasure to inform you Mr. Eli Greer, the senior partner and majority owner of the Chicago and Northwestern Railroad, will be gracing our small town with his presence this afternoon. I encourage you, the citizens of Huron, to be at the train station at four o'clock to offer Mr. Greer the warm welcome he deserves for all the railroad has done for our community." The man paused to glance at his pocket watch. "By the time you're done with Miss Denny's punch and cookies the train will have arrived. There will be another man with Mr. Greer. Mr. Allan Pinkerton of the Pinkerton Detective Agency."

People were clapping, whispering, and nodding at one another. Molly wasn't. She had no desire to meet the owner of the railroad, and she'd heard of Pinkerton detectives. Read about them in newspapers. Brutes. Bounty hunters. Guns for hire. Despite her sister's hold, Molly slid off her chair and walked out the door, keeping the little paper program listing all the children and their poems over her stomach. It wasn't much, but along with her shawl—which was lightweight but hot—she hoped it was enough.

Molly was almost to the buggy when someone said her name.

Remorse showered her and she stopped, turned around to face the girl—woman—who, up until a few months ago, had been her best friend for years. Emma's smile was so unsure, all sorts of things softened inside Molly. Unable to stop them, her eyes went to her friend's stomach.

"Just last week I had to take out the seams in a few dresses." Emma, dressed in mint green, including the feathered hat perched on her russet-colored hair, was the epitome of pretty, even with a larger than normal waist. "Ivy did an excellent job," Emma then said. "Her poem was beautiful."

Molly nodded. "She loves school."

"So did we." Emma continued to approach, stopped when they were less than a foot apart. "Remember?"

"I remember," Molly whispered, shaken.

"I've missed you," Emma said. "Our friendship."

They'd shared so much in the past, especially support when her parents had passed, and she couldn't help but wonder how different things would be if the two could share what was happening now. Their pregnancies. "Me, too," Molly choked out.

Emma flung her arms around Molly's neck, an impromptu hug. Molly's response was to hug her friend in return, and did so until she realized their stomachs had bumped and Emma had stiffened.

"Molly?"

She knew exactly what her friend had discovered. "I've got to go." Spinning, she hurried toward the buggy.

Buttercup, the mare who used to be gentle in the days when she was ridden consistently, hadn't pulled the buggy in over a year, and started tugging at the rein securing her to the post. The wild rolling of the horse's eyes slowed Molly's approach and she struggled to find her voice in her burning throat to calm the animal.

Emma, however, was rushing behind her. Molly heard the steps, and her name being repeated, and recognized the movement and sound were disturbing the spooked animal more. She was almost at the horse, reaching out to clutch the leather rein, when Buttercup reared.

A hoof came down and caught Molly's shoulder. The force and sharp pain unbalanced her. Knocked to the ground, Molly curled into a ball and rolled, avoiding the hooves coming down on both sides of her.

Emma was screeching for aid, and Molly wanted to tell her to be quiet, but all her concentration was set on timing her next rotation. Buttercup reared again, and Molly rolled, over and over until convinced she was clear of the hooves.

She was, and took a moment to catch her breath. When she opened her eyes, a crowd had gathered around her. Emma was still shrieking, "Get Dr. Henderson! We need Dr. Henderson!"

Molly groaned. Her shoulder was throbbing, but it was her position, flat on her back staring up at blue sky, that was excruciating. Her stomach had to stick out like a Swiss Alp.

"I'm here! Let me through!" Dr. Henderson's face appeared then, contorted with concern. "Molly?"

She closed her eyes. Kept them that way when Emma said, "I think she's pregnant."

"Of course she's pregnant," the doctor replied.

The crowd went silent, or maybe the swooshing in Molly's ears was just too loud to hear around.

Nope, she could hear. Heard someone ask, "How can that be?"

How indeed.

"She's been married to Carter Buchanan for months."

Molly snapped her eyes open. She'd recognized Pastor Jenkins's voice, but what he'd said proved her ears weren't working. He was kneeling beside her, next to Dr. Henderson, and while the doctor was examining her shoulder, the pastor was looking up at the crowd.

"Mr. Buchanan is a Pinkerton operative," Pastor Jenkins said. "He's been working undercover on a case for the railroad, therefore he and Molly had to keep their marriage a secret."

"It's true," Dr. Henderson added. "I've known about it for a long time."

"So have I." That was Mrs. Rudolf, now kneeling on Molly's other side.

"You did?" the doctor asked incredulously.

"I do now," Mrs. Rudolf whispered. "It certainly explains Carter's protectiveness, and his concern for Ivy. Besides, weeks ago I recognized the way they looked at each other." The woman then raised her head, and her voice. "We all know Molly would never have let a stranger move onto her property. That would have been scandalous." She patted Molly's cheek. "No wonder you weren't acting yourself all these months. Worrying about him."

Molly was wishing Buttercup had kicked her in the head. Then she wouldn't have heard any of this. Wouldn't hate Carter Buchanan to a level she'd never reached before. A Pinkerton operative? Undercover? He'd been that, all right. She bet the mercantile she wasn't the first woman he'd completely fooled, either, with all his secrets. Lied to. Hoodwinked. Deceived. The list went on and she didn't mind adding to it.

"J.T.!" Dr. Henderson shouted. "Take that horse back to the mercantile." Then he instructed the pastor. "Caleb, help me get her in my buggy."

By the time Molly arrived home, she'd cursed Carter so severely her soul was halfway to purgatory. He may have once claimed to have an angel on his shoulder—another lie—but Molly had a demon in her ear, and it was shouting while the doctor and pastor aided her into the parlor, fussing exhaustedly.

It's what you wanted, the devil repeated over and over.

No, it's not, she argued. True, at one time her plan had been to ask Carter to marry her, but that hadn't worked. She'd moved on. Had a new plan. She'd written a letter to Robbie, told him about her condition.

"Here, Molly, lie down," Dr. Henderson said. "Let me look at that shoulder."

"It's fine," she insisted, but did lie down. She had to. Her life was on another downhill slide.

The doctor didn't take her word for it. After shooing everyone from the room, he unbuttoned her dress, exposed her shoulder. "Nothing's broken," he said after a thorough examination. "Where else are you hurt?"

"Nowhere," she said. Hearts don't count.

"That shoulder's going to be sore for a few days. I want you to take—"

"I'll take it easy," she interrupted. Sitting up, Molly gathered the neckline of her dress together, noted how the sleeve seam had been ripped open. "I have to go change."

"I'll get Karleen to help you."

"No." How was she ever going to face her sisters? She cursed Carter again, and sent her soul a bit deeper into fire and brimstone by vowing to kill him if she ever set eyes on him again. "No. I'll be fine by myself."

The voices in the store meant she didn't encounter anyone on her escape to solitude, which would be short-lived. The doctor said he'd wait until she returned downstairs. With her other gray dress hanging on the clothesline out back, Molly took down a navy blue one. The skirt of this one started just below her breast line, which hopefully meant it would fit.

The dress with its embroidered white collar did fit, and Molly then set about removing the pins from her hair. Her shoulder ached, more so when she lifted her arm, so after brushing the grass from her hair, she left it down. Braiding it would hurt, too. The window was open and the noise said a crowd was approaching. Unable not to, she took a peek to see if they carried torches and stakes.

They didn't, but two tall, well-dressed men, along with Mr. Wilcox, led the mob.

Hell hath no fury like a woman scorned. She now knew what the English playwright meant. They could ridicule her all they wanted, but no one would scorn her sisters. Her hand went to her stomach.

Her family.

Molly spun, and called upon all the dignity she'd ever possessed.

The store was packed, people spewing out the door and peering through the plate-glass windows. Mr. Wilcox and the two other men were at the counter, shaking Karleen's hand.

"This," Karleen said as Molly moved to stand with Ivy between them, "is our other sister, Molly."

The first man, with a friendly smile, introduced himself as Eli Greer. The second man, tall with a beard and mustache, also smiling, made her shiver when he said his name was Allan Pinkerton. That shouldn't surprise her, Carter being a Pinkerton agent. He'd been a bully since the first day they'd met. If not for the crowd, she'd have asked where he was, and then dug out the shotgun. She knew how to use it.

Mr. Greer, his eyes, kind and sincere, was looking at Ivy. "I'm here," he said loud enough for all to hear, "to see Miss Ivy Thorson." He pulled an envelope from his breast pocket and extended it across the counter. "To offer her a reward for finding and returning property belonging to the Chicago and Northwestern Railroad."

Ivy looked up, and Molly, as confused as the child, gave permission for Ivy to take the envelope. When it was opened, the contents displayed, Molly gasped at the bank draft, and again at the amount of it.

"That's ten percent of the property recovered. A fair amount, don't you agree?"

Karleen answered in the affirmative, but Molly understood Mr. Greer was waiting for her response. "That's more than generous, Mr. Greer, but...actually, I—we—"

"Please," he interrupted, "don't say you can't accept it."

Molly bit her lip. She couldn't take this away from Ivy no matter how unconventional it seemed. "Thank you."

"I'd also like to assure you, all three of you, that the C&NW respects all merchants," Mr. Greer said. "We understand the commitment and devotion it takes to run a business successfully." He cast a rigid gaze toward Mr. Wilcox before looking at her again. "You ladies can be assured, from this day forward, no member of the railroad will make any attempt to prevent you from managing your affairs, nor will they make an offer to purchase this fine establishment from you." He smiled, especially at Ivy. "As a matter of fact, the railroad will be doing a considerable amount of business with Thorson's Mercantile going forward."

The ambience surrounding Molly had taken on a dreamlike quality, where there were happy endings. She returned Ivy's broad smile, and laughed aloud—along with many others—when her littlest sister said, "And we'll gladly let you."

Carter smothered a chuckle from where he stood in the hall, peering around the doorway. His heart was probably in Montana, only because it was pounding hard enough to cover the distance to there from Huron in record time. He, however, had no desire to go to Montana. Now or ever. Or anywhere else. He'd figured out where he needed to be, and who he needed to be with. Now he just had to come up with a way to be welcomed.

That wasn't going to be easy.

Molly was more than fetching every day, and, unfortunately, her laugh, the way her hair cascaded down her back, simply her—knowing she was within reach—had him aroused. Thoroughly, and unfortunately, because now wasn't the time for that.

Allan Pinkerton started to speak then, and Carter held his breath. Not to hear the man's words, but to watch her reaction. Allan knew all there was to know, and though he'd said he hated to lose Carter as an operative, he'd do all he could to ease Carter's transition.

"I wanted to personally thank you, Molly," Allan said. "I can only imagine how difficult the past few months have been on you and I sincerely appreciate your willingness to maintain complete secrecy. My entire agency is indebted to you."

Her back had gone stiff, and that was what Carter needed to know. She hated him.

While Greer shared the railroad's appreciation to her, Carter backed up. The desire to go to her boiled inside him. He'd like to just carry her out of there, but had to think of her. How embarrassed she might be by that. They needed privacy to say what he had to tell her, convince her he was right.

On the back steps, he paused, wondering how to fill his time until the crowd thinned. In the end, he went to get Sampson settled. The horse was still saddled, standing outside the barn door where it had gone once Carter had jumped off to run to the back door of the store. With more pressing things to do, he hadn't stayed at the rail station, listened to Greer give his speech. He'd known they'd all be coming down to the mercantile, and had hoped to arrive in time to see Ivy get her reward. He had, and now just needed to wait to see Molly.

The young kid, J.T., was in the barn, having a heck of a time trying to back the buggy into the narrow slot allowed for it. After assisting him, while Carter walked toward Sampson— the animal remembered which stall was his and seemed relieved to be home—the kid offered his thanks. He'd been trying to get the buggy parked for an hour.

"Why was it out?" Carter asked, loosening the cinch on his saddle.

"Molly and Karleen took it to the school, to hear Ivy's recital."

Disappointment washed over Carter. "That was today?"

"Yes." J.T. brushed his damp hair back, picked a bowler hat off the floor. "Is Molly all right? She didn't get hurt too bad, did she?"

Carter froze and spun to face the kid at almost the same time. "Hurt?"

"Yeah. Buttercup got spooked. Reared up and knocked Molly down."

Carter was already running for the door when J.T. shouted, "Doc and the pastor brought her home."

That was just like her, hurt, but too stubborn to admit it. In his rush, Carter forgot the crowd. After shoving aside the first few, he merely needed to elbow his way. Then as if an invisible Trojan horse ran before him, clearing a path, he was in the center of the store. Face-to-face with Molly.

She was behind the counter, and her mouth formed his name. Carter didn't hear what she said, didn't attempt to read her expression, because in the end, it didn't matter. He rounded the corner, swept her into his arms and carried her out the doorway to the hall. There he paused briefly, unsure where to take her, but knowing Molly, complete privacy would be best.

Noise, shouts from the crowd, or perhaps protests from her, filled his ears. He ignored it all, carried her through the kitchen, across the yard and didn't set her down until he stood beside the bed in the soddy. There he laid her gingerly on the bed, and rather shook up, half fearing to look closely, he asked, "How bad were you trampled?"

She sat up as if spring-loaded. "I wasn't trampled!" Hopping on her bottom to the edge of the bed, she shouted, "I was just fine until I was accosted!"

"Accosted?" He checked, made sure his gun was on his hip. "By who?"

She bounced to her feet. "You!"

Carter took a good long look then. He had to—she was right before him. A stunning sight. The dark blue dress enhanced her breasts, showed off her elegant neck, reflected up into her soft eyes, and stole away every bit of his control. He took her face, held it between the palms of his hands and kissed her lips, even while they were moving. Calling him several names he'd heard before.

In due course, for Molly was stubborn, she stopped talking and started kissing, and Carter went in with all he had. He ought to take it slow, but there had been a lot of things he should have done at one time or another. Tasting her, feeling her, loving her took him someplace between heaven and earth, where "ought to," "should have," and "would have" didn't exist.

They had to come up for air—leastwise Carter did—and as he stepped back, he once again held her face with both hands.

"How dare you?" She obviously hadn't needed air.

"I'm a brave man," he replied.

A grin almost formed on her lips, and that was enough to plant the largest one he'd ever displayed on his lips. He kissed her again, and this time when he drew back, she said, "I still hate you."

"I know," he answered, letting her show him

how much with another good bout of lips and tongues.

He could go on kissing her forever, but there were things she needed to know. The best way to start a conversation was with a question, so Carter did that, or maybe it was a command. "Marry me, Molly."

She bowed her head, and then lifted it, shook it so her hair fluttered about her shoulders, down her back. "Half the town believes we *are* married, Carter." She took a few steps backward. "Probably all of it by now."

Not much he could say, other than, "I was afraid that would get out."

"Get out?" She flapped both arms. "Why would you tell people that? When? Pastor Jenkins said we'd been married for months. Since last spring."

"The pastor has been telling people?" He shook his head. "The doctor told him."

She glared.

He shrugged. "The night you were ill I may have suggested I'd been out here last spring, undercover, and only you knew about it."

"Oh?" She was pacing, as she always did when riled. "And Mrs. Rudolf. How'd she know?"

"Mrs. Rudolf?" He stepped forward, took her arms. "I never said a word about it to Mrs. Rudolf."

Some of the steam had left her. "I don't think she knew before today—just wanted to get her two cents in."

"Today?"

"Yes, when Buttercup got scared she knocked me down and Emma started shouting for the doctor, told him she thought I was pregnant. Dr. Henderson confirmed it and Pastor Jenkins said he knew, too. Mrs. Rudolf said…"

Carter had stopped listening, was examining her instead, from head to toe. When her explanation ended, he laid a hand against the firm, round bump her belly had become. "You're all right? Both of you?"

She closed her eyes as she covered his hand with both of hers. "Yes, I—we are fine."

"I worried about you, Molly, while I was gone." He had. More than he'd expected to. More than he ever wanted to again. "Both of you." Searching for her grin to return, he said, "I even worried about Karleen, and of course Ivy and her recital." When her smile appeared, he said, "I'm sorry I missed it."

"She did very well."

"I'll be at her next one," he vowed.

Molly was searching his face, reading him, and Carter didn't mind. Not in the least. He was reading her, too, and liked what he saw. "How badly were you injured?" he asked.

"Just a bump on the shoulder," she answered quietly.

"This one?" he asked, taking his fifty percent odds by pointing to her left one.

She shook her head.

He never had been a good gambler. His fingers went to the top button of the pretty white collar resting just below her throat. Several fasteners later, the gown was open enough for him to push her right shoulder free. A circular red line marred the delicate skin and he leaned forward, kissed it softly. "I don't know how it happened or where it came from, Molly."

"Buttercup hasn't pulled the buggy in a long time," she whispered. "She got spooked."

"Not this." He grinned while kissing the injury again. "I'm talking about how something so strong can grow out of nowhere in the harshest conditions. Where there was no light, no tending, no acceptance."

"What?"

Baffled himself, he kissed her furrowed brows. "I'm talking about love, Molly. I can't explain it. Don't know exactly when it happened, or why, or how, but it did. I don't even know how to describe it. That's why I know it's real. I didn't have to find it. It found me."

Her eyes fluttered shut, and it seemed the perfect moment to declare, "I love you, Molly." The smile on her lips was precious, but when she opened her eyes, his heart took a major tumble, corroborating all he'd said. All he felt. "I love you, and your sisters, and the baby. I'll be good to you. I'll take care of you. All of you. If you'll give me the chance."

"We love you, too, Carter." Biting her bottom lip, she shook her head slightly. "I love you." Then, lifting her chin, she repeated more firmly, "I love you."

He wanted to leap in the air, shout with joy, do all sorts of silly things kids do when intense jubilance overcame them, but he was an adult, and she was hurt, therefore, he kissed her shoulder again, softly.

She let out an encouraging little whimper, and Carter continued, ran kisses along the slender slope of her shoulder and back up to her neck. His hands went to the buttons on her dress again, undid them all to expose more room, more space to touch, taste.

A little shove sent the dress to the floor and he started on her shift. The buttons were so tiny he had to stop his kisses to find them. Allan Pinkerton knew everything, knew what his plan was, and therefore Carter wasn't worried about someone knocking on the door, yet he glanced around, assuring their privacy. That's when he noticed how empty the soddy was. "Where's Buster?"

The man had decorated the place with his belongings when he'd moved in.

Floating next to the clouds, Molly's mind took a moment to gather Carter's question. "I don't know," she answered.

"Isn't he still here?" he asked. "Sleeping in the soddy?"

He'd stopped unbuttoning her camisole, and she didn't want that. Not right now. He loved her. He. Loved. Her. Her, and that had sun shining inside her. Bright and beautiful. She'd never been anywhere like this before. This perfect, spectacular place, full of sunshine and dreams. Other things were appearing inside her, too. She wanted Carter beyond imagination. A growing need that went beyond all earthly desires. It, too, was lush and beautiful. There was no way she was going to step out of this uncharted dreamland, not right now. People could pound on the door, but she wouldn't answer. Not right now.

Taking a step back, she waited until Carter's fingers fell away before she began unbuttoning. "Buster's still here. I asked him to start sleeping in the house over a week ago."

"Why?" Carter asked. "What happened?"

He was so handsome, his features so perfect, his hair so dark, his love so strong it welled all around her. "Nothing happened," she said. "I asked him to sleep in the house." Opening the shift, she shrugged both shoulders at once, let the garment fall to the floor. "So I could sleep out here."

His eyes gave her a slow appraisal, taking extra time between her hips and chin, before, shimmering, they rose to meet hers. "Why?"

"Because it smells like you."

He gave a slow, even shake of his head as if unsure of what he'd heard.

"And," she whispered truthfully, "I could pretend you were here. With me."

Swiftly, just as he'd done in the mercantile, while she'd thought she was imagining things, he swept her into his arms. Then he twisted, set her on the bed and stretched out beside her, all in one enchanting movement.

"I was with you," he said. "In my heart, I'd never left." He kissed her, softly, briefly. "I love you."

Molly never considered herself greedy, but at this moment, she was insatiable. She wanted Carter, every last bit of him. "I love you, too. Very, very much."

In time their clothes were gone. Carter, his hands, his kisses, already had her mind reeling, her body humming and her blood simmering, yet he continued, kissing and caressing until she thought she might expire from the agony burning deep within her. She was to blame, too, his flesh, so hot and slick, was incredible, and she couldn't touch it, taste it enough.

But, still, she needed more. Her breasts were throbbing, her nipples taut and damp from his mouth, and she was wet other places from his touches, ready and waiting impatiently.

"Carter, please," she groaned. "Please."

He positioned himself above her, and her heart tumbled sweetly when she noticed the hesitancy in his eyes. "It's all right," she whispered, fully understanding. "The doctor told me it's safe."

"You asked him?" he asked, clearly astonished.

Wiggling her hips, lining them up with his, she shook her head. "No, he just told me. Must have figured I'd want to know."

His grin was priceless, as was his lifted brow. "Did you?"

Lying beneath him, naked, wasn't embarrassing, neither were all the things they'd been doing to each other, yet answering that question brought heat to her cheeks. "Yes," she admitted.

He laughed, and in a lusty, fantastic movement, he rolled, landed on his back and held her, hips aligned, above him. "I did, too," he said, licking the tip of one breast. "And was told this is the safest way."

Her knees straddled his thighs, and enticed

by the power the position gave her, she asked, "It is?"

"That's what I was told." His hands gripped her hips, pulled her downward.

With a single, slick, hot thrust, he was inside her. Molly was immediately gone, or close to, but Carter, holding her hips, wouldn't let her cross the invisible threshold. He controlled the pace with several, slow, long and delicious strokes that had her trembling and cooing his name for an extended length of time.

She held on to his shoulders, relished his mouth teasing her breasts. Cherished their union, an even pace she now understood was delaying what would be an ultimate finish for as long as possible. Slowly, perfectly it carried her toward that brilliant moment on the horizon.

When it became too much, she was too close, Molly arched her neck, felt a shudder race down her back where it got caught up in the now-feverish tempo Carter was directing. Faster, more intently, he drove her forward.

She held her breath as a tense yet wild power overcame her. Moments later, in the midst of their somewhat frantic union, a tremendous joy erupted between them, a fierce liberation that had both she and Carter gasping and repeating each other's names as if senseless. Their spirits met, then became one in an ultimate finale that consumed her, filled her with ecstasy.

Spent, yet still experiencing the aftereffects spreading through her system, Molly sagged. Fell upon Carter as if her bones had turned to water. He laughed, a fabulous sound, and held her tight, their bodies still linked.

Chapter Seventeen

Having Carter help her dress was as stimulating as having him undress her, and Molly had to step away, take a breath. Yet, she let her smile and eyes show it wasn't because she wanted to. In return, he let her know he understood, silently.

Once they were both fully clothed, him standing beside the bed, her sitting on it, tying her last shoe, he asked, "When are we getting married?"

The real world shattered around her like a window hit by a rock. Trying to block it, she covered her face with both hands.

Carter pulled her hands away. "I'm sorry, Molly, for what I said before I left, for how I hurt you. I thought it was the only way—"

"It's not that. You didn't say anything that wasn't true." Tears had started to fall, painful, burning ones, and she had to fight to get enough air to say, "Nothing I didn't already know."

He kissed her knuckles. "Then what is it?"

She'd done some stupid things the last year, but what she'd done last week, what she had to own up to, was by far the worst. Stupid. So, so stupid. Pulling her hands away, she stood, took a step away. "I can't marry you, Carter."

"Why not?"

Her throat burned, yet she pushed out, "Because I wrote Robbie a letter. Told him about the baby."

The hissing sound, that of Carter breathing, ripped her in two. Justification wasn't much, but she didn't have much. "I had to do something. I didn't think you were coming back."

His silence shamed her, took away all the elation he'd filled her with just minutes ago. She'd known he'd be back—this man who not only loved her but her family, too—yet, at the time, she couldn't believe that. Not with all that had happened. Not with her past record. She'd had to do something. A touch of fury returned then. "Were you ever going to tell me you were a Pinkerton agent?"

The silence between them grew thicker as he continued to stare at her. Finally, when her throat had started to burn all over again, he said, "No."

A shiver sliced her in two. "No."

"I didn't plan on it, no," he said. "I couldn't. It would put you and the girls in danger."

His answer unleashed a bit more anger. "We were never in danger, Carter. Not with the way you threw your weight around. Every male customer walked on eggshells around you." She was trying to defy him, but the truth of what of she said only reminded her of all the things she loved about him. Trying harder, she said, "You acted like you'd rather shoot them than wait on them."

"That was the only life I'd ever known. Always on the defense," he said. "I didn't want you and the girls exposed to it." Stepping close, he lowered his voice, "I'll try harder, in the future, not to be so insensitive."

Turmoil was swirling inside her. Little more than an hour ago, when she'd first heard he was a Pinkerton man she damned him to hell for lying to her, for how she'd accepted him into her home, but in reality, that was a part of him she loved. "I don't want that, Carter."

He ran a hand through his hair and Molly couldn't bear the uncertainty in his eyes.

"Your confidence, your attitude is what was missing around here," she admitted. "It's who you are, the very things I love." Her deceit was eating at her again now. How she'd blown any chances of the two of them being together a second time. "I don't want you to change a single thing about you, but I still can't ma—"

"When did you write to Robbie?" he asked.

"Last week," she answered, sick to her stomach. "I sent it in care of the railroad. Figured they'd know how to get it to him."

"He's here. In Huron."

"Robbie?" She wrapped her arms over her waist. Protection.

"Yes. I took him and his father to the town's jail as soon as we arrived. Allan and Greer will see them to Chicago."

"Jail?"

Carter rubbed a hand over his mouth, and Molly held her breath until her lungs burned, sensing he struggled with what he was about to say.

"I understand how important it is for a child to know their parents," he said, "but, I believe your child will be better off not knowing Robbie. Or any of the Fredricksons."

"That's not why I wrote him, Carter. So my baby would know him." She trusted Carter and had no qualms telling him everything. She should have done it before now. "I wrote him because I couldn't lose everything. I couldn't do that to Karleen and Ivy, and I couldn't do it to myself, either. Yes, I made a mistake. I acted foolishly. I lied. Mainly to myself." She shook her head. Still not completely understanding why she'd done it. "I was so…lost, I guess. I can't explain what I felt that night, but I was frustrated. Fed up with everything, and I—I…I wanted something different and I was so tired of fighting for it. Foolishly, I thought Robbie could provide it. I thought I could learn to lov—"

After what she and Carter had just shared, what had happened months ago was so painful it hurt to breathe.

Carter took her hand. Kissed the back of it. "We all make mistakes, honey. We all have regrets."

She nodded. Breathed. "I know." Sighing, letting it cleanse her if possible. "I knew it was going to be painful, that I wouldn't come out unscathed, but I thought I could do it. That it might convince me to leave with him. Find schools for Karleen and Ivy to attend and leave all my troubles and worries behind. That's what he'd told me I should do, said it was what others would do. But even before…" She refused to think about it. "Afterward, I told him to leave. That I would never go anywhere with him. Never give up."

"Do you love him?"

"No. Never." A bitterness built inside her and she tried to shake it off. "I wrote him because I still won't give up everything I have. The letter tells him about the baby, and that he has a choice to either marry me, make this child legitimate, or I'll sue him."

"Sue him?" Carter asked, wide-eyed.

"Yes. I know it was all lies. The things he'd said, promised, and I can face what I did, as long as my baby has a name."

"Molly, that's commendable," he said, "but—"

"The Fredricksons have money," she interrupted. "Lots of it, and lawyers, and they could fight me until I lose everything." Pride was with her now, and she carried it on her shoulders, in her chin. "Robbie used that threat before, and that's why I also told him, in that letter, that I knew about the train robbery. That he'd done it, and that I'd go to the authorities."

"How did you know he stole the money?"

"Buster told me about that night. I put the rest together." Placing a hand on her stomach, she said, "I wrote that letter for justice. For the baby. For Karleen and Ivy. I don't want Robbie as my husband. I don't love him." Her throat was on fire again, burning. "But I didn't see another choice."

Carter, a bit surprised by all she'd said, was also in awe of her strength. He'd been prepared to tell her about Robbie's dealings. About the false back in the wardrobe that had concealed the stolen money. About the other women carrying Robbie's children. How Eli Greer claimed he'd never allow his daughter to marry someone so immoral, corrupt and dishonorable. Carter also wanted to tell her that once in Chicago both Robbie and James would be imprisoned for years, and that her child would be better off never knowing who their real father was, but there was no need. Not for that.

"I was working on the robbery, Molly."

"I know," she said. "But I—we—the baby and I weren't part of the case. It wouldn't give my baby a name."

She was right. He'd given her no reason to believe he'd take care of everything. After hearing what Greta and the other girls said Robbie and James had told them, promised them, Carter also understood how trapped Molly must have felt—still felt.

He picked up his hat, put it on.

"Where are you going?" she asked.

Hope was all he had, and he'd hold on to it, that the mail was slow. "To find that letter before it reaches Robbie." Carter placed a hand on her stomach. "I want to be the only father this baby ever knows. I want you and the baby to be Buchanans."

Uncertainty dulled her eyes. "You'll take us to Montana?"

"Montana was just a word," he admitted. "One I used to describe what I wanted, what I was looking for. I've done a lot of thinking the past two weeks, Molly. About you, about us, and I discovered I'd found my Montana. Right here in Huron. It offers more than I ever dreamed of having."

Her lips trembled as they tried to smile. "What about your ranch?"

He shrugged. "I don't mind being a merchant."

A tiny grin appeared on her lips. "You're a cowboy, Carter."

"Will that be enough for you, Molly? A cowboy—" he caressed her stomach "—and a baby?" While she held her breath, looked up at him with those glowing eyes, he added, "And maybe two or three more babies? I want to be the father of all your babies, including this one."

Tears shimmered in her eyes. "That's what I want, too, b-but it's too late, I—"

"No." That wasn't an option he was willing to accept. "Robbie hasn't received that letter yet, I'd have known. I'll have Allan intercept all future mail. Destroy it."

Molly bowed her head and her silence tore at him. So did her eyes when she lifted her head. "I have to tell him, Carter. I have to face it. I can't live my whole life wondering, fearing…"

Carter gave the only answer he had. "All right." In her shoes, he'd have felt the same way, actually did. "We'll do it together."

She eyed him critically. "You aren't going to shoot him, are you?"

A grin tried to form. "I can't promise that." Taking her hand, he led her to the door. "Let's go get this over with."

Carter questioned her ability to walk to the jail, but eventually accepted her assurance she'd be fine. He also nodded toward those still gathered at the mercantile, watching as they strode past. His mind tossed wildly, spewing possible outcomes that had his nerves ticking.

At the jail, he held the door as Molly entered.

Two cells, one on each side of the room, each held a man, and he gestured to the left, where Robbie was. James was in the one on the right.

Molly, about as petrified as she'd ever been—she'd never had so much to lose before—lifted her chin and moved forward. The sheriff tipped his hat as his gaze went to Carter.

"We're here to see a prisoner," Carter supplied.

"That one's been quiet," the sheriff answered, "but his old man hasn't shut up."

The man in the other cell started shouting that she couldn't talk to Robbie. That no one could, and the sheriff walked in that direction, telling Robbie's father to be quiet. Molly chose to ignore it and made her way across the room.

"Get out of here, Molly," Robbie whispered

before she stopped next to the iron bars he stood behind.

"I need to talk to you," she said.

"No."

Robbie looked shorter and thinner than she remembered, and was clearly unsettled by the way his father kept shouting. The sheriff was still trying to quiet the older man, and Molly's hand went to her stomach. Robbie caught her movement and wrapped his hands around the bars as he stuck his head between two of them.

"Don't say it, Molly," he whispered. "I'll deny ever touching you."

Molly thought she'd seen all sides to Robbie, but this one surprised her. He sounded almost desperate.

"You," Robbie continued quietly, "need to marry that Pinkerton man with you and forget you ever knew me." His gaze shifted across the room, to where his father was still shouting. "He'll destroy you if he knows."

Shivers rippled her, but she forced herself to continue, "Robbie, I—"

"No." He shook his head regretfully. "You're different, Molly. You made me want more. A life I know I can never have. My father knows that, and he'll never give me up. He can't ever know you're the reason I stole that money. To take you away. Take me away. It can't ever be, so please,

Molly, pretend it never happened." His tone and gaze grew pleading. "Please, Molly, for you, for your baby, for me, pretend it never happened. I'll never contact you again, ever, I swear."

"I wrote you a letter," she whispered, growing more fearful than ever.

Robbie shook his head and glanced toward Carter standing behind her.

"We'll find the letter and have it destroyed," Carter said.

Robbie nodded and turned around, walked toward the tiny cot inside the cell. "Take her out of here."

Molly wasn't exactly sure why, but compassion filled her. She believed him and could almost understand why Robbie was the way he was, especially when his father shouted, "What did you say to him? What did you say to my boy?"

Carter took her arm, and as they walked across the room, he said, "I just wanted to introduce him to my wife."

An indescribable bout of pride swelled inside Molly, and that made holding her chin up no work at all as Carter led her out the door. The sheriff walked onto the boardwalk beside them where Carter explained any mail delivered to the prisoners was to be confiscated, and asked for a deputy to be sent to the railroad, informing the same thing.

The sheriff agreed and congratulated them on their marriage before they left.

A bit giddy, yet nervous, for things were turning out too good to be true, Molly asked, "Now what?"

Carter laughed and kissed the tip of her nose. "I'd say we need to find a preacher."

Her heart leaped. "But if the letter—"

"If we don't intercept it, Robbie will destroy it."

"How can we be sure of that?"

Carter shrugged. "I believe him. You have the ability to bring out the best in people. You did it to me, and I believe you did it to Robbie." Once again holding her elbow, Carter started down the road, toward the mercantile.

Molly couldn't say she believed that, but she did believe in him. He had the ability to bring out the best in people. He simply demanded it. Walking beside him, she asked, "Can you be a Pinkerton agent from Huron? Or—"

"I've resigned," he said. "I have a feeling you and the girls are going to take all my attention."

Molly did like that idea, but felt compelled to say, "You don't have to resign."

"Yeah, I do," he said. "That part of my life is over. I'm ready for the next chapter." He folded her hand around his elbow. "When I said I love you, Molly, I meant it. You, the girls, the baby—you are my life now. My family."

The entire world was suddenly bluer. She'd been wrong. Someone could sweep into her life and change it all for the good. His name was Carter Buchanan. "I meant what I said, too, Carter. I love you, and I always will."

Carter leaned over to place a tiny kiss on her temple as they walked, utterly convinced he had made the right choice. Loving Molly was going to be all he'd ever dreamed.

At the edge of the mercantile yard Ivy, Karleen and a barking Bear met them. He hadn't forgotten about the girls, and was touched by how good it was to see them. How complete he felt. It was amazing, and fitting. Once a person experienced being whole, they couldn't go back to being half again. This was his family. The one thing he'd never had, but did now. He'd been adopted without knowing it.

"Carter, did you hear about my reward?" Ivy asked.

He scooped the child up, gave her a hard hug and a kiss on her cheek. "Yes, I did."

Never one to be left out, Karleen said, "Carter, did you hear about this?"

He frowned as she waggled something in front of him. "What is that?"

Karleen grinned and stretched on her toes to kiss his cheek. "A letter Molly thought she mailed, but I intercepted."

Molly gasped and Carter grabbed the envelope. He had believed Robbie, but the Pinkerton agent in him had said he still wanted to intercept that letter.

"Someone recently told me," Karleen said, "that an adult knows how to balance caring about others with staying true to themselves." She moved to wrap an arm around Molly's shoulders. "My sister wasn't balancing things, nor was she staying true to herself." Beaming, Karleen proclaimed, "I, however, know love when I see it."

Carter already liked this new role, that of being a father, and just so Karleen would know there would be no falling in love in her immediate future—not for years actually—he said, "You're still not too old for me to paddle."

She rolled her eyes, but joined the rest of them as they laughed.

Carter ripped the letter into tiny shreds and threw them into the air. The pieces rained down as all four of them hugged, and Bear attacked the fallen scraps while Carter and Molly kissed.

Karleen, clearing her throat, broke them apart. Both he and Molly turned to her. "Pastor Jenkins is in the kitchen. He'd like to know, now that it's no longer needed to be kept secret, if you and Molly would like to renew your vows this Sunday in church." Nose in the air, Karleen turned, started marching toward the house. "I'll tell him you'll be in shortly to make the arrangements."

They were.

They did.

* * * * *

A sneaky peek at next month...

HISTORICAL

IGNITE YOUR IMAGINATION, STEP INTO THE PAST...

My wish list for next month's titles...

In stores from 2nd August 2013:

☐ Not Just a Governess – Carole Mortimer

☐ A Lady Dares – Bronwyn Scott

☐ Bought for Revenge – Sarah Mallory

☐ To Sin with a Viking – Michelle Willingham

☐ The Black Sheep's Return – Elizabeth Beacon

☐ Smoke River Bride – Lynna Banning

Available at WHSmith, Tesco, Asda, Eason, Amazon and Apple

Just can't wait?

Visit us Online

You can buy our books online a month before they hit the shops! **www.millsandboon.co.u**

Special Offers

ery month we put together collections and
nger reads written by your favourite authors.

ere are some of next month's highlights—
d don't miss our fabulous discount online!

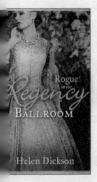

sale 2nd August   On sale 2nd August   On sale 19th July

Save 20%
on all Special Releases

ind out more at
ww.millsandboon.co.uk/specialreleases

*Visit us
Online*

0813/ST/MB428